D0057229

NANTUCKET COUNTERFEIT
The Fifth Henry Kennis Mystery

"The narrative flows along at a good clip, with eddies of philosophy and humor. The witty dialogue perfectly matches the multifaceted characters. That Henry believes in an 'old school, low-tech version of police work' allows the reader to readily follow the clues."

—*Publishers Weekly*

"The fifth in Axelrod's clever series casts a cynical eye on Nantucket's decidedly diverse denizens. Only the most careful readers, undistracted by his satire, will figure out whodunit."

—*Kirkus Reviews*

NANTUCKET RED TICKETS
The Fourth Henry Kennis Mystery

"Nantucket's many charms fill the pages..."

—*Publishers Weekly*

"Axelrod and his protagonist bring an amused, judicious, and ultimately tolerant eye to the foibles large and small of a mixed Santa's bag of characters."

—*Kirkus Reviews*

NANTUCKET GRAND
The Third Henry Kennis Mystery

"*Nantucket Grand* has everything I look for in a crime novel—tight, vivid prose, a sharply-drawn setting, an intricate plot with lots of unexpected twists, well-crafted characters, and an appealing protagonist in the person of Police Chief Henry Kennis, a dogged investigator you're going to enjoy following on all of his adventures."

—Bruce de Silva, Edgar Award-winning author

"Using his screenwriting background to good advantage, Axelrod packs plenty of layers and surprises into this intelligent, twisty tale. Henry's wry humor as well as his affection for the residents he serves exude warmth and will appeal to fans of Bill Crider's Sheriff Dan Rhodes."

—Amy Alessio, *Booklist*

"Axelrod's characters span the spectrum from homey and nice to proudly nasty. Fans of Spencer Fleming's Russ Van Alstyne and Frederick Ramsay's Ike Schwartz will enjoy Henry's literary leanings and dogged determination to protect his island and its residents."

—*Publishers Weekly*

"A beautiful island made ugly by class warfare makes a convincing backdrop for Chief Kennis' third case."

—*Kirkus Reviews*

NANTUCKET FIVE-SPOT
The Second Henry Kennis Mystery

"Axelrod crafts an enjoyable, fast-paced read."

—Publishers Weekly

"In the second Henry Kennis mystery, the summer tourist season on Nantucket is under way when a threat to bomb the Boston Pops concert disrupts the holiday feeling, although the poetry-writing police chief suspects this may be a distraction to cover up a much bigger and more dangerous conspiracy."

—Library Journal

NANTUCKET SAWBUCK
The First Henry Kennis Mystery

"*Nantucket Sawbuck* is a rare delight—a well-written small-town mystery that feels like life, complete with suspects who are the sort of people who commit murders and a police chief who's capable of catching them at it. Read this book."

—Thomas Perry

"Axlerod is a full speed, powerhouse of a writer."

—Domenic Stansberry, Edgar Award-winning author of *Naked Moon*

"Kennis is an honorable small-town cop whom readers will root for."

—Karen Keefe, *Booklist*

"...this is a promising start for a new author."

—*Publishers Weekly*

"Axelrod has a gift for characterization and a strong lead in Kennis. Nantucketers might bristle at the cynical portrait of their home, but his mystery debut gives the island as much personality as its varied inhabitants."

—*Kirkus Reviews*

Nantucket Counterfeit

Books by Steven Axelrod

The Henry Kennis Mysteries
Nantucket Sawbuck
Nantucket Five-Spot
Nantucket Grand
Nantucket Red Tickets
Nantucket Counterfeit

Nantucket Counterfeit

A Henry Kennis Mystery

WITHDRAWN

Steven Axelrod

Poisoned Pen Press

Copyright © 2018 by Steven Axelrod

First Edition 2018

10 9 8 7 6 5 4 3 2 1

Library of Congress Control Number: 2018940611

ISBN: 9781464210396   Hardcover
ISBN: 9781464210419   Trade Paperback
ISBN: 9781464210426   Ebook

All rights reserved. No part of this publication may be reproduced, stored in, or introduced into a retrieval system, or transmitted in any form, or by any means (electronic, mechanical, photocopying, recording, or otherwise) without the prior written permission of both the copyright owner and the publisher of this book.

Poisoned Pen Press
4014 N. Goldwater Blvd., #201
Scottsdale, AZ 85251
www.poisonedpenpress.com
info@poisonedpenpress.com

Printed in the United States of America

For Annie Breeding,
who puts Jane Stiles to shame.

Acknowledgments

Thanks to William Pittman and his superb Nantucket Police force. As usual, all of Henry's mistakes and poems are my own. Thanks also to The Nantucket Theatre Workshop, which would never allow a rat like Refn in the door. A great Nantucket institution, sixty-two years old and still going strong.

I have heard
That guilty creatures sitting at a play
Have by the very cunning of the scene
Been struck so to the soul that presently
They have proclaim'd their malefactions;
For murder, though it have no tongue, will speak…

—*Hamlet*, Act Two, Scene Two,
William Shakespeare

Part One:
Around the Point

Chapter One

D.R.T.

The day we found the Artistic Director of The Nantucket Theater Lab murdered in his basement, I was too busy to respond.

Haden Krakauer, my Assistant Chief, and I were in the middle of busting a cockfight on Essex Road—thirty-two thousand dollars in the kitty, eight birds in cages, two more in the dirt, thirty men, six extra cops, and three translators working five languages in the angry crowd.

Haden sighed as the ringleaders were cuffed and hauled away. "This isn't my Nantucket."

"Really?" I said. "Wasn't that your old pal Nick Folger, calling the fight?"

"Don't remind me."

Back at the station, I could see it was going to take hours to untangle the mess, with advocates and family members and a team of veterinarians for the birds. Just sorting through the confusion of dialects—Belarus, Spanish, Portuguese, Russian, Jamaican patois and, this was a new one, Vietnamese—slowed the process to a crawl.

At one point Haden leaned across the interview table where we were dealing with the five Ecuadoran brothers who owned the cockfight property, and said, "Let us go down, and there confound their language, that they may not understand one another's speech."

I nodded at the Biblical reference. "But the point of the Tower of Babel was to stop this kind of shit. Humans all talking the same language was the whole problem, right? 'They have all one language and now nothing will be restrained from them, which they have imagined to do.' God didn't like that idea—people imagining stuff to do. Mostly bad stuff."

"Wicked stuff."

"Yeah. So he made everybody speak different languages."

"And yet…we still have cockfights on Essex Road."

"At least He made the effort."

"How about just, like, making people nicer? That would have worked. We could all speak Esperanto and help each other. But, no. He'd rather just sit around like Tolkien, making up those weird languages and writing in Elvish."

I smiled. "God as a crackpot English academic. I like it."

The Ecuadorans stared at us. Their lawyer continued texting. He knew his clients would be back on the street in an hour, once the bail was set.

We stood and stepped out into the main hall. I felt a tug at my shirt. It was Barnaby Toll, out of breath. He must have taken the stairs to the basement booking room, deserting his dispatch desk. He knew better, after four years on the job, so something big must have happened. His round pale face confirmed it. I could see the excitement in his eyes. Some authentic crime had brought out the animal in him, that fight-or-flight jolt straight from the adrenal gland. I could feel it, too—the clutch of danger, the thrill of the hunt—when he whispered, "Chief! Chief! Somebody killed Horst Refn!"

Haden was already on his cell phone. "Charlie Boyce is out there. Fraker and the Staties got the call. They beat us to the house and sealed it. The vic is D.R.T., head-first in his meat freezer. Charlie rallied the troops, talked to the neighbors. Looks like the T.O.D. was less than an hour ago."

D.R.T.—dead right there. Haden had picked up the term from me, but I hadn't heard anyone use it on a crime scene since I left the LAPD. A witness with a solid Time of Death report would be a huge help. My boys were already canvassing the neighborhood, just as I'd taught them to do. Maybe the NPD was turning into a real-life police department, after all.

I scanned the milling crowd of mostly Hispanic cockfight aficionados. They would all be processed by the end of the day, placed in holding, released or turned over to ICE if they had criminal records. Our work was done. I nodded to Haden. "Let's go."

On the way out the door I recognized a face and almost turned back. But there was nothing I could do for him at that moment, and my singling him out would only make trouble for him with the others, marking him as an informant or a rat. As far as I knew, he was neither. He ran a big landscaping company he'd built from scratch and wrote agitprop plays about the Nantucket class war. His name was Sebastian Cruz, father to Hector Cruz—my daughter's new boyfriend. It was a small world on Nantucket.

And getting smaller all the time.

The last time I saw Sebastian, he was having a shouting match with Horst Refn on Main Street.

"*Same Time, Next Year? Good Vibrations?* What is this? Jupiter, Florida, dinner theater? At least those audiences get to eat!"

"We have a great season," Refn sputtered.

"You have crap! *Who Dun It?* A 'black box,' no cables, bring-your-own costumes *Spider-Man: Turn Off the Dark?* Why bother? *Aida* with a papier-mâché pyramid and six kids in Babar costumes left over from Halloween?"

"That's not fair! We're doing a great job with—"

"With what? I give you a serious piece of theater and you shit all over it."

"Yeah! Because it was bad!"

"No, because you are bad! Because you are an ignorant, gutless, low-class punk! You're useless. You're a suit from Walmart. You're a chicken nuggets Happy Meal!"

"I'm the Artistic Director of The Nantucket Theater Lab!"

"You're a corporate stooge! Everyone hates you! You think the girls like it when you come on to them? You're pushing fifty and you're getting fat!"

"Say that again"

"Fat! You're fat! Your fat piggy face makes them sick! You're ripping the seams of that fancy jacket. Look in a mirror! You're an overstuffed sausage."

"Shut up!"

"Make me."

Refn shoved him. That was where I stepped in.

I blocked Refn, twisted around to flat-hand Sebastian's chest. "That's enough, boys."

Refn glared at me. "Did you hear what he said?"

"I don't care what either one of you said. Break it up right now or I'm locking both of you up for disturbing the peace."

"That's the most ridiculous thing I ever—"

"Show some dignity, Horst."

Sebastian laughed. Refn lunged again and I had to grab his arms. I turned to Sebastian. "Go. Now."

Sebastian looked past me at Refn. "You ever lay a hand on me again, I'll fucking kill you, *culero*."

He turned and walked off down Main Street. "What did he say? What did he just call me?"

"You don't want to know."

Literally, the term meant "ass salesman" but "asshole" was the most useful translation. The small crowd that had gathered started to disperse. The show was over. But Refn still struggled against me. "You're just letting him walk away? He threatened my life! That's assault in this state."

"And you pushed him. That's battery. And this is late June on Nantucket, going into the biggest holiday of the year. So we're all going to live and let live."

But someone obviously had a different plan in mind for Horst Refn.

As we pulled into the driveway of the Killdeer Drive house, I felt relieved. Sebastian's arrest was one piece of good news—if the coroner's report confirmed witness statements for the time of death, his presence at the cockfight would be an unbreakable alibi.

I killed the engine, just as the WACK disc jockey who called herself J. Feld was about to identify the song she'd been playing. The imagery of the "bargain-priced room on La Cienega" had made me briefly homesick for Los Angeles. The repeated line "You, or your memory" was probably the title. I'd look it up when I had time.

I stayed in the silent car for a moment or two, studying the house. It exuded a bristling sense of danger, cruel but sluggish, like the giant yellow-jacket nests you found so often under the eaves of Nantucket mansions. Police and crime scene techs moved in and out like insects, bound on inscrutable random business of their own.

Neighbors had gathered on the sidewalk, curious but keeping their distance. Local alternative newspaper editor David Trezize was interviewing one of them, scribbling intently in his spiral-bound notebook, glancing up occasionally through his thick glasses, looking like an intelligent otter, reaping the first quotes for his front page story. I looked around for someone from the *Inquirer and Mirror*, but David had beaten them to the story, once again.

Past the yellow crime scene tape, Lonnie Fraker had his troops fully mobilized, working crowd control at the perimeter, guarding the doors and loitering with squinting intensity inside. They reminded me of the paint crews Mike Henderson had pointed out a few weeks before, with one guy on a ladder scraping listlessly at a window casing, another one standing at the base of the ladder for no particular reason, a third guy dabbing at the fence as if he were touching up a self-portrait, with the rest of the crew pointing up at the second floor, studying each car as it drove by or staring at their smartphones. "How do those crews make any money?" he had asked me. "I actually work, and I can barely make ends meet."

The answer was easier for Lonnie's storm troopers. Malingering in the most threatening way possible was their basic job description. The real action was happening in the basement, where the Boston crime scene techs were working.

We climbed out of my cruiser and started up the driveway. Just inside the front door, a new hire I'd never seen before blocked the hall. "This is a restricted area, sir. I'm going to have to ask you to vacate the premises."

I wasn't wearing my uniform—I rarely did. Still, he should have known better. I had participated in an orientation day for the new State Police recruits less than a month ago. But I'd been wearing my uniform that day.

I shook my head at the stilted jargon. "Is that like 'leaving the building'?"

Haden laughed, but the kid didn't see the humor. That's my cross to bear. The kid moved a step closer. "Don't make me ask you again, sir."

I decided to speak his language. I pointed out the open door to where my official Ford Explorer with full police markings and big antennas was parked at the curb. "I'm the operator of that vehicle. Get it?"

"Let him in, O'Donnell," Lonnie called out from the kitchen. "He's Chief of Police Henry Kennis."

O'Donnell's face pulled tight and his eyes opened comically wide. He reminded me of an L.A. burglar pinned by the floodlight from a police helicopter.

I patted his shoulder. "No problem, O'Donnell. Now you know." I tipped my head toward Haden. "This is Assistant Chief Krakauer. He's allowed to be here, too."

"Yes, sir. Sorry, sir."

We moved past him into the kitchen. I turned to Lonnie. "What have you got?"

Lonnie pulled his heavy-framed, Buddy Holly-style glasses from the front pocket of his uniform, extracted his wallet-sized spiral blue pad, and flipped a couple of pages. With his high-pitched nasal voice and a hunched posture that tried to minimize his awkward height, he could have been a geek at ComicCon, haggling over a mint condition Steve Ditko Spider-Man comic.

"Okay, so, the forensic team reconstructed the incident this way. Front door was open, the perp knew that, and they're thinking it had to be someone who knew Refn. No sign of struggle. Two coffee mugs out on the kitchen counter—nice friendly chat. Eventually Refn and the perp go down to the basement."

"Any idea why?"

"Well, clearly it's pretext, not 'reason,' you know what I mean? This individual had a plan. Refn had lots of stuff stored down there—art books, vintage clothing, plaster maquettes, antique quilted pillows—he had put a lot of the merchandise up at the ReUse exchange website. Seems like he wanted to unload a lot of personal baggage fast. Maybe he was planning to make a move? Which is weird because the Theater Lab just renewed his contract for three years. Anyway, we're taking his computer and we'll track the e-mails, see if anyone was in touch about the stuff he had for sale. So, let's see…they go downstairs, there's a struggle, we have signs of blunt-force trauma. The perp knocks him out, then jams him into the meat freezer. There's serious pre-mortem frostbite on the face."

"Cause of death?"

"Looks like strangulation, as the perp held him in place. Nasty way to die."

"Time of death?"

"We lucked out there, Chief. The next door neighbor was listening to the Red Sox game and heard sounds of struggle right after a Pablo Sandoval home run. And, hey, if you follow the Sox, you know any home run is a big deal this season. Am I right?"

"We could sure use Ortiz right now," I offered. I didn't really follow baseball but you couldn't help absorbing the basics, here in Red Sox Nation.

Lonnie flipped over a page. "The body was found by Donald Harcourt, he's on the NTL Board, some kind of industrial packaging big shot, WASP, big money, house in Shimmo."

"What was he doing here?"

"He says he got a call from Joe Little. They were supposed to meet at the house. Some kind of big pow-wow with Refn. But Little was a no-show. Or he split before Harcourt arrived."

"Joe Little…" I was trying to place the name.

"Joseph Frederick Little, Lotus Capital Management? Loaded, like all the rest of them. He's on the NTL Board."

I put it together. "Yeah…he had a big fight with Harcourt at some charity cocktail party a couple of weeks ago. One of them pushed the other into an antique hutch that turned out to be a replica from Pottery Barn. The owner was going to sue until the decorator confessed—a perfect Nantucket story."

"I never read about it," Lonnie said. "Were you there?"

"Right. I always get invited to these fundraisers because they know I'm an easy touch."

"Okay, okay, so how did you find out about it?"

"Jackson Blum told me."

"You're all chummy now?"

"Actually, we are. He turned out to be a pretty decent guy."

I had arrested Blum for murder last Christmas, on the night he found out he'd driven his gay son to suicide. It was a horrific one-two punch, but we dropped the murder charge and the son survived. Still, the night Blum spent in jail and the ecstatic family reunion the next morning had scrambled his brain chemistry like a course of electro-shock. Here, I thought only a lobotomy could redeem him! Seriously, though, Blum had become so humble and friendly, I suspected an ulterior motive, but the wolf really had transformed into the wolfhound. If only I could pull the same trick on people like Donald Harcourt and Joseph Little. As it stood right now I might have to console myself with arresting one of them for murder.

"Is Harcourt still here? I need to talk to him."

Lonnie grinned. "He's in the Great Room. Pissed as hell. This dead guy is ruining his whole day."

"Let him wait. Did you talk to the neighbor?"

"We talked to all the neighbors. Or, I mean—we are talking to them. The canvass is ongoing. They all hate each other and they all hated Refn the most. Parties late at night. Police call-outs—you can dig up the records. Cigarette butts in the yard. Apparently, he smoked outside, and the wind blows those butts all over the place."

I shook my head. "It's hard to believe anybody still smokes."

"Yeah," Lonnie grinned. "It could seriously shorten his life. Though four out of five doctors agree it's not quite as dangerous as being strangled and stuffed into a meat freezer."

"That's catchy. You should write ads for Big Tobacco."

He shrugged. "There was more. Refn let his hedge grow too high and never trimmed it. The homeowners' association was bitching about that as far back as last summer. And he built his fences wrong-side out. That had the abutters screaming. This guy definitely puts the 'butt' into abutter."

"Inside out?"

"It's a rule. I thought it was one of those unwritten rules, but it's also a bylaw. You build a fence on the property line, the structural part of the fence, the cross pieces, have to face your property. The neighbor gets the good-looking side, the slats. Refn ignored the law, and the—you know, the custom, the neighborly agreement—and put up the fences so the neighbors have to look at the bad side. Best part is, it's not even his house! The Theater Lab owns it and the Artistic Director just lives here. Like the President in the White House."

I nodded at the casual way Refn had trampled the community's mores. "He seems more like the President in the White House all the time."

"Hey! Refn was good looking—and smart, supposedly. With actual hair. Anyway, the Theater Lab was pissed off at him, too—but they wouldn't pony up the dough to take down the fences."

"Is that all?"

"Are you kidding? Not even close." Fraker flipped another page. "Let's see…he parked his car blocking other people's driveways and he had a car alarm that went off at all hours. People love that! Someone was flattening tires with a knife and everybody suspected Refn. No one filed a complaint; there was no proof—but it gives you the idea. Next big hurricane they'd have been looking for the wind machine in his basement. He'll be off the hook for that now. And they have to admit he didn't commit this murder. Unless he killed himself—to frame one of the neighbors!"

Lonnie laughed. I held up a hand. The gallows humor was necessary to vent the tension of the crime scene, but we were getting off track. "Down, boy. Where's the one who heard the murder go down?"

"That would be Paula Monaghan. On the other side of the mega hedge. Seventy-two years old, founding member of the Garden Club and probably everything else around here. Deeded her pile on Baxter Road to the kids last year, and moved into this place."

"I'm going to talk to her first."

"Be my guest. She's at home. I have Wylie and Steinkamp in there with her."

"In case she makes a break for it?"

"Just following procedure, Chief."

"Whatever. Keep this place buttoned up until I get back."

Paula Monaghan was a perfect Nantucket type. I could have picked her out of a lineup: slim, regal, white-haired, sharp-eyed, dressed down in grass-stained khaki trousers, untucked blue Brooks Brothers shirt and well-worn espadrilles. This was old money personified. My girlfriend came from the same stock. She had educated me on the particulars of the Social Register set and their ostentatious hatred of display. Paula's tarnished Tiffany silver service would be treated like Walmart flatware; her toilet paper would be one-ply, her reading glasses straight off the drugstore rack.

"Well, well, well," she stood in her doorway, shaking my hand in an alarmingly solid grip. "Our poetry-writing police Chief. Quite a rarity! I suspect you're the only specimen extant on the length of the Eastern Seaboard."

"I hope not."

"Optimism—that must be an essential shortcoming for a police officer."

I smiled, "You may be right."

"How agreeable you are! Please, I'm being terribly rude, come in. I was just having a cup of tea. Would you like one?"

"No thanks."

She stepped back and I saw Wylie and Steinkamp, two crew-cut tubs of testosterone, lurking uncomfortably by the door into the living room, big guns on wide leather holsters bristling with mace and ammunition, perpetually longing for a declaration of martial law that never came. They made me nervous—I couldn't image how Paula Monaghan felt.

"Okay, guys," I told them. "I've got this one."

"But Captain Fraker said—"

"This is my case and my witness." I flicked a dismissive wrist toward the door. "Scat."

I stared them down and saw Mrs. Monaghan fighting a smile as they shuffled out.

She closed the door behind them with a sigh of relief and I followed her into the kitchen. The big sunny room distinguished itself from the average Naushop setup by a few key details—the hanging rack of All-Clad pans ("A wedding gift") and a block of Wusthof knives ("You need a good knife to cook properly."). She maintained a small garden in her small tidy backyard—herbs and shallots, heirloom tomatoes.

"There's no room for much of a flower garden here," she said. "But I do have a weakness for hydrangeas. And some marigolds in the window box. Have you seen the window boxes in town this year? So overdone, so awful. The plants at that Graydon House look like they're about to eat the hotel! That whistling sound you hear is generations of New England Quakers spinning in their modestly unmarked graves. But excuse me. You have much more serious matters to discuss."

"No problem, Mrs. Monaghan. This kind of crime makes people talkative—like whistling through the graveyard."

"My father made us hold our breath."

"That works."

We sat down at the kitchen table. She sipped her tea. "I'll tell you exactly what I told those awful State Police people. I was weeding my garden, I actually do it myself, unlike some of the ladies in the Garden Club who have their gardens—I don't know how else to say it—*installed* by very expensive landscapers, down to the last speck of mulch. Anyway, it was very quiet, the occasional car going by, birds jabbering as they do. I had my faithful old transistor radio on for the ballgame, of course, softly. I love my Red Sox, but I don't like to annoy the neighbors. So, let me see…the first strange thing I heard was a dog whining—some miserable little creature forced to walk around on the leash, no doubt. Then a few minutes later a man walked up to Mr. Refn's front door. Walk outside and check for yourself—you can see it through the hedge. Rather a short, stout man. He knocked, but the door was unlocked, and he went in. A little later I heard some sort of scuffle and shouting from the basement—the casement window in the foundation was open. I stood up, I wasn't sure what to do. And that's when I heard the gunshot!"

No one had mentioned any gunplay, and Fraker hadn't mentioned blood spatter, shell casings, or ballistics. But I didn't want to interrupt Mrs. Monaghan. I made a mental note and let it go for the moment. "Did you see anything else?"

She nodded. "I saw a woman."

"I'm sorry?"

"She was running away down the street."

"When was this exactly?"

"I—wait a moment. I...yes, when I stood up after the shot, I was holding my breath listening. I was standing as still as a rabbit in the *rosa rugosa*. I saw something out of the corner of my eye—someone running. It was a small person. My first thought was, 'Oh my God, this is the killer.' Why I didn't think about the weapon she was carrying, I don't know. I suppose I couldn't imagine being gunned down in my own front yard. Anyway, I got to the street just as she disappeared around the curve in the street to Kittiwake Lane. I could tell it was a woman then."

"Do you remember what she was wearing?"

"Blue jeans, and a long-sleeved t-shirt. It was light blue. And she had sneakers of some kind. Running shoes, I suppose you'd call them now."

"How about her hair?"

"Shoulder-length, frizzy. Oh, and she was wearing a red hat with a visor. One of those baseball caps. I couldn't see any insignia on it, she was too far away, and she was moving too fast."

I felt a momentary chill, and it wasn't just Mrs. Monaghan's air conditioning. Her description sounded ominously like my girlfriend, Jane Stiles. The thought was absurd. I shook it off, changed the subject. "Did you notice anything else unusual on the street?"

"Well, yes, actually. There was a house painter working two houses down, painting the front clapboards. I had noticed him because it was unusual—one person, obviously a local, instead of a big...diverse...crew. We have tremendous diversity on

Nantucket now, as I'm sure you know. Especially in the building trades."

"And that was all—that he was working alone?"

"No, no, no—the strange thing was that he was gone. I mean…it must have been what? Two-thirty, two forty-five in the afternoon on a spectacular summer day. And suddenly he was nowhere to be found. It struck me as quite suspicious."

"But the woman with the gun—"

"I didn't see her carrying a gun. She might have thrown it down. I'd check all the bushes if I were you."

"I'll make a note of it."

"She could have handed the gun to the house painter. They could have been in it together! There's something shady about those people anyway. I mean, we pay them to loaf on our property, they're poking around inside our houses when we're not home. I heard one of them was arrested for stealing last year."

She was talking about a friend of mine, and I had to set the record straight. Rumors spread on Nantucket faster than poison ivy. "That was Mike Henderson, and it turned out that Sheriff Bob Bulmer was stealing from the houses Mike had open in the winter, figuring Mike would take the blame when the owners arrived in the spring."

Mrs. Monaghan stared at me. "That's diabolical!"

"Well, it wasn't very nice. But he made quite a few mistakes, fortunately, and we caught him quickly. So really, it didn't—"

"Henderson! That's his name!"

"Excuse me?"

"The painter. I remember now. His name is right there on his truck."

This was getting worse by the second. Next, it would turn out that my ex-wife was showing a house in the neighborhood, and Billy Delevane was building a deck next door. The hammer was a classic murder weapon, and a missed swing that connected with something hard could easily sound like a gunshot.

Enough. I felt a pang of nostalgia for the rough dirty world of Los Angeles. In my eight years on the LAPD I never turned up anyone I knew at a crime scene. A city is lonely and isolating and full of strangers—and that may be the best thing about it.

Clearly, I needed to interview Mike Henderson before Lonnie and his goons got a chance. But that would have to wait. I wasn't finished with the crime scene yet. First, I needed to get a look at the body, brace Donald Harcourt, and talk to the neighbor on the other side of Refn's house.

As I was brushing past Wylie and Steinkamp on the driveway, Mrs. Monaghan offered a parting shot. "It's not surprising."

I turned. "Excuse me?"

"The murder. It doesn't surprise me, at least. Refn ran a non-profit."

"So?"

"Over the years, I've served on the boards of the Dreamland, the Nantucket Historical Association, and the Basket Museum, Chief Kennis. I know the nonprofit world quite well. Too well. The rage and hate and backstabbing and slander would turn your hair white. I think it may have done mine! Honestly, it's like the last days of the Nixon White House in those boardrooms. Or the first days of this one. Anything's possible."

"Including murder?"

"They say the second time is easier."

Wylie and Steinkamp exchanged a look of skeptical contempt. But there was steel in her voice.

"You're saying that one of these people has killed before?" She met my gaze calmly. "Perhaps you should look into that."

"If you have information pertaining to—"

"I have no such thing. What I do have is a boundless faith in human nature. Roughly ninety percent of all the people you'll ever meet are unredeemably bad, young man, greedy and selfish and cruel. Most of them would commit the most heinous crime you could possibly imagine, if they knew for certain they could get away with it. I sometimes think the fabric of society is held together by nothing more than the daunting awareness that it is, in fact, quite difficult to get away with murder."

I had no time for her preening nihilism. "Thanks for your thoughts, Mrs. Monaghan. If you remember anything else that might aid the investigation, please call the station."

The forensic team was finishing up in Refn's basement when I came downstairs. Our own forensic tech, Monica Terwilliger, fat but remarkably graceful and light on her feet, stood as I came down the plank stairs. She had cut her thick blond hair short and once again it struck me that she was forty pounds away from being a dangerously beautiful woman. But she seemed to like the distance.

Carl Borelli was leaning over the body. Short, balding, dumpy, nearing retirement age and counting the seconds, he worked for the State Police out of Barnstable. As he pushed off the edge of the freezer to straighten up, I could tell he wasn't exactly thrilled to be on Nantucket. As I recalled, he hated flying, and they would have had to jam him onto one of those Cape Air Cessnas to get him here this fast.

Monica spoke first. "Hey, Chief, we're looking at—"

"I'll handle the briefing, Ms Terliger."

"It's Terwilliger."

"It's irrelevant."

"Not to me," I said. "Try to learn people's names, Carl. It helps foster the useful illusion that you give a shit. Go on, Monica, sorry."

"I was just going to say…we have signs of a struggle, defensive wounds on the arms, blunt-force injuries to the ribs, lots of mess and chaos—" She waved her arm around the basement floor, which was scattered with old books and magazines, small broken plaster statues, crockery and coins, spilled from boxes when a big metal shelving unit tipped over. "Someone threw someone into that," Monica said, "and the perpetrator had what I think was probably a bat, judging from the width of the bruising. No sign of struggle upstairs, though, which makes me think the assailant entered freely and came downstairs with no interference."

"So, a friend."

"Well, not an enemy at least. And not a stranger. Though Mr. Refn obviously…well, he didn't know the person quite as well as he thought he did."

Borelli spoke up, still sullen from my rebuke. "There's strangulation ligature on the neck, if I may add an observation. Refn was held down in the freezer long enough to get a serious case of frostbite on his face. The freezing is all ante-mortem. He felt it while it was happening. We're talking about torture. Someone really, really didn't like this guy."

I thought of Paula Monaghan's comment. But this would be taking bureaucratic infighting to a whole new level.

I left them to finish, and went upstairs to find Donald Harcourt.

He was not in a great mood. "Am I under arrest?"

"No. Of course not."

"Then why am I being detained here?"

He was a short, stocky man with an unruly mop of black hair that he obviously colored, despite the token gray streaks he had left at the temples. He wore Nantucket Reds—trousers that turned pink with repeated washings—and a blue blazer over an expensive-looking gray crewneck t-shirt. He looked like he was on his way to a cocktail party, not a meeting with his Artistic Director—but he obviously had further plans for the day. I knew the type. Call it profiling, Nantucket-style. The physical profile was an aristocratic one, if you ignored the spider web of burst blood vessels on his cheeks. The man obviously liked to drink, and my guess was he'd started early today—a shot of vodka in the morning coffee, perhaps. Or a couple of Bloodies with breakfast.

"I need you to tell me what happened this afternoon."

"I've already told twenty different people! And they're all

waiting for me to slip up so they can pounce. 'You told Deputy Dog that you parked in front of the house but we located your car halfway down the street,' they say. It's insulting. I had a senior moment about my car. Does that make me a murderer?"

"You found the body, Mr. Harcourt. They have to ask these questions. And so do I."

A shudder of resignation. "Fine. Ask away."

"Shall we sit down?" I knew the conversation would seem less confrontational if we were both settled in Refn's plush-looking armchairs. And I was right: the tension broke as Harcourt got comfortable. He pushed his hands down his thighs, as if he was working out a cramp.

I began. "So what brought you here today?"

"A text."

"From?"

"Joey Little—Joseph Little, of Lotus Capital Management? I'm sure you've heard of it."

"No, sorry. I manage my own capital. Which basically comes down to balancing my checkbook."

He ignored me and pushed on. "Joey married a much younger woman several years ago, a model named Laura Gutterson. Charming girl. You must have seen pictures of them in the *Foggy Sheet.*"

This was our version of a society page, featured in *N Magazine* and the Mahon About Town website—over-exposed photographs of overdressed Nantucket gentry under the tent at various cocktail parties and fundraisers, mostly belying the cherished myth that the rich were thinner and better looking than the rest of us. Laura Gutterson-Little would stand out in those crowds. I made a mental note to check the back issues. But I'd need Gene Mahon's help to make a solid ID. "Those photos are never captioned."

"Of course not. People in the know, know already. Everyone else can just watch and wonder."

"So, Little texted you this afternoon. Why?"

"There was an issue that had to be resolved." I waited. "It was personal."

"It's going to come out eventually, Mr. Harcourt. Here or at the station, or during the trial."

"Trial? What do you mean—trial? I did nothing! I was just trying to help."

I sat forward a little. "Convince me of that."

"Apparently there had been some sort of…dalliance. Refn was quite the ladies' man. There were photographs. Refn was threatening to put them online, unless Joe paid him off. The man was making close to a hundred and fifty thousand dollars a year for doing next to nothing. Why did he need to blackmail people?"

"Lots of reasons. A gambling habit. A drug habit. I hear he does a lot of high-end shopping. That stuff adds up."

"I suppose. It's privileged information, by the way—about the salary."

"Don't you have to post all your financial information? You're a nonprofit."

He smiled at my naiveté. "We do as we like, Chief Kennis. We haven't had an open annual meeting for three years. And no one makes a peep. They say money talks. On Nantucket it talks very loudly indeed."

I almost said, yeah, and it never shuts up.

But Harcourt was moving on. "Refn said an amusing thing about those bylaws and regulations, a while ago. He was paraphrasing Oscar Wilde. 'Rules are like hymens—made to be broken.' I'm sure Refn has broken more than his share of both."

"So you and Mister Little are close? He confides in you?"

"Well…I wouldn't go that far. I certainly wouldn't murder some random extortionist for him, if that's what you mean! He's an acquaintance. We've been texting each other since I convinced him to double down on his investments after the election. He was shorting the market, preparing his clients for the big crash! But I knew it would be a bonanza for business if the election went to the GOP. So Joe reversed himself and, needless to say, it worked out quite nicely. I became his mentor after that. I told him to sell before things got really crazy, and he did, at the top of the market as it turned out. Hence the text messages. He won't make a move without me."

"I'm confused. What were you fighting about?"

"Excuse me?"

"At the charity affair a few weeks ago."

"Oh, the Sanfords. Nothing is private anymore."

"Especially a brawl in front of two dozen witnesses."

He shrugged. "Point taken. It was an awkward moment."

"What was going on?"

"I told him about my suspicions. I had seen Refn and Laura together at Faregrounds, of all places! They must have assumed that no one who mattered would see them." Faregrounds was a mid-island working-class sports bar. Little had probably been right. But he hadn't counted on Harcourt slumming.

"So you confronted him at the fundraiser?"

"I admit it was an inappropriate moment. But I had just been listening to Laura lecture a group of women twice her age about the sanctity of truth in marriage. 'Lies between a husband and wife are black mold! They spread and they poison the air. They make your home toxic. Scrub the walls with the bleach of honesty, rinse them with the pure water of forgiveness, before it's too late.' She calls herself a 'life coach'! Can you imagine? Preaching that sanctimonious crap while she's cheating on her husband with…with that despicable creature in the basement."

"So you decided then and there to tell Little what was really going on."

"He looked so proud and adoring. Like a one-man cult."

"And you couldn't resist a little deprogramming."

"Something like that. Pointless exercise. He called me a damn liar. I called him a damn fool. He threw a punch and I pushed him. End of story."

"Until the blackmail letter arrived."

"Exactly. We both agreed—the time had come for action. He texted me to meet Refn with him—here today, this afternoon. We were going to close Refn down for good, unless he backed off. We could get him fired, contract or no contract. We could tar and feather the little dandy. There have been other incidents—sexual harassment, public drunkenness, even suspected embezzlement. He was hanging from a thin thread and we were more than willing to snip it."

"Why not do it before?"

"No one wanted the publicity. And Refn could be a charmer—like every other sociopath in the world. Great fund-raiser—he had a knack for tricking money out of tight-fisted matrons. Also, for the record, he happened to be quite a talented director. So I'm told. I don't go to the plays, I just wanted a handsome figurehead on the cover of *N Magazine*, and Refn delivered on that score. No one wanted to tarnish the theater's image."

"So Little arranged this meeting. But he never showed up?"

"I'm not sure. I heard footsteps on the bulkhead stairs when I went down to the basement."

"Back it up a little for me. You got here—what time was it?"

"A little after two-thirty. I was running late."

"Can anyone verify your whereabouts?"

"I was sitting in traffic on Old South Road! Do I really need to verify that? Have you driven anywhere on this island lately?"

I dropped the subject. He had no alibi, but I wasn't ready to accuse him of murder, and I wanted him on my side. "So… you knocked?"

"The door was open. I went inside but there was no one home. Then I heard noises from the basement, banging and choking, bad noises. I ran down there but whoever it was took off and there was just—Refn, in the freezer. I didn't even check to see if he was dead. I mean—he looked dead, he wasn't moving. But that was none of my business. I called 911."

"You did the right thing."

He shook his head. "Joe Little, my God."

"So…Little killed Refn?

"There was no one else here."

"You didn't see him, though."

"No, but—"

"And the text got you here, all alone with the dead body when the police arrived."

"Are you saying he tried to set me up?"

"It's possible."

"But I called the police myself!"

"It often happens that way. The killer calls the police to report the crime. It makes sense. You expect a killer to flee the scene. Reporting it makes you look innocent. It's what an innocent person would do."

"But I am innocent! I could never kill anyone! I couldn't even spank my own children. And my father had no trouble taking the paddle to me."

I sat back, studying the bewildered plutocrat on the other side of the coffee table. I believed him. "So why would Little want to frame you for murder?"

"I have no idea. Besides, you said it yourself—it could have been anyone down in that basement. All we know for sure is that I didn't see Joe when I got here. He could have—I don't know. He could have forgotten the meeting."

"I don't think so. Not this meeting."

"Okay, right, sure. But I don't know—maybe he got stuck in traffic, too. Maybe he's still stuck in traffic. Maybe his car broke down."

"He would have texted you."

"Unless his phone died. Or—or, he could have left it at home. Everyone does that. He could have had a heart attack! He could be in the hospital right now. Have you seen Joe Little? He's a coronary waiting to happen. And besides…we have no quarrel with each other anymore. I was helping him with the Refn matter. Not to mention, I probably made him a million dollars this year."

"I'll be talking to him soon." I stood up. "We're done here, Mr. Harcourt. Sorry to inconvenience you. One of my detectives will be in touch if we have any more questions."

"So that's it?" He seemed disappointed. I've noticed that reaction many times—a sort of reluctance, often with witnesses and even exonerated suspects. The spotlight is shifting, the investigation is moving on, leaving them behind.

He stood and I shook his hand. "For now, anyway. Thanks for your help."

I had one more stop to make before heading back to the station—the neighbor on the other side of Refn's house, Betsy Gosnell.

A dentist's widow from Scarsdale, she was planning to sell the Naushop place, and move full-time into her Coral Gables condo. She didn't like what Nantucket was becoming. "And this is a perfect example," she said as we stood in her doorway. She seemed reluctant to let me in. I could see the messy living room over her shoulder and she had already broken out the wine. She drank her Chardonnay out of a highball glass, with plenty of ice.

"This?" I prompted her. I assumed she meant the murder next door, but I'd followed some productive tangents over the years by setting my assumptions aside.

"People going crazy!"

"Actually—"

"The population is out of control! There's just too many people. You put ten rats in a cage meant for five? They start eating each other."

"Mrs. Gosnell—"

"I mean, I expect crime from these…from the immigrant people. I don't even blame them! Life is tough here. They work like sled dogs. They get treated like dirt. Of course they're going to do something desperate. But this is different."

"I'm sorry. Are you saying—?"

"I saw the killer. With my own eyes. A white woman! She was running like her life depended on it, running away from that house, the death house. No one runs around here, Chief Kennis, except little kids and joggers. This woman was no kid, and she wasn't jogging! You know, I always say if you spend enough time making up scary stories about death and murder, it gets under your skin eventually, like…like fishing something out of a public toilet with a paper cut on your hand. That's how the MRSA virus gets in. And once it's there, antibiotics don't work. And it's contagious, Chief—that's what you need to think about."

"Excuse me?"

"She's your girlfriend—the mystery writer. The Madeline Clark mysteries! How many people has she killed in those books of hers? More than all the murders since we bought Nantucket from the Indians, put together! That has to affect a person."

I took a step closer. "What are you saying?"

"Jane Stiles! I recognized her from the dust jacket picture. She's the one that killed him."

Chapter Two

Motives and Opportunities

"I don't know what's worse," Jane Stiles said. "Being accused of murder, or someone actually recognizing me from that horrible dust jacket photograph!"

"But they didn't." I pointed out. "Since you didn't actually kill anyone and you weren't even there."

She had spent the afternoon in question with her son, Sam, picking low bush blueberries from one of her secret spots near the Miacomet Golf Course. They had a big china bowl of fruit to prove it. "But that doesn't mean much," she said. "A suspect's nine-year-old son is considered unreliable corroboration at best. No one saw us out there. I could have picked these berries any time. And I have a motive for the killing."

We were standing in the weedy, junk-strewn yard of her ex-husband's house in the Friendship Lane development, off Bartlett Road. Joe's Equator Drive house needed a new roof, some fresh sod, and a dozen trips to the dump. The top of a 1986 Mercedes 560 SL he had vandalized for parts rested in a tangle of poison ivy and it looked like the car was sinking into the ground. Old lobster traps, torn waders, aluminum ladder sections, and rolls of chicken wire completed the picture of hillbilly squalor.

But Joe Stiles was anything but a redneck squatter. Croatian by descent, his original last name was Vrsaljkjo, pronounced VersaLeeko. He changed it to Stiles when he got married and kept the name after the divorce, partly because he wanted a name people could pronounce ("Everyone was always saying what the hell are those 'J's doing there?") and partly because he thought the name Joe Stiles sounded cool. "Like a private detective in an old movie. Joe Stiles, PI."

In fact he was a computer savant. He built websites and designed the lighting for local theater productions, along with doing various eccentric car repair jobs for a select clientele. He was currently obsessed with a white Volkswagen Vanagon, and had been trying to unbolt the coil from the engine mount when we pulled up. A gaunt, shambling man with a skimpy beard and an unflattering ponytail, it was hard to imagine him with Jane, but they had stayed married for twelve years—just like Miranda and I had. Genial and placid, mostly living in his own head, Joe perked up when Jane mentioned the murder.

"I have a motive, too," he said cheerfully, wiping his grimy hands on a rag while Sam hugged his leg.

"Hey, me first!" Jane snapped. "What an attention hog."

"Okay, okay." He turned to me. "Janey wrote this book."

Jane explained, "It was one of the first Maddie Clark books. Refn had just started at the Theater Lab. I hated him instantly and so did Joe."

Joe nodded. "Oh, yeah. That slimy little punk! He took over and everything from then on they did the cheapest, easiest, crummiest, ugliest way possible. Who needs lights? All he really wanted was a couple of halogens—or maybe just a kid with a flashlight! I had to buy my own gobos when we did *Moon for the Misbegotten*, which was the last decent production I can remember in this town, and we only did it because Bud Caxton went to the mat and Lucille Waters wanted to play Josie. Then Bud died and Lucille moved to New York. She's doing real theater now! Strindberg, off-Broadway. Good for her."

I nudged him back on track. "What's a gobo?"

"Ah, it's—the word stands for 'goes before optics.' It's kind of like a stencil? For lighting effects. I wanted leaf shadows on the porch, and Refn fought me about it. Not in the budget—and then he buys himself a brand new Ducati motorcycle! What a turd."

I turned to Jane. "So…you wrote a book about Refn?"

"Not exactly. I mean—he was the murder victim. Well, not him exactly. I made the character as different from him as I could. But Refn heard about it and he still went crazy. Sued me, sued my publisher. It cost a lot of money and I had to totally rewrite the book."

"I don't remember reading that one."

"It was the one with the paraplegic black transgendered Basket Museum guy."

"Oh, right. Where the wheelchair got pushed down the steps at Steps Beach, *Battleship Potemkin*-style."

"Mmmmm, Eisenstein. And everybody thought I was ripping off Brian DePalma."

I nudged the conversation again. "So…are you saying you'd kill Refn over something like that?"

Jane shrugged. "Somebody might."

"How about getting fired because some New York critic praised the lighting and didn't give Refn credit?" Joe asked.

"Sounds flimsy."

"I also demanded a raise."

"That's it?"

"Well, he said I was already overpaid, it was just a part-time job. I told him I was leaving and I was taking my light board with me and he said he'd have me arrested if I did that, and I told him I'd shove the board so far up his ass his eyes would light up and he said 'Are you threatening me?' and I said what kind of clueless dipshit doesn't even know when he's being threatened? And he said, 'I could have you arrested just for that,' and I said

'Don't worry. I wouldn't wreck my lighting board for a grand gesture. Unlike you, it's functional.' The whole cast was there, Chief. They heard it all. Put 'em on the stand, they could send me straight up to Shirley for life."

He was talking about the maximum security Sounza-Baranowski Correctional Center in Shirley, Mass. The question was worth pursuing. "So, tell me, Joe—do you have an alibi?"

"Rock solid, Chief. I was in Madaket, helping Hugh Billings with his website. We had the ballgame on. Hugh was standing over my shoulder. I remember we high-fived after the Sandoval home run. I remember feeling lucky I wasn't driving in town right then. I'd already missed part of the game, on the way to Hugh's house."

"How so?"

"I like to listen to the Red Sox in the car, but sometimes you get stuck under those power lines and you totally lose reception."

"It's true," Jane added. "The worst is the hill going up Orange Street. You can't hear anything but static. Someone should map those areas for dedicated AM radio sports fans."

Joe grinned. "I already did."

She sighed. "Why does that not surprise me?"

Sam piped up. "Can I go inside? I just got *Lego Star Wars* on my PlayStation. I'm already on the Battle of Takodana!"

Joe waved at the house. "Go on in. Take the left corridor, destroy everything you see. And watch out for Imperial Storm Troopers."

"Thanks, Dad!" Sam scampered away.

"Listen, Janie…could you take him tonight? I just got a couple of computer house calls. They pay cash and I could really use the money."

Jane looked at me. I shrugged. A solvent Joe Stiles was in everyone's best interest. "Well…"

"Otherwise he'll just be here eating cornflakes, and playing video games by himself all night."

"That's child abuse."

"My point exactly."

"I can't believe you let him play those games."

"I love that stuff. I spent two years working my way through all the *Ages of Myst*. Remember *Myst?*"

"How could I forget?"

"Ah, she just hates non-linear storytelling."

Joe looked like he expected some comeback from his ex-wife—this must have been a vintage argument, fermented to an intoxicating refinement of acrimony over many years. But Jane's mind was elsewhere. She touched my arm. "Remember that woman I pointed out to you last Christmas—when the kids were caroling at Sam Trikilis' house?"

"Uh…"

"My supposed look-alike? Marcia Stoddard?"

"Right, but she didn't really look like you."

"I know that! Because people don't pay attention. Still, I can't tell you how often people come up to me and say, 'Marcia, how's Ken?' or 'Marcia, so sorry to hear about the operation.' I have no idea who Ken is and I've never had an operation in my life! I still have my appendix. It's infuriating. She's so ugly."

"But you just said—people don't really notice things."

"People used to say you looked like Philip Seymour Hoffman."

"Before he got fat."

"And before he died. Did you like that?"

"No, but nobody likes being compared to anyone else, even if the other person is much better looking. Everyone thinks they're better looking than they are. Except you."

"I always told her that," said Joe. We touched fists. "For all the good it did."

"Anyway," Jane cut in, "the point is, Marcia Stoddard is the production designer for the Theater Lab. Or she was. I heard she quit. I don't know why."

"She wasn't happy," Joe said. "She had all the responsibility and none of the power, you know? She wanted the official title—production designer. And that useless prick wouldn't give it to her. Refn's like, 'These are my concepts!' whatever the hell that means. Just like the lighting. It was all about him. Which was hilarious, because that douchebag couldn't tell a gel string from a diffusion filter. His idea of a blacked-out mansion was some kind of blue LED luminaire that made everyone look embalmed. I mean, Jesus Christ, are you fucking kidding me?"

"So this Marcia Stoddard was angry."

"She was furious. I mean, she was…you should have heard the things she said she wanted to do to that fucking guy. She'd get drunk at the White Dog and just go wild."

"Did that include stuffing him in his own meat freezer?"

"I'm not sure she mentioned that idea."

"It's just talk, Joe." I put in. "The people who actually commit crimes don't talk about them. That's how you know the *Bad to the Bone* guy isn't really bad to the bone. He's just singing about it. If he were really bad to the bone, he'd be kicking the crap out of someone because they looked at him funny."

"I guess."

"Except for one thing," Jane said quietly. "Marcia Stoddard was seen running way from Refn's house a few minutes after he got killed. It had to be her. She's my look-alike, Henry. Someone mistook her for me."

I called in to the station and asked Haden Krakauer to pull Marcia's address. She had rented a cottage in Codfish Park for years, a five-minute walk from the house where my ex-wife was living with her fiancé, Joe Arbogast.

It occurred to me that I could pick up the kids while I was out there, and trade nights with Miranda, which would give Jane and me a free night tomorrow. These ad-hoc custody arrangements needed fixing, anyway. The way it stood, Jane and I had one night alone every week, without either Sam or my kids at the house. We hadn't gotten around to reorganizing the schedule, and it was based on extinct priorities. I had Tim and Caroline on Monday nights because of Miranda's yoga class, which she hadn't attended in years; she took them on Wednesdays because I had taken a midweek night shift when we first got to the island. Today's simple exchange, if it became permanent, would give Jane and me an extra night alone together every week. It was worth a try.

I called Miranda on the way out to the east end of the island and she was happy to get rid of "The Bickersons" as she called them, referencing one of her grandmother's favorite radio shows, featuring relentless verbal warfare between a combative married couple played by Don Ameche and Frances Langford. My kids made them look like the Coach and Tami Taylor on *Friday Night Lights*.

It made me think of something our genial divorce lawyer, Moe Rinaldi, had told us when we were arguing over custody. "In two years, you'll be fighting over who *doesn't* have to take the kids." Miranda was outraged at the idea. Moe said, "This is your first divorce, honey. It's my four hundred and sixty-third." And Moe was right, though it would be cruel and—more to the point—futile pointing that out to Miranda, who was basically incapable of admitting she was wrong on any subject.

Years before, during a bizarrely memorable homework session, she had denied that "pterodactyl" was spelled with a "p". Following our sensible family rule "Don't Argue Over Facts," Tim looked up the word in the dictionary—first under "T", out of deference to his mother. When he finally found the word in its proper place, Miranda shifted without missing a beat to "Obviously it starts with a 'p'. Everyone knows that." I'd been reading the kids *1984* at night and Tim whispered, "We are at war with Eurasia, we've always been at war with Eurasia." Caroline giggled. I shot him a murderous look, but, luckily, Miranda missed the reference. Her reading in those days was limited to biographies, fashion magazines, and Diana Gabaldon.

Given all that, it was unlikely that she'd be willing to confess that she and Joe enjoyed their nights off as much as Jane and I did. Anyway, Miranda was stuck with the kids for a little longer. I was determined to see Marcia Stoddard before I picked them up.

Marcia's little cottage, steps away from the beach, was a rare and precious year-round rental, but she was obviously preparing to abandon it. Marked moving boxes ("Linens," "Dishes," "Sketchbooks") crowded the floor, presided over by empty bookshelves, windows without curtains, and pale squares on the walls where her pictures had been hanging, probably for years. Paint fades slowly, especially in a dark little shack in the shade of the 'Sconset bluff.

The door was open, but I knocked as I stepped inside. "Hello?"

Marcia glanced up from a box. She held an aluminum saucepan in her hand. She wore paint-spattered khaki shorts and a horizontally striped "French" t-shirt—one of Jane's favorite outfits. No ballcap today and the frizzy hair was another point of similarity. Slim, five-four or so, curly hair—was that all it took to trick the inattentive eye? Apparently.

"Hi, Chief."

"Going somewhere?"

"My parents left me a little house in Rhode Island, outside Providence. It's not much bigger than this but it's not like I have a family. So…"

"Can we talk for a minute?"

She set the pan in the box and stood. "Would you like a coffee? I've got nothing here but we could walk over to the mark-up."

"The mark-up?"

"It's what locals call the 'Sconset Market. A term of endearment. A family tease. We would band together and soundly thrash any tourist who called it that!"

"Me and my brother against the world."

She smiled. "Exactly. Come on, let's go. I need to get out of this house for a few minutes."

As we approached the old town pump in its little square off

Shell Street, I said. "I have to ask…what were you doing near Horst Refn's house this afternoon?"

"He had offered me a going away present. Can you imagine that? When Harry Bowman left, he got a NTL mug. Thanks so much for twenty years and more than two hundred shows as TD—don't let the door hit your ass on the way out."

"TD?"

"Harry was the technical director. He built the sets, in the old days when the Lab cared about sets. He had just gotten divorced and he wanted his kids with him for the summer. All he wanted was housing for them. Instead, they took away his own housing and he wound up quitting. The lesson was pretty clear—don't stick your head up, don't ask for anything. Don't give them a reason to notice you. Just go along, doing all the work for slave wages and be happy you have a job."

"But you didn't learn the lesson."

"No." We walked along. "I could have run the Theater Lab, you know," she said suddenly. "I could have. I've been part of the place for thirty years. I don't care. I'm out of here. I'm gone."

The market looked busy, with cars in all the slots in front and facing the little park, and people hovering around the bulletin board in tennis clothes. All the activity made Marcia flinch. "Do you mind if we just keep walking for a while? I'm hating people right now."

We skirted the rotary and strolled downhill to the beach, under the pedestrian bridge. "I wanted more money and a little recognition after a decade of eighty-hour weeks. The money was just a token. I live pretty simply. But I wanted the title. They promised me. Then they said no. The Theater Lab is like an abusive boyfriend, Chief Kennis. You keep thinking they're going to change, but they never do. Finally, you just have to leave."

"For some reason I'm thinking about *The Burning Bed*. Did you ever see that old movie?"

"I read the book. Faith McNulty. Wonderful writer. She was

on staff at the *New Yorker* for many years. She wrote children's wildlife books. One was called *When I Lived with Bats*—that's a much more appropriate title for my time at the Theater Lab. At least, since Refn showed up. You know, I remember at the time, so many of us old-timers kept asking how did this even happen? Where did he come from? How did he wind up in charge? It's so crazy. I've been with NTL since it started. Harry, too.

"Barton Anderwald was like a father to me. I applied for the Artistic Director job three times. I never even got an interview! No, they'd rather do one of their 'nationwide searches' and turn up a creep like Refn. Heaven forbid they should ask a local. No, it always has to be someone from around the point. From away. From anywhere but here. But nothing good ever comes from around the point, Chief. That's what I've learned.

"They keep looking, though—and this is what they get. Junk plays and low attendance and running in the red. And now they have sleaze and scandal and murder to deal with. It serves them right. I'd say I was feeling *schadenfreude*, but there's no *schaden*, only the *freude*. I hope this murder brings the whole crummy corporate mess down around their ears and we can start all over again and build ourselves a real community theater." She shrugged. "Fat chance. The talk when they hired Refn was they wanted someone cool and hip to revitalize the Lab. With old Neil Simon chestnuts and a production of *Jersey Boys*? Seriously? It's pathetic."

"So…you despised him. But you didn't kill him."

"Of course not."

"And you never threatened to kill him."

"No."

"And you never said 'Don't attack the king unless you know you can kill him.'"

"Who told you I said that?"

I shrugged. "Just a rumor."

"It's a figure of speech. I meant if you try to get Refn fired and fail, you're worse off than before. Obviously. But I mean... killing people? That's crazy." We started up the steep hill to Front Street. "Do you believe me?"

"For now. But I'm going to have to ask you to stay on island for a while."

"I have boat reservations."

"Change them."

"You think I'm running away from a murder charge?"

"Let me clear this case. Then you'll just be running away."

"Until then, I'm...what do you call it? A person of interest."

I smiled. "I imagine you've always been a person of interest."

"Well, thank you for that. I try not to be boring. But it's hard when you spend most of the day feeling sorry for yourself."

"Go home. Unpack. With Refn gone, things will be different at the Theater Lab. There might even be a place for you there again."

She pressed her lips together. It wasn't quite a smile. "Another motive."

"Everyone I've talked to has a motive. Suspects and motives—they're everywhere, like ticks in the moors."

"Don't get bitten, Chief. Not everyone involved with this business is as harmless as I am...if you really are convinced about me."

I was. But I hadn't read her letter yet.

It was waiting for me at the station—my senior detective Charlie Boyce had found it in one of Refn's desk drawers when he was working the crime scene. Lonnie Fraker's Staties had stayed on the obvious path of the perpetrator, from the front door down into the basement, every inch of which they were studying like archaeologists at a dig site. They had all the bells and whistles a hefty state budget could offer, from the Omnichrome blue light filter cameras that revealed subcutaneous bruising to the new Faro 3-D laser scanning system that captured the whole crime scene in perfectly rendered three-dimensional images.

I preferred the old school low-tech version of police work, and encouraged my men to poke around and follow their hunches. Charlie's curiosity had led him to Refn's home office, and his desk drawers, which the victim had left unlocked and accessible.

He found the letter and texted me:

> M. Stoddard murder threat on paper.
> evidence on your desk this pm. C

I thought briefly about swinging by the station on the way home—of course it wasn't actually on the way home—but Miranda's voice in my head stopped me. "You upend everyone's night to take the kids and then spend the whole time doing police work? I guess nothing ever changes." Her theory of "false urgency" in law enforcement had always irked me during our marriage, but now that there was no catastrophic power shift in losing the argument, I could admit that she, most of the time, had a point. Whatever evidence Charlie had found wasn't going anywhere tonight, and neither was Marcia Stoddard.

Besides, my son had some interesting evidence of his own to share. We had enrolled him in the NTL summer theater camp, a cunning racket whereby parents paid for their kids to rehearse and appear in a minor musical production (*Newsies*, in this case) for which the theater charged top dollar…to the same parents, along with assorted family members. With more than twenty parts for kids and none of the usual Actor's Equity ringers from New York to pay, the summer show was both a juggernaut money machine and a genuine "Let's put on our own show" community theater experience. It was hard to argue with that. And we didn't. Both our kids, along with most of their friends, were involved, either on stage or behind the scenes. I liked it because it got them working together and off their phones for a few hours a day.

Tim had enlisted as a desperation move, so he could spend more time with his fickle girlfriend Debbie Garrison, and wound up working the light board under the tutelage of Jane's ex-husband. That put him backstage and privy to some sinister-sounding private moments. For instance, that very morning he had witnessed another flare-up between Sebastian Cruz and Refn. Cruz had stopped by the church to pick up the copies of his play, *Fundamental Attribution Error*, which he had given to Refn when he thought NTL was going to produce it.

"That's the title?" I asked.

"I guess."

"It means assuming you're special because you're rich," Carrie piped up.

"So…"

"Or thinking some inner city kid got bad grades because he's dumb, not because his school is falling down and there's no chalk and they stopped serving the one decent meal a day the kid ever got."

"And Sebastian wrote a play about this?"

"He wrote a play about Nantucket! And all the entitled smug awful people here."

"Like the ones who support NTL."

"Totally!"

"And imagine them not wanting to put it on."

"You have to speak truth to power, Dad."

"Refn obviously didn't feel that way. And speaking truth to money is a little more difficult, especially around here."

"That's basically what Hector's dad said to Mr. Refn," Tim said. "Along with how bad this *Who Dun It* show was, and then Mr. Refn said they'd probably be taking it to Broadway in the fall, or anyway off-Broadway. And Mr. Cruz said—" Tim laughed.

"What? "

"He said…'How far "off-Broadway" can you be and still call it that? The basement of a homeless shelter on Staten Island?' And then he said, 'I'd kill you but no one would know the difference.' And Refn said, 'Talk, talk, talk—you're all talk and no action, just like your plays.' I guess they've been arguing a lot."

"Wow. So what did—?" I stopped short, finally realizing the obvious.

"Dad? Hello?"

"Sorry."

"You just thought of something."

"No, I—"

"Was it about Hector's dad?"

Think fast. "No, no…it was about—I was thinking I wanted to take a look at the play they actually are doing—*Who Dun It*. I saw a picture of the writer and Mark Toland on the cover of *N Magazine* last week. I should talk to them both."

Since he had last been on-island, and briefly a person of interest in an arson case, Mark Toland had released what looked like was going to be the first of a "tent-pole" series of block-buster summer movies. Based on a Young Adult trilogy titled *Acid Reign* and retitled *Smog Mutants* for international movie markets, the film, set in the required dystopian future, presented a segmented America where all industrial production and the requisite pollution were isolated under a giant dome that strad-dled several fly-over states. The work was done by slaves who had been genetically engineered, or perhaps simply evolved, to safely breathe tainted air and drink tainted water. The teenaged hero and heroine, Trall and Trayla, escape and find that they have superhuman physical abilities and exponentially increased mental acuity when they finally breathe fresh air. They become curiosities and briefly celebrities before going back home to organize the revolution that takes up the second installment.

The books were fun. Jane introduced me to them. I loved the evocative first sentence: "The sky was on fire again, all last night." The movie was surprisingly good, too, and my kids were obsessed with it. Mark Toland, a youthful-looking fortyish clotheshorse, was clever and candid and good-looking enough to become a minor star in his own right.

That explained Carrie's mouth-open, wide-eyed stare—a

human shock emoji. "Oh, my God, you're going to meet Mark Toland?"

"I almost arrested him last year. Jane's known him since they were kids."

"I can't believe this."

"It gets better. You could have met him last summer. He was right under your nose for weeks! But you had no idea who he was. The only movie he'd made at that point was a lost-love romance called *Turns in the Wauwinet Road*. He was here scouting locations for a sequel." And thinking seriously about making his girl-who-got-away fantasy come true with Mike Henderson's wife, Cindy. But that was nobody's business—not even mine. A small-town cop keeps a lot of secrets.

I needed one more conversational pivot. "We have to hit Stop & Shop on the way home. Who's up for a round of Grocery Gumshoes?"

The kids loved that game—studying the purchases of the customers ahead of and behind us and extrapolating the details of their lives by the food on the conveyor belt.

We pulled into the newly expanded (but still inadequate) parking lot of the big store (the most profitable one on the whole East Coast, supposedly), my ominous silence long forgotten. But the questions remained: according to Tim, Cruz had been squabbling with Refn while the cockfight was going on two miles away. An hour later Refn was dead. So who had we arrested at the cockfight? And, more importantly, where was Hector's father when Refn was being killed?

As of this moment, Sebastian Cruz had no alibi for the crime.

Chapter Three

Misdemeanors

The case was stalking me—into the car with my kids, even into the grocery. I half expected someone to confess in the dairy aisle. In fact, I saw Charlie Boyce and his wife, Sandy, picking over the broccolini, but I gave him a warning squint when he started walking toward me. I shook my head; he nodded. No police business in the produce section. I had to enforce the same rule on myself when I saw Mike Henderson picking up a loaf of Pain D'Avignon bread from the bakery's rack at the other side of the store. I noticed a couple of Theater Lab board members and visiting film director Mark Toland wandering the over-lit food lanes, chatting on cell phones, comparing pasta sauces. The Stop & Shop had always been an exhausting social club, but today I saw suspects everywhere and every one of them looked guilty.

I was glad for the distraction of our little detective game. There were three people ahead of us in the check-out line. The kids examined the first load—a guy buying hamburger and tofu, kale and frozen French fries. "A vegetarian!" Carrie said. "And he's having a meat-eater over for dinner."

"Not necessarily," Tim said.

"A new container of ketchup? What are the odds?"

"Nice catch,' I said.

The next shopper was a harried-looking woman with a pile of Lean Cuisine frozen dinners, diet soda, packaged greens, sugarless ice cream bars—and potato chips, sugar-frosted flakes, juice boxes, and lunch meat.

"Single mom," Tim said. "On a diet. Looks like she has the kids tonight."

The last customer before us was a middle-aged man wearing a gray suit a little too warm for the weather. He had a box of store-made fried chicken, a package of pre-cooked barbecued ribs, and a box of Entenmann's chocolate donuts along with the usual staples of milk, bread, eggs, shell noodles and sauce, bananas, and bagged lettuce.

"Single guy?" Tim ventured.

Caroline studied the items as they moved toward the register. "Nope. Married guy. His wife is out of town for the week and he's getting to eat all his favorite foods." She turned to me. "It looks like the kind of shopping you used to do when Mom went away."

The guy turned with a sheepish look. "Good guess, kid."

"Be sure you clean up the fried chicken crumbs," I said. "They were my downfall."

Back in the car heading home, I asked Tim about his sometime girlfriend Debbie Garrison. I hadn't heard much about her lately, despite their working on *Newsies* together.

He studied the oncoming traffic. "She's okay."

Carrie jumped in. "She thinks he's a wimp because he's afraid to go surfing."

"Shut up."

"He took a bad wipeout and now he's scared of the ocean. Plus sharks."

"There are sharks! There's tons of sharks! There was one in Welfleet Harbor. I saw the video on YouTube."

"And there's this boy, Brandon-something—"

"Brandon Colter."

"Billy Delavane met him last winter in Costa Rica and invited him to Nantucket for the summer. He wants to go pro. Like—travel around for all the contests and get sponsors and stuff."

"He's a moron," Tim said.

"I think he's cute."

I remembered: "Billy mentioned him. Apparently the kid is disappointed in the waves. He should be gone soon. That's what Billy told me. He may come back in the fall for hurricane season but he wore out his welcome with Billy pretty fast. Billy hates 'wave snobs'—he'll surf anything. And the kid was a rotten houseguest—lots of twenty-minute showers, wet laundry everywhere, bad music, skunk weed, fender-benders. And that kid can eat."

"It doesn't matter," Tim said. "They can still stay in touch. They Snapchat all the time. He even sexted her."

Carrie bunched her mouth like she'd just bitten into a mealy peach. "Ugh, gross."

"Really? Well, Hector sexted you."

"He did not!"

"Somebody did."

"It wasn't Hector."

"It came from his phone!"

"Somebody stole it."

"Are you kidding?"

"It's true! He told me."

"Wait a second," I said. "Someone sexted you?"

"It was Snapchat—it's gone."

"That is so not true," Tim said. "There's a million ways to retrieve Snapchat pictures. Everyone knows that."

I pulled over across from the old red brick mansion built by Jared Coffin in 1829, and abandoned for the Jared Coffin House, now a storied hotel at the top of Broad Street, supposedly because his wife hated the ten-minute walk into town.

I twisted around to face the kids in the backseat. "So you really believe Hector, that he didn't do it?"

"I know he didn't," Carrie said. "It's just not the kind of thing—he would never…"

"Maybe someone wants to break them up," Tim offered. "I mean…Carrie's like the biggest prude ever, she totally dropped Cathy Hannock when she started smoking weed, and everybody knows she's the world's biggest fancy-Nancy—"

"The world's biggest what?"

"You know…she has to be better than everyone else, and—"

"I do not!"

"Fancy Nancy?"

"It's just something kids say."

"Yeah—in 1906."

"They say it now, Dad. Sorry."

"No, no I like it. Anyway…a sext would break up Carrie and Hector. So…you have to ask—who wants that to happen?"

Carrie sat forward. "You have to figure it out, Dad. You're the detective."

"You can do it," Tim said. "You're awesome."

"But you can't tell anyone about it or you'll get Hector in trouble."

"You could get in trouble, too," I pointed out. "I'll have to check, but I believe it's illegal even to have the picture on your phone if you're underage. The State of Massachusetts considers it child pornography."

"But I'm a child! So is Hector!"

"I never thought I'd hear you make that claim. Usually, it's 'I'm not a child any more.'"

"Well…it's—I'm not! I mean, in a lot of ways, but…I'm not some…some smut monger because I got a private picture on Snapchat!"

I started to laugh—smut monger? But I clamped it down. "I'll check this out."

"You promise?"

"Absolutely. We'll get to the bottom of it—discreetly."

"Thanks, Dad."

I pulled out into the street and started the zigzag from Summer Street to Pine to Darling that took us home. I felt a craven parental relief that Carrie hadn't offered the obvious defense—that she knew the picture was false from firsthand experience. She really was a fancy-Nancy, thank God—and she'd finally stopped being friends with that creep Cathy Hannock! So it wasn't all bad news. Still, solving the mystery without making things worse for everyone was going to be a challenge.

And it would have to wait. Back at home, Jane had her own investigation going on, and it connected to my murder case, though you'd never have guessed that from the way it began.

Early in May, she had been cleaning up her grandmother's grave in the Catholic cemetery. The small decorative juniper tree, planted twenty years before, had grown into an unruly dome of green, spreading beyond the Stiles plot, which itself was starting to sink because her family had been too cheap to lay a cement foundation for the grave. The work was mostly pruning and landscaping, with numerous trips to the dump, hauling branches. I had helped with some of the heavy lifting, regaled by stories of her family history on the island.

Her grandmother had wanted to be buried in the Protestant cemetery across the road, and compromised with a plot close to the fenceline so she could look over and chat with her friends.

On this particular day Jane noticed something odd. The earth around the nearby Tarrant plot had been disturbed. At first she thought the ground crews had just roto-tilled the area before re-sodding it. But that work had to be paid for by the families, and the Tarrants were notoriously cheap, even for Nantucket. Also the earth was dense clay, not the loamy topsoil a roto-tiller would churn up. Someone had excavated Dorothy Tarrant's grave. But why? Someone knew the answer, or rather two people did: she found a used condom near the Folger family burial plot, ten yards or so away and up a slight rise in the ground: ringside seats for the crime.

"Busy night at the Catholic cemetery," I said.

Jane nodded. "I didn't think anything about it until a couple of days later, when I stopped by Becky Harper's store. Just browsing, I can't afford her prices. But it was a slow afternoon. We were chatting about various things. Some rich guy had come in and ordered a hundred and twenty miniature gold lightship baskets for a wedding, but he wanted them in two weeks, so that was never going to happen. They sell for around two hundred dollars apiece, so it would have been a twenty-thousand-dollar sale and he offered to pay double. Forty thousand dollars for wedding favors! But she couldn't make this man grasp the fact she actually had to *make the things*, one at a time, weaving little gold threads. He stalked out of the store. He was furious. Becky had to laugh—all in a day's work on crazy island. Anyway…she also mentioned the ring."

"A Tarrant family heirloom?" I guessed.

"Don't wreck my story!"

"Yeah, Dad," Carrie scolded. "Don't wreck her story."

"Sorry."

"It had a lapis lazuli stone. Becky's mother had worked on it years before, and Becky helped repair it as part of her apprenticeship. The prong had warped, the stone was coming loose and they replaced the whole setting with platinum. Twenty years later, Otto Didrickson comes in wanting to sell it."

"Did she ask how he got it?"

"Yeah. He told her he bought it at one of Raphael Osona's estate auctions, back in the nineties. He wanted it for an engagement ring but the woman dumped him. That was the story. He always hoped she might change her mind, but she finally died and he had to give up the dream."

"Otto's a good storyteller."

"Well, it's his job, when you think about it."

For years Otto Didrikson had led "Ghost Tours" of Nantucket haunted houses, spinning yarns and inventing uncanny supernatural incidents as he led packs of tourists through the winding streets of the town. He had speakers set up in one abandoned pile where supposedly the "whistling carpenter" had lived, and he could key a suitably spooky recording from a remote in his pocket. He had shills he paid to faint at the sight of ghosts who only revealed themselves to "the chosen."

In his most audacious coup Didrikson took the crowd into the kitchen of a crumbling mansion on Main Street and left them there to "feel the vibrations." After a few minutes the lady of the house stormed downstairs, cursing and yelling, "Get out of my kitchen! This is trespassing. I've told Otto a million times! He can't just bring people in here willy-nilly! This is my home! I'm calling the police! I'll have you all arrested! Get out! Before I start swinging my rolling pin!"

When the cowed and humiliated tourists found Otto in the street and told him what happened, he blanched and said, "Oh, my God. You saw Mrs. Starbuck. She's been dead for twenty years!" It gave the credulous an authentic chill down the spine until word got out and he had to change his act.

His explanation about the Tarrant family ring—unrequited passion foreclosed by death—sounded exactly like his kind of tall tale. Apparently the NSA can now identify anonymous bloggers without tracking servers, tracing URLs or struggling with elaborate encryptions. Instead, they analyze prose styles, and a writer's habitual sentence construction and word choices give them away every time. I suspect the same is true of narrative, generally: Otto's brand of morbid melodrama was as definitive as a fingerprint.

"Did she buy the ring?"

"No. She felt weird about it. She told him to put it back into one of Osona's auctions. He didn't like that much. "Everyone walks out of here in a huff,' she told me. 'What am I doing wrong?' I said, 'Nothing a sweatshop full of gold-basket-makers in the basement and a willingness to traffic in stolen jewelry wouldn't fix.' She gave me a hug, closed up the store and bought me a latte. But I just couldn't let it end there."

I smiled. "Of course not."

"Maddie Clark wouldn't."

"She is fictional," I pointed out.

"Maybe to you."

"Okay, so you investigated it. What was your first step?"

"I checked with Rafael, went through all his records. He put everything onto a hard drive a few years ago, so it didn't even take that long."

"No record of the sale?"

"Nope. Plus he didn't remember it and neither did Gail, and they remember everything. I saw him at a yard sale one time, he was holding a sterling silver butter knife, practically dancing in place, saying, 'It's the missing piece from the Jepson Tiffany service!' He was talking about a lot he sold *fifteen years ago*. He'd had to let it go cheap because it was incomplete. Drove him crazy. So he bought the knife and sent it to the people as a gift—he remembered them, too. "

I recalled the incident of a silver porringer a few years back. Jane was right. "So Otto's a grave-robber."

She nodded. "And Rafael did what Becky suggested. He put the ring up for sale at his last auction."

I watched her attentively, my face studiously blank. I knew this part of the story. But I didn't want Jane to find out, at least not yet. She went on: "The ring sold after a bidding war. My old pal Mark Toland bought it. But the ring found its way home anyway. He gave it back to the Tarrant sisters. Whoever he was proposing to must have said no. And I have a pretty good idea who that was."

So did I. So did most of the island, I was willing to bet.

"The Tarrant sisters. I've heard of them. They live in a falling-down old house in Quaise. One's a shut-in and the other walks around town all the time, talking to herself."

"She should get a Bluetooth unit,' Carrie offered. "She wouldn't even have to hook it up. People would think she was on the phone like everyone else."

Jane laughed. "That's a pretty good idea. Anyway, they may sound crazy but they're not. They're just a little peculiar. I talked to Mark. When Otto showed up, Edith called Rafael and checked the provenance of the sale. She put two and two together, wanted to call the police and have Otto arrested. 'He desecrated my grandmother's grave!' She was furious. But Paula talked her down. She was thrilled to have the ring back; she hated the fact that they buried it in the first place.

"The fact is, they've known Otto since he was a baby. 'He's never been right but he's never been bad,' that's the way Paula put it. He helps out at the food pantry and coaches Little League, and reads to the old people at the Salt Marsh Center. But he's always short of money and it turns out he's hooked on some kind of painkiller. So they got him into a treatment program at the hospital, and all is forgiven.

"I see Paula's point, by the way. It's a gorgeous ring. It deserves to be out in the world, and part of someone's life. It was a lovely gesture…Mark giving it back to them."

"Yeah."

"People can change. I never really believed that, but maybe it's true."

We were drifting a little, but I had a knack for grasping the thread of a conversation and returning hand over hand to the point, through all the tangles of digression. "So you went back to Prospect Hill? The condom meant someone had seen Otto at work."

"Right."

"So did you fingerprint it?"

"Dad!" Carrie said.

"Ugh, no. How would I do that anyway?"

"Haden would have helped you out."

"Maybe, but it was gone when I got back."

I pounced: "So you looked for it."

She shrugged. "Kind of."

Carrie said "This is gross."

Tim piped up: "I think it's cool. Can you get fingerprints off rubber?"

"With the right equipment. But we're getting off topic here." I turned back to Jane. "So what was your next move?"

"I canvassed the neighborhood, just like a good cop."

"And nobody saw anything or heard anything, most of them didn't want to talk to you, and a good percent took off out the back door when they saw you pull up. Plus dog bites."

"Speaking from experience there, Chief?"

"I advise plainclothes and a can of mace."

"Well, I don't live in a big dangerous city like Los Angeles and neither does Maddie Clark. So the whole tone of the investigation was completely different. For one thing, I know most of the people who live out on Milk Street Extension, Hummock Pond Road and Mt. Vernon Street. The Praegers are off-island, Louise Crawford is in bed by ten every night, and old Bob Barnett has arthritis in both knees. He wouldn't be poking around the Prospect Hill Cemetery at night."

"Sounds like you were done before you started."

"Except for Frieda Bissinger. She was one of my mom's best friends. She looks right over the graveyard and calls her house 'High Spirits.' She's an insomniac and her old lab has bladder problems. She walks him a couple of times a night."

I frowned. "If she heard something, wouldn't she call the police?"

"She doesn't like the police. She grows a little weed in her backyard." She put her hand to her mouth. "You didn't hear that."

"Didn't hear what?"

"Thanks."

"So, what did she say?"

"Well, that's where it gets interesting. She didn't see anyone digging up Dot's grave—Dorothy Tarrant, sorry…But she heard the lovers going at it, loud and clear. The woman called out a name—several times."

I grinned. "Horst!"

"You're pretty good at this. You could even do it for a living."

"Horst Refn."

"I hear he's quite the ladies' man."

I put the rest of it together. "No one said a word to the police, which means Refn turned down the chance to be a town hero. Why? He had to be blackmailing Otto Didrickson, too."

"Otto had to sell the ring to pay off Refn. He'd burned his savings on Vicodin. He was desperate. Little did he know he'd be off the hook in a week."

"He should have waited."

Jane narrowed her eyes. "Maybe he didn't."

"Whose side are you on?"

"I'm just trying to find the truth, Chief."

Carrie stood and delivered her verdict. "You both have extremely devious minds. But luckily you found jobs where that's a good thing."

We dropped the subject after that. I had other concerns.

Perhaps it was my devious nature, or a peerless attention to detail and a cold, insectile thoroughness—my own explanation… but I couldn't shake the feeling that we'd all missed something at the murder scene. My eye had snagged on some irksome little detail, caught like a blackberry thorn in my sock. It hadn't even started to bother me until the middle of the night, and when I stopped by Refn's house on my way to the station the next morning I didn't really know what I was looking for.

I didn't try to figure it out in advance—the mind plays tricks that way. I just slipped under the yellow police tape, let myself in the front door and stood still, looking around.

A short hallway leading into an open plan living room/kitchen, stairs mounting to the second floor on the left. Two spindles per tread, lathe-turned, stained to match the oak railing, ugly red-and-brown floral runner flowing down the middle of the steps, tacked to the risers with a series of brass clips. No dents, chips, smudges. No sign of struggle. Everything looked freshly painted, in the same earth tones, coffee-colored walls showing a faint sheen and on the trim, "cottage red," an HDC-approved color, usually seen on house exteriors. The effect was dark and funereal.

I remembered that Mike Henderson had painted the place a few months ago, through Cindy's theater connections. He had laughed about the ugly colors when I ran into him at Fast Forward, sipping coffee in the parking lot: "It's hilarious. How to knock a hundred thousand dollars off the price of a house with a five thousand-dollar paint job."

I stood, barely breathing, as if I expected some visitation from the spirit world. The shade of Horst Refn, perhaps, touching my shoulder. Otto would have been pleased. But I wasn't interested in ghosts. I was looking for pattern-disruption. Crime took a physical toll on the environment, beyond the evidence you can pick up from UV light or fluorescein, fingerprint analysis, or gunshot-residue testing. People managed to solve murders in the days before this technology, and even my forensics professor at the Academy had his misgivings about our brave new world of scientific crime scene investigation: "All these gadgets make people lazy." It was true across the board. How many people remembered a phone number anymore? Everything's stored in your phone, and God help you if you lose it.

So I was probing for the signs an observant eye could catch unaided. In fact I had noticed something the day before—that little bramble spike—but what was it? Something about the runner? The carpet leading deeper into the house showed the same pattern, burgundy and russet buds and leaves tangled in dark olive vines. I went down on my knees, pushed my fingers through the nap of the rug. Lonnie had said the intruder walked straight through the hall, into the kitchen, and down the basement stairs. His tech guys had ignored this part of the house.

I inched along the rug on my hands and knees, looking for what? Shell casings? A coin or receipt or loose key that might have fallen from a pocket when the perp pulled out a weapon?

A footprint, a scuff on the baseboard? But the place had been trampled by the State Police and the floor was clean.

I pushed to my feet in the living room. Big French doors leading out to the flagstone patio flooded the dark-painted room with morning light. The high-ceilinged chamber was calm and tidy, revealing no sign of violence or even human habitation. It held me still, like one of the bubbles in the faux antique windowpanes. I listened to the muted racket of lawnmowers and leaf blowers from various houses around the neighborhood, music from someone's radio. J. Feld again, telling us we'd just been listening to Mark Knopfler and EmmyLou Harris singing "Beachcombing," off their *All the Road Running* album. Good song. Good station—97.7, "True Island Radio." The slogan irked me. Where would mendacious island radio come from? Martha's Vineyard, no doubt.

I breathed in. The only smell was sun-warmed fabric and furniture polish. I checked my watch—eight-fifty. I liked to be at work by eight-thirty and I had a meeting scheduled with my detectives for nine. I hated people who showed up late, and I was turning myself into one of them. What was I doing here?

I had given up, had actually turned to leave, when I finally saw it.

A bloodstain had altered the pattern on the armchair next to the couch. One of the muddy scarlet berries was fractionally larger than the others. At first I thought—wine, ink, cranberry juice? I kneeled down for a closer look. I had seen a lot of bloodstains in my career, and there was no mistaking this one. A struggle had taken place in this room. Someone had ending up bleeding. Refn or the killer? A blood test might not give the whole answer, but it would be a start, and I needed one badly that morning.

I stopped by Monica Terwilliger's lab in the basement to drop off the pillow and took the stairs to the second-floor conference room two at a time. I was more than half an hour late, but no one seemed to care. They were all on their phones. Kyle Donelly was hunting for fantasy football "sleepers," hoping to draft a backup who could become a regular starter and help get him to the play-offs. Charlie Boyce was burning data, watching YouTube surfing videos. Haden Krakauer was mooning over the Birdforum galleries, looking for photos of Tennessee warblers or Nankeen night herons, and Karen Gifford was catching up on her Instagram feeds.

I had a six-year-old Nokia flip-phone and I used it for phone calls. "Fun's over." I walked over to the Keurig. "Phones away."

After some grumbling and rustling and shifting in the seats, largely covered by the hiss and grumble of the coffeemaker, everyone had their folders in front of them and their pens in hand.

I sat down at the table. "What have we got?"

Chapter Four

Suspects

After a quick recap of the day's police business—a fender bender in the Stop & Shop parking lot, a kid saved from a fentanyl overdose by a shot of Narcan, and a break in at a retired judge's house where nothing was stolen, Charlie cleared his throat and addressed the murder.

"You know those cases where there's, like, two suspects and one of them has a great alibi and the other one signs a confession after fifteen minutes in the box?" Charlie asked.

I didn't like where he was going. "Yeah…?"

"Well, this case is the opposite of those cases."

"Okay."

"Tons of suspects, everybody has a motive, Nobody talking, no one confessing, nobody has an alibi. Maybe they all did it. Like in that Agatha Christie movie."

"It was a book first. Just for the record."

He nodded. "Right. A book."

"Nantucket's a small town," Haden said. "You piss off enough people, it complicates things for the constabulary."

"You mean us."

"Well—no. Just you, Chief. You're the boss. We're your minions. We do what we're told."

"I wish." We sat staring at each other. I glanced around at the others. "Okay—who wants to start?"

"I think you should read the letter," Kyle said. Nods of agreement around the table.

"It's in your folder," Haden added. "First sheet on the top."

"We can wait," Karen offered, with a helpful smile. She obviously wasn't finished with her Instagram contacts.

I pulled out the letter—two typed pages:

Dear Horst:

So the battle is over, and you won. I knew the first moment I saw you that an enemy had come into my life, and the life of the theater I love. I could see the future in a flash. The bold, experimental company that Howard Anderwald founded was going to become cheap and tawdry. The people with talent and vision would be pushed out, as you pushed out Tag Reemer, Joe Stiles, Harry Bowman—and me. I could see you making a beloved institution over in your own image, and the theater that gave us *Cabaret*, *Long Day's Journey into Night* and a new translation of *The Lower Depths* would eventually be reduced to Neil Simon revivals and cheeseball musicals like *Jersey Boys* and *Good Vibrations*.

I understand you, Horst. It wasn't because you disliked my work that you strived so hard to undermine me behind my back. Just the reverse. Because I had ideas and you didn't, because I was creative when you weren't, because I could work hard and you couldn't, my efforts made you feel bad. My talent proved your lack of it, my energy proved your sloth, my passion proved your indifference to everything but the trappings of success. I've kept an extensive record of the abusive way I was treated last season, which would make fascinating reading—in a boardroom or a courtroom, or the local newspaper.

Many more people than you can guess have said to me, "How can this self-important, lazy, inept two-faced huckster be running The Nantucket Theater Lab?" I think I know the answer. It started with Donald Harcourt and continued with Judith Barsch: the corporate take-over of our theater.

I almost laughed when you mentioned a nascent HR department. Our sometimes dysfunctional but always loving and
caring family has become a soulless corporate entity.

Ironically, much of your despicable behavior would be
considered unacceptable in today's corporate culture, if it
was made public. Sexually harassing the people you work
for is frowned upon these days. Sticking your hand up an
actress' dress—in front of numerous witnesses? That's the
kind of mistake that could cost you that absurdly overpaid
job. Lucky for you, the individual involved refused to press
charges. She didn't want to be connected to you by scandal.
I liked the way she put it—"You don't want to walk through
a leper colony. You don't know who's going to brush up
against you—or what will fall off later."

Lepers are afflicted, tragic victims of circumstance. You
have no one to blame but yourself. When I visited Howard
at the Island Home last week, he said, sadly, "I wish I had
died before I had to see this, what my island and my theater
and the whole country have come to." But Howard's death
would solve nothing. Yours is the death I pray for. May it
be slow and painful and cold. I know you hate the cold. I
like to think of you buried by an avalanche, suffocating and
freezing in the icy dark.

That's a comforting image.

I'll take it with me when I leave.

Sincerely,

Marcia Stoddard

I looked up from the page. "Holy shit."

Karen slipped her phone into her pocket. "I like the 'sincerely'."

"Freezing in the dark?" Haden added. "She came pretty close."

Kyle socked Charlie on the shoulder. "And you said we had
no confession."

"Well, technically…"

"He's right," I pointed out. "All we have is a hysterical letter
from an angry woman. Who weighs like a hundred and two
pounds. I don't see her forcing Refn into that freezer."

"Not alone," Haden said.

"So it's a conspiracy?"

"It sure could be. Refn pissed off a lot of people—not just Marcia Stoddard."

I set the letter aside as Haden started going through the list. "Right, so…first of all, there's Donald Harcourt and Joseph Little, both board members, both with grudges against the guy, one on the scene, the other one summoned him there, no alibi…but we ought to be looking at all the board members. There are six others who really make the decisions. Judith Barsch is the board president—we should touch base with her, in any case. She hasn't lived here long but she knows everyone, she hears all the gossip, she's up to her neck in all the nonprofit trench warfare. She'll want to weigh in on the case, and she may have some ideas of her own. The other board members…the names are in your folder. Talking to them is more or less of a formality, but this is a big blow for the Theater Lab, and a little small-town hand-holding would go a long way."

I nodded. "Right, good point. Do you have Harry Bowman on your list? Marcia Stoddard told me they fired him. Could be some bad blood there."

Charlie scribbled a note. "Thanks, Chief. I'll check him out. We also have Sebastian Cruz, who got into a couple of shouting matches with Refn. He has anger-management problems, couple of misdemeanor beefs, and an assault charge that got dropped over some tussles at the Chicken Box. Could be a political thing with him. His play is crazy—some over-educated immigrant guy just like him kidnaps all these rich Nantucket summer people, tortures and interrogates them. 'What have you done to deserve this wealth,' kind of thing. I could see him killing Refn just to advertise his play. No alibi, of course. The other writer is worth looking at, also—Blair Hollister? The Lab is doing his play *Who Dun It* this summer and he's here for the season."

I squinted down the table "That makes him a suspect?"

"It's a play about a murder, he shows up and a real live murder happens? You're the one who doesn't believe in coincidences, Chief. Besides…people who write about murder all the time… it's on their minds, it's normalized. It's a plot point. Take it one step further and there's no turning back."

"Somebody made that same point about Jane yesterday."

"Hey, listen, sorry! I'm not—I didn't mean—"

"Forget it, Charlie. We'll talk to him. I've already talked to Jane. Who else are we looking at?"

Charlie shuffled his papers. "There's Joe Stiles, fired for no reason, hated Refn and couldn't keep his mouth shut about it. Your friend Mike Henderson was in the neighborhood, someone swore they saw your girlfriend, but we're pretty sure it was Marcia Stoddard, and that crazy letter speaks for itself. Three interns say he harassed them sexually, let's see…Kelly Ramos, Terry Poole, Dana LeBreux, all blond, all cute, all of them together supposedly yesterday afternoon. But no one saw them. Kelly says she showed them her 'secret beach' in Squam. The whole point is no one ever goes there. You can have it to yourself even on the Fourth of July. It's true. The steep drop-off means no waves, and it's pebbly. Lots of seals in the water. Not a great beach. But private. Who else? Kelly is gay and her lover is kind of a prominent person around here. Jenny Feldman, you know her. Or you've heard her, anyway. She's the main DJ at ACK radio."

I drew a line through her name. "She was working yesterday afternoon. We heard her when we were driving over."

"Right. Well, that's a relief." He turned a page. "Next, we've got Fred Hamburger, the NTV guy. Says he was at home editing tape all day. Saw nobody, nobody saw him. Of course. So, he did some big promotional video about Refn and never got paid. He sued and won, but at the time of his death, Refn still hadn't paid him a dime. We have the usual public shouting matches and death threats. Refn really brought out the best in people."

He turned a page. "Onward. Next is Tag Reemer. He got

pushed out when they hired Refn and he's been seething about it ever since. No death threats or fistfights, but no alibi, either. He's been seen at the Island Home, visiting Barton Anderwald and Miriam Talbot. They started the organization; they wrote letters of protest at the time; made a ruckus at a few board meetings. You could have a conspiracy there. Reemer's acting career fizzled after he got sick and the MS diagnosis could give him a who-gives-a-shit attitude about murder. Same with Anderwald and Talbot. They're almost dead anyway, so there's that. Reemer says he took his boat out to Coatue yesterday. Of course no one saw him."

"Don't forget Otto Didrickson." I said. "It's possible Refn was blackmailing him." I explained the grave-robbing, sex-in-the-graveyard scenario, as Jane had laid it out for me. That earned a moment of silence.

"Speaking of blackmail," Kyle said, "we have to talk about the Kohls."

I heard a collective sigh, like the moment when everyone realizes that the last warrant article at Town Meeting is unexpectedly controversial and the debate might go on for another hour.

I blew out a tired breath. "Tell us."

"Howard Kohl is on the board. He used to act, but not since Refn took over. No, no, it's not that! I wish. Refn was having an affair with the wife—Bess Kohl, you know the type, professional trophy wife, Pilates and yoga, jogging with the Labradoodle, picking out new faucets for the guest bathroom at Housefitters. And sleeping with the Artistic Director, it turns out. He filmed the sex, and extorted her. She paid him a lot, but she eventually ran out of her own money. Refn confronted the husband, and then started pumping them both for a total of something like thirty thousand dollars, as of last week. They were terrified of the scandal. They cracked when I braced them. It was almost like they wanted to talk about it."

Karen nodded. "That could be the 'thirty racks' in Refn's

notebook."

Haden eyed her. "Thirty racks?"

"What notebook?' I asked.

Karen hitched her chair forward. "It's a moleskine, there were about twenty of them on his desk. Most of them had notes for productions, budget estimates, daily diaries. One recorded his food intake. He'd started on the paleo diet. One was all catalogue item numbers. I matched them up with the Nordstrom, Orvis, Neiman Marcus, and Williams Sonoma catalogues scattered around the house. He hadn't bought anything, as far as I could tell, but it added up to almost twelve thousand dollars' worth of aspirational retail porn. Pardon my language."

I shrugged. "Don't worry about it. I was married to a real estate agent."

"Anyway, the one that matters was tucked in there, kind of hiding in plain sight, using the other notebooks for camouflage. That's how it seemed to me, anyway."

"What did you find?"

"Well, so, there were these kind of nonsense words or phrases with notations next to them—two racks, three racks. One had two racks crossed out and replaced with three racks and that crossed out and replaced with four. My dad works for Citibank. He uses the term all the time—it's the packets of hundred-dollar bills, sealed into ten thousand-dollar bundles."

"What are the 'three rack' notations?"

"I have two of them. One says 'Amok halo.' The other one is 'Eat crab'."

Kyle blew out a breath. "Well, that's useful."

"No—they're anagrams," Haden said.

I was already working them. *Oklahoma* and *Cabaret.*"

Karen grinned. "Laurie and Sally!"

She was ahead of me. "What—?

"The female leads. That was his code. Laurie, from *Oklahoma.*"

And Sally Bowles, from *Cabaret.* That would be Sally Howe."

"How many racks had Sally paid him?"

"Just one."

Haden pounced. "Laurie Little!"

I nodded. "We have confirmation on that one." I filled them in on my conversation with Donald Harcourt—his suspicions, the sighting at Faregrounds, the fight at the fundraiser. I turned to Karen. "How many more names on that list?"

"Four."

"Christ, Refn was a busy boy."

"Yeah."

"Can I take a look?" She passed her list over to me and I saw what I was looking for right away: 'Spongy Beards.' *Porgy and Bess*…That would have to be Bess Kohl. And the Kohls had paid out three racks, thirty thousand dollars, just as they had described it to Kyle. Everything snapped together like Lego pieces. But what exactly were we building? I handed the sheet back to Karen. "Decrypt the other names. That will give us a total of six more suspects."

Charlie sighed. "Great."

Karen closed her folder. "Maybe it really was all of them. You know what I mean? All that psychic energy mounting up, like gas fumes in a closed garage. Then boom. Like Mao and Stalin. They both got mysteriously sick…Stalin basically died in bed. They say it was a stroke, but nobody knows. It could have been all those wounded angry bereaved people just hating him *so much*. That could kill you."

"But it couldn't stuff you into your own meat freezer," Haden pointed out. He despised what he referred to as woo-woo thinking—Ouija boards and astrology charts.

Karen shrugged. "I guess not."

I'd heard enough. "Okay, everyone, spread out, talk to these people. Bring them in if you have to. I want full reports, transcripts, and documentation on my desk ASAP. Meanwhile, let's get photographs of every suspect at every counter in the airport as well as the FBO/General Aviation terminal, the Steamship, the Hy-Line, with copies for the Harbormaster's Office and all the Boat Basin personnel. None of these people leave the island until we've cleared them."

"They're not going to like that," Karen said.

"All the more reason to sort this mess out quickly. So get moving."

Back in my office a few minutes later I paged through the file on Refn that Kyle had gotten from Nantucket Theater Lab—W-2 forms, performance evaluations, and his original application. I needed some contact information. I had to inform the next of kin.

Rudolf and Maria Refn, 2024 Woodland Avenue, Ojai, California. 805-632-9948. I poked in the digits and got a grating three-note electronic fanfare: the number had been disconnected. I checked the address: the house was for sale.

On a hunch I called the local police and talked to a detective named Ed Trank. "Yeah, they're gone," he told me. "Moved to Florida, that's what I heard. They just couldn't take it anymore."

"Take what?"

"Well, their son disappeared five years ago. Went for a drive and never came back. We never found the car, we never found the body. Guy just vanished off the face of the Earth. We figured he was running away from something. Dude was a vet, PTSD issues, hassles with the VA, couple of DUIs. Not a happy camper. I mean—living with your parents at forty? That's a red flag right there. Good riddance, far as I was concerned. But they wouldn't leave it alone. Hassled us constantly, put signs up everywhere, like the guy was a stray cat or something. They finally hired a detective, he nosed around for a while, but I guess he gave up. Or maybe they just ran out of money. A PI can run up a big tab fast. Anyway, they left. That's what I know. Check the listings in Florida."

They were living in Sarasota. Rudy picked up after the second ring. I explained who I was. "I have some bad news for you, sir. Your son passed away yesterday. I'm very sorry for your loss."

"You're wrong,"

"I'm—excuse me?"

"That's what the Ojai cops were trying to tell us. But we hired a detective and we tracked Horst down—we found our son! It wasn't even that hard to do, Chief Kennis. He was using his credit cards again. We got the billing address and wrote him but he never wrote back—or, at least not yet. Horst is his own man, he goes his own way. He'll get back in touch when he's ready. That's what Maria says, and I think she's right. He'll come home. He has our address here now. He knows he'll always be welcome."

I took a deep breath and let it out slowly. "I'm afraid that's not going to happen, sir. Horst was murdered here on Nantucket Island yesterday afternoon."

"It wasn't our son. There's been a mistake."

"I wish that were true, but—"

"I'll prove it. I'm sending you a picture right now. It's five years old, but it's him, people don't change that much. Wait. All right. Here it is. I'm texting it to you now."

"Mr. Refn, I really think we should just—"

My phone chimed. "There it is. Check your texts. Just look at the picture."

The resolution on my flip-phone wasn't great, but it didn't need to be. The Horst Refn in the family photograph was huge, red-haired with a prominent wart beside his nose and a prosthetic arm. He dwarfed the piano he was leaning against, and his crooked smile showed a full mouth of dentures. A scar from the IED that must have taken out his teeth ran up from his chin to his temple. He was attempting a smile, but that was a mistake.

I stared at the picture. I was absolutely speechless.

Rudy couldn't stand the silence. "Your murder victim—it's not our Horst, is it? Is it?"

"No, sir. It is not. I'm sorry I troubled you this morning."

"Don't be. This dead body of yours not being my son? That's the best news I've had in years."

"All right, then. Thanks for talking to me. You've been a huge help."

I hung up, cravenly eager to end the conversation before Rudy figured out that our corpse had been using their son's credit cards for the last five years. The real Horst Refn hadn't needed them because he was dead. Not disappeared, not AWOL, not in the Witness Protection program—dead. My murder victim had played the real Refn's family perfectly, after making sure the body was never found—allowing them the toxic kernel of hope that would keep them away from the police. They wanted to believe their son was alive and they still did. They had all the answers they needed. Not me.

All I had were questions.

They kicked up at me like highway slush from an eighteen-wheeler—my windshield smeared, the cleaner fluid tanks dry, the wipers working full tilt, but still losing the battle. I was driving blind. Time to find a rest area, pull over, and call it a night. But the questions kept spewing at me.

Who was the man who'd called himself Horst Refn? Why had he come to Nantucket? And more troubling—had someone followed him here? Where had they come from? Why had they killed him? And was he the only intended victim?

I set my elbows on my desk and rested my forehead on my palms. This was getting out of control. I thought of Marcia Stoddard, saying, "Nothing good ever comes around the point." Many people thought that included me, that I had brought the curse of big-city crime with me when I moved to Nantucket. I used to scoff at that idea.

But maybe they were right.

Part Two:
Who Dun It

Chapter Five

Conspirators

I pulled myself together, stood, and pocketed my phone. Maybe I was some kind of Typhoid Mary of urban crime and corruption. All the more reason to get the situation under control and set things right. That meant finding Refn's real identity.

I took the elevator to Monica Terwilliger's domain in the basement.

She literally danced across her lab when I knocked on the frosted glass door—two steps on tiptoe, a leap, and then another one where she scissored her calves together, landing in a perfect turnout with her hands reaching out, palm upward.

She grinned. "An entrechat, a jeté, finished off with a cabriole, Chief!" She took a modest bow. "I'm studying ballet!" I couldn't help thinking about *Fantasia*, and Ponchielli's Danza delle Ore from *La Gioconda*. Monica moved with startling poise and grace…but then so did Disney's Hyacinth. "It's just for exercise, but I love it."

"Looking good, Monica."

"You should try it."

"I'll stick to poetry. There's less chance of killing myself."

"Two left feet?"

"Two right feet, actually. Which is only a marginal improvement."

She half sat on one of the lab tables and allowed herself a couple of deep breaths. "So what brings you down here this morning?" I told her about Refn. "So you want me to run the fingerprints by IAFIS."

"That would be great."

"And you want the results ASAP."

"Well…"

I knew what she was going to say. The FBI's Automated Integrated Fingerprint Identification System was a miracle of modern technology—as long as your subject had a clean police record… and a set of prints in the system. No matches, no "human intervention"—that is, no actual person has to do any work. You can get those results back in a couple of days, depending on the number of requests working their way through the DOJ biometric database, navigating the complications of the M40 algorithm, with all its Galton points ridge extraction-analysis and matching protocols.

The delays come when the prints belong to an authentic criminal.

That's when actual people get involved. It seems odd, like visiting a big city newspaper and finding wizened old guys setting the type by hand. But there are still some things that computers can't do as well as people can. The DOJ technicians have to pull records and rap sheets, contact various police departments, talk to booking cops, detectives, district attorneys, prosecutors, court clerks, probation officers. So I was fully expecting the standard "delay notice" and the usual estimated time for a full response: "indefinite." The important thing was to set the process in motion.

I had plenty to do while I waited.

Top of the list: Paying a call on Joseph and Laura Gutterson Little.

I drove out of the station parking lot, and eased myself into the bumper-to-bumper traffic on Old South Road. I was pleased to note the tiny woman in the giant Chevy Tahoe ahead of me putting down her phone and buckling her seatbelt. I could feel her inventorying her parking tickets and moving violations as she leaned sideways, no doubt double-checking her glove compartment for her registration. At times it made me sad to strike such irrational terror into the hearts of the most powerful people in the country. Today it felt good.

I was calling on a couple of billionaires and I needed every advantage I could take. I cleared the rotary and headed down Lower Orange Street past the bustling hive of Marine Home Center, thinking—"take" advantage, how apt. You have to take it. No one's giving it away.

I skirted the bottom of town, edging the harbor, loving the clear light over the water, then along the "strip" at the bottom of Broad Street, past all the double-parked cars (people grabbing coffee and a muffin, or a sandwich for lunch) and the spill of Young's Bicycle shop kids in their bright yellow shirts demonstrating mopeds to the tourists. Next, the long straight stretch of road to Jetties Beach, past the clutter of mini-mansions built on what Jane told me had been marshland until the real estate boom of the eighties. I took the steep, narrow Cobblestone Lane up to Cliff Road. The cobbles were the same as they had always been, laid by Portuguese artisans in the nineteenth century, but someone had bought the property that climbed the hill beside the narrow street and turned it into a gaudy wonderland of stone walls, hedges, granite slab stairways, and massive new construction. It got me thinking about the rich people again. It's hard not to think about them during a Nantucket summer. This is their world and the sheer density of them as a population makes any extremity of affluence seem bizarrely mundane.

I remembered my father's lawyer in the old days, who contributed a pittance to his infirm mother's living expenses, but never cancelled a vacation or stinted on his wine cellar, and the billionaire Dalton father who left his struggling kids only a few sticks of furniture.

Nothing changed; it all felt the same here, today—Mike Henderson's wealthy customers who assumed everyone was trying to rob them, the rich divorcee I took up with when my own marriage ended, who stuffed cash in my pockets before we went to dinner so that no one would suspect she was paying the tab. The guilt, paranoia, and mendacity, predictable as a Nantucket parking ticket.

So, at some point I started to wonder—is this nature or nurture? Do the rich people learn this behavior from their parents? Or is it hardwired into the lizard brain of the human species? Is it a mental illness, or an atavistic hangover from the caveman days when an extra pelt hidden under a rock could mean the difference between life and death?

I knew this much—rich people needed to conceal the gulf that separated them from the rest of us. To admit their true status would be catastrophic. They'd have to cope with unbearable guilt or attempt unsustainable acts of reparation. They would be set upon by the jackals of the underclass and torn to pieces. Better to build walls and moats, live in gated communities, dress down, and only speak the truth to other members of the tribe.

Much of this is learned behavior. Jane's billionaire uncle, who made his brother-in-law split the tolls on the drive from New York to Connecticut, who called his party guests "freeloaders" because they were drinking his liquor, clearly learned his mean-spirited parsimony at a parent's knee. It might have been the same parent, in the same tight-fisted culture, that taught J. Paul Getty to install a pay phone in his house so that greedy guests wouldn't run up his phone bill.

So perhaps this stinginess is not inherent in the human psyche. I had always believed that—until I came into some money myself.

Actually, the story was even better. I only thought I was coming into the money—I never actually saw a dime. The true-crime book I wrote in Los Angeles was going to be a movie until the LAPD fired me and forced me to abandon it. The big deal fell through—most Hollywood deals fall through, except the drug deals. Still, for a few weeks there I saw a vision—the true prospect of a windfall. No more debt! No more overdraft fees. No more punishing eighty-hour workweeks.

Instead—travel, freedom, peace of mind.

And what was the first thing I thought of? How to hide my new fortune from my friends. How to protect it from my needy brother and my greedy in-laws. How to use it without giving myself away, what story I could concoct to explain a new car or a flat-screen TV? Small inheritance? DOJ auction? Scratch tickets?

I was behaving exactly like all the rich people I hated—and I was still broke! Just the thought of money had poisoned my mind and kick-started all the same bullshit I'd been denouncing for years.

That memory gave me an insight into Joe and Laura Little. It humanized them. I needed that, just as much as I needed their irrational fear of me, to conduct a useful interrogation. That's why I was both wearing my uniform this morning and remembering those brief few weeks when I thought I'd never have to wear it again. The gentleman poet! I had to smile—what a pretentious clown. But there was real value to my failure. It brought me to Nantucket, and taught me the single priceless lesson of my adult life—I love my work.

I love the hunt, I love the hidden fact that turns a case, the lie that doesn't quite add up, the true story in the shadow of the fake one. I love deciphering the hidden patterns of motive and decision, the hidden logic in the chaos of a crime scene. But mostly I love catching the criminals, outsmarting them, and, I might as well admit it, solving their puzzles, setting the world—my world, my tiny part of the bigger world—to rights.

And I was on my way to do that this morning, uniform and all. I climbed out of my cruiser, crossed the crushed-shell driveway and took the wide steps up to the columned front deck with my confidence refreshed. I was formulating my first questions as I rang the bell.

I heard steps from inside and the glossy forest-green six-panel front door swung inward revealing Laura Gutterson Little—a small, perfectly presented woman, from her short-cropped bottle-blond hair to her Botoxed and surgically tightened face to the pleated khaki pants, short-sleeved white blouse and expensive sandals. Her arms showed the evidence of hard daily workouts. A gym membership at Westmoor? Or a private trainer? Probably both. I guessed her age at just over forty. Her much larger husband, moon-faced and balding, loomed behind her. He wore tennis clothes purchased ten pounds and a couple of years ago, clearly headed out to the Yacht Club for a match.

"Mrs. Little—Mr. Little…thanks for agreeing to see me today. I know you're busy."

Laura stepped back, forcing her husband to move out of my way. "Don't be silly. You're the busy one. Please come in."

They led me into the living room—the Great Room, I'm sure they called it—with its spectacular view over the edge of the cliff to Nantucket Sound, blue and sparkling under the dome of the cloudless, early summer sky. I picked out a couple of sailboats, a windsurfer or two, and the ferry inching away in the distance toward Hyannis. The cool, dry house was silent except for the faint whisper of the climate-control system.

We sat down, them on the white silk couch, me on one of the facing white silk armchairs. Everything was pale, squared-off, impossibly clean. I hated to think what my kids and our dog would do to a house like this if they were turned loose in it. Questions teemed to mind: how to vacuum the sand out of the Berber rug, how to scrub the food stains off the elegant chairs, and the dog fur off the perfect couch. The Littles didn't have these problems. Joe's children, if he had any, were grown and gone. And more kids weren't part of the trophy wife equation.

But, then again, neither were infidelity, blackmail, and murder.

"So tell me about Refn," I began.

Laura studied the Steuben whaling sculpture on the glass-topped coffee table—the white crystal whale in breaching flight above a four-man whale boat with peg-legged Ahab wielding a harpoon in the bow. It probably cost as much as my yearly salary. Laura had a nice life here on Cliff Road. She didn't want to lose it.

"He's a terrible—" they started to say together. Joe turned to her. "Sorry. You go."

"I was going to…It's—he's a terrible person—was a terrible person. I just wish I'd figured that out before."

"But charming?" I offered.

"He—yes, I suppose. At first. That killer smile of his. People don't realize how important a good smile is in this world. Unless you don't have one. Then you know. You feel it. And you feel yourself being taken in by this totally superficial meaningless *arrangement* of facial features, and you know what's happening but it doesn't make any difference at all."

"Darwin said smiling is the only universal body language across all primate groups."

"So I suppose we're all just apes."

I shrugged. "My mom always says, 'we're not down too long out of the trees' whenever someone does something particularly awful. She has a point."

"I suppose."

"Anyway, you fell for him."

"Yes."

"You had an affair."

She pressed her arms together, clamped them between her legs, hunched her shoulders. It was like someone had cranked up the air conditioning. But no one had. She spoke to her knees. "Joe and I…We have an open marriage,"

Joe coughed up a laugh. "She has an open marriage. I have ED and a Viagra allergy."

"Joe!"

I glanced over at him. "I had no idea—"

"It's real. There's lots of side effects they don't tell you about."

This was none of my business. But murder opens up peoples' lives, the way a twister tears the roof off their house. One quick flyover and you can see everything.

"So…Donald Harcourt saw you together. And told your husband."

"Yes."

"There was a brawl at the Sanfords' fundraiser."

"Yes, well…Joey had to make a show of it."

"No one knows about our arrangement," Joe added.

Laura explained, "I have a book out on the sanctity of marriage, and monogamy and how to make life work in a traditional marriage. It's called *Vows*."

"Like the wedding announcements in the *Times*."

"The subtitle is *Living Your Ever After—Happily*. A revelation like this could wreck my sales."

"Or double them. Scandals sell books."

She gave me a look of prim distaste. "My reputation sells my books, Chief Kennis. And I will not have it sullied."

I spoke directly to Joe. "You couldn't pay Refn off forever, or even be sure he'd keep quiet, no matter how much money you gave him. But there was an obvious solution."

"Not that we could see."

"Here's how it looks, Mr. Little. You killed Refn and then called Donald Harcourt to the Naushop house. He has his own reasons for wanting Refn dead, and he's caught red-handed at the scene of the crime."

"Why would I want to frame Don Harcourt?"

"You tell me."

A toxic silence spread between us. The knife was out of the drawer. Joe said "I think I need to call a lawyer."

Laura spoke up. "No! That's ridiculous! This is all about one cell phone call. Someone must have cloned Joe's phone."

"Come on, Mrs. Little. That hardly seems—"

"It's easy to do. Anyone can buy the equipment online. And my husband lost his phone the week before the murder. Remember, Joe? We were having lunch at Ventuno." She turned back to me. "It was like an informal meeting of the executive board of the theater—The Kohls, the Harcourts, Judy Barsch, Ken and Sally Howe. Who else? Oh, the Callahans. Anyway…What an awful lunch! Joe got food poisoning. The point is, he had his phone out the whole time, he was checking for likes about some idiotic thing he had posted on Facebook, ranting about the Supreme Court."

"I just said—they take a case, you know the decision in advance. The very fact that—"

"Please, Joe. Not today. I'm trying to explain something to Chief Kennis." She touched his knee to focus his attention then withdrew her hand to her lap. "The phone was out on the table for most of the meal and when we were walking back to the car Joe reached into his pocket and it was gone."

"We went back into the restaurant," Joe added. "We asked the waiters and the people at the tables near us. But no one had seen it."

"There was an odd moment at lunch, though," Laura said. "Just before Joe started to feel sick. That writer, Blair Hollister? I guess he was a few tables away. He strolled over to say hello, and we were all chatting and then everything seemed to happen at once. Someone knocked over a glass of wine, and Joe just—"

"I thought I was going to puke. I jumped up and ran to the bathroom."

Laura shuddered. "Ugh. I followed him into the men's room—it was awful…and when we got back there were waiters cleaning the floors and changing the tablecloth and—sort of controlled chaos? But it all worked out all right. And we all got free desserts. Which is a nice treat at Ventuno."

"I must have picked up a bug somewhere," Joe said.

"Anyway, like I said, the phone was gone after lunch and then the next morning, I found it on the deck. Just sitting on the table where we have our coffee! How did it get there?"

I shrugged. "Someone noticed the phone at the restaurant later, recognized you and returned it."

"Exactly! After they cloned it!"

I took a breath. "So, let me try to piece this together. This individual followed you into the restaurant—or had access to the reservations list…and knew Joe's Facebook addiction…and lurked nearby hoping for the moment when they could snatch the phone off the table? With no one in a party of eleven noticing?"

"Well, I…it's—I don't know. How do you explain it?"

"I think I already did."

"But humor me. If the phone's sim card really was cloned…"

I met her steady gaze. "Then someone in that restaurant took it."

"Thank you."

Joe jumped in. "But no one would! The waitstaff has nothing against us, and no one at that table—I mean, they wouldn't try to frame me for murder. And also—I mean…those people…our friends…they're not criminal masterminds, swiping phones and performing all this high-tech magic and luring people to crime scenes. It makes no sense."

I offered Laura an apologetic smile. "He has a point."

"But he's missing the real point, as usual. Joe didn't make that call. Which means someone else did. And it's your job to find them."

"I wonder how you can be so sure Joe didn't make the call. Were you together?"

"No, but—"

"Where were you?" It had to be someplace public she couldn't lie about, or she would have.

"As a matter of fact, I had a tennis date with Sally Howe yesterday afternoon. At the Yacht Club."

I caught Joe's eye. "And you?"

He looked away, studying the wall of books behind me. "I'd rather not say."

"Try again."

"It's—I was in a meeting. At the Chicken Box."

The Box was a low-rent mid-island bar, a local hangout leftover from a very different Nantucket. It was hard to imagine Joseph Little in there.

"The Box? Really?"

"I didn't choose the location."

"Who were you meeting there?"

"Two Bulgarians, brothers—Dimo and Boiko Tabachev? They've done work for me before—moving furniture, dump runs, things like that."

I knew the Tabachev brothers. They were smart and shrewd, always careful to stay on the right side of the law, like drag racers on the right side of the road, one wheel riding the yellow line. We suspected them of everything from opioid-dealing to low level protection rackets and even running the (mythical?) Eastern European prostitution ring. But we'd never managed to catch them doing anything worse than operating a betting pool on Whalers' football games. I brought Dimo in on that one a couple of years ago—just for a warning, which I hoped would be enough. When the interview was finished, the big man, who must have weighed close to three hundred pounds at that point, loomed over me and said, "I am loving this country, Mr. Police. Don't make me feel unwelcome here."

The threat was veiled, but then so is a grieving widow's face at a funeral. That formal concealment reveals more than it hides.

"I know Dimo," I told Joe. "He does a lot more than move furniture. We just haven't been able to prove any of it. Yet."

"I don't want to get in trouble, Chief."

"Then tell me what the two of you were talking about."

"This is off the record. I'll deny anything I say to you right now. So will Dimo. And Laura will back us up."

Then I got it. The irony would have been funny, if irony was ever funny. "You were conspiring to commit murder while someone else was actually murdering your intended victim."

"It was just…exploratory."

"Here's some free advice, Joe. Next time you're exploring the idea of committing a capital crime with a known felon, don't meet in public. And choose a more reliable felon. Dimo would turn you in for a free round of beer."

"We did nothing! It was just—talk. Someone else killed Refn."

"Lucky you."

I'd had enough. Police work shows you the worst of everyone. Forty-four years old and I still preferred my illusions. Well, who doesn't? I stood. "That's all for now. Don't leave the island. I'll be in touch if we need to talk again."

I was suddenly overcome with the fatigue of dealing with horrible people.

And my day was just beginning.

Chapter Six

Weeding the Garden

"Weeding the garden." That was what Chuck Obremski, my old boss and mentor in the LAPD, used to call getting rid of the false suspects, and "persons of *no* interest," as he called them, trimming back the little plot of land that constituted your case to find the foxglove or the water hemlock you were looking for.

"Lots of deadly plants out there, Hank. But those weeds'll confuse you. Make sure you wear gloves when you pull them out. Lots of prickles and thorns. They'll cut you up good if you're not ready for them."

I remembered that advice, so I was ready when I drove out to Almanack Pond Road to meet the Callahans. Good thing. Chuck Obremski was on the money, as usual.

Almanack Pond Road is a winding dirt track that meanders away from Polpis Road into the moors. I often wondered why the immensely rich people whose houses were tucked away among the pine woods and brambles never paved the narrow lane. Its ruts, washboard sections, and "thank-you-ma'ams—deep craters usually filled with standing water that you edged past with one wheel in the mud, the lip grazing the undercarriage—had probably wrecked quite a few expensive suspensions. As usual, when it came to the habits and peculiarities of Nantucket's ruling class, Jane had the answer. "They like the bad road. It discourages the riffraff."

That would be me, I thought as I pulled into the Callahans' winding driveway and approached the massive, columned, gray-shingled pile at the end of it. I saw a "guest cottage" the size of a normal house to the left, and a horse barn with a split-rail-fenced paddock behind the mansion to the right, screened by a line of beech and holly trees.

When I killed the engine on the cruiser, the silence settled on the car like fog. I could pick out tiny individual sounds—a bird calling *twitter-twitter-twitter-twee* somewhere deep in the woods, the ticking of my cooling engine, a horse harrumphing at my arrival—but they defined the silence, the way a lone figure gives perspective to an empty landscape. That's what money buys in today's world—this dense abiding quiet I could feel in my pulse. Of course, what money really buys is isolation. People make noise. There were no raucous shouts, no braying laughter, no radios blaring "House" music. How much land separated the Callahans from their nearest neighbor? Five acres? Ten? And a mile and a half of rutted dirt road.

A car suspension you can replace. Nothing could replace this.

As for the Callahans themselves, they fit the mold perfectly— A Victorian copper mold, no doubt like the fish, lions, and scallop shell examples that hung on their kitchen wall.

I checked off the standard inventory when they came to the door. Walter, a whale in Nantucket reds and white polo shirt, white-haired and well-fed, with a broad suspicious brick of a face set off by scholarly black-rimmed glasses. Marge, a small smart smiling little smelt, the perfectly poised pilot fish, at least twenty years his junior. Second wife? Third? I thought of Jane dismissing women like her as "professional wives." Marge Callahan looked like a seasoned pro, complete with a set of formidable equestrian skills. No doubt she had some second- and third-place eventing ribbons, along with her squashed Olympic ambitions, stashed away somewhere.

Walter scowled at me. "Will this take long?"

I scowled back. "Let's hope not."

"Please come in." Marge said. Of course the tactical application of her expert social graces was part of her job description.

When we were seated in the wide sunny "Great Room," with the required clipper ship model and the flock of wooden herons and gulls crowding the tops of the built-in bookshelves, Walter came right to the point. "Are we under suspicion?"

"Should you be?"

"I resent your tone, sir. It was a fair question."

I took a breath, let it out slowly. "Everyone who had dealings with Horst Refn is of interest to the investigation. At this early stage, we really don't—"

"Refn was blackmailing my friends. Are you saying he was blackmailing us?"

"I'm trying to understand exactly what—"

"Are you saying my wife was having an affair with Horst Refn?"

"Walter," Marge attempted.

"Let me handle this! I want an answer."

I glanced over at the hideous sculpture of Queequeg heaving a harpoon at the picture window from the white brick mantelpiece. *The whale's over here, buddy*, I thought. Though it occurred to me that Walter would give anyone chasing him quite a "Nantucket sleigh-ride." All you could do was hang on tight and let him exhaust himself.

"I'm not ruling anything out yet, Mr. Callahan."

"Well you can rule that out. We're happily married and have been for a decade. I have six children and fourteen grandchildren. I'm a pillar of this community. I've donated more money than you'll see in your whole lifetime to the new hospital fund, the Boys and Girls Club, the NHA, and a thousand other charities which I have no interest in disclosing. We fully fund ten college scholarships for Nantucket High School students every year. We saved the Theater Lab when it almost went under a few years ago. That's what we do. When we are called, we serve. When we are asked, we give. When we promise, we deliver. If your baseless allegations damage my reputation in this town, where I have lived and prospered for more than forty years, I will sue you and your police department for slander and see that you are fired and never work in law enforcement again. I will make you a pariah. I will break you in pieces and step on the pieces. There will be no second chances for you. Not like last time."

I let the storm of words buffet me. But the final blow hit home. "Last time?"

He leaned forward, elbows on his knees, squeezing his left fist in his right hand. "Oh, yeah, I know all about you, Kennis. I did my research when the town wanted to hire you. I was against it."

"I appreciate that, but—"

"I dug up the copies of *L.A. Weekly* where your little 'true crime' story ran before the LAPD yanked it, and slapped you with a lawsuit and kicked your ass into the street. Main Street, as it turned out—our Main Street. That piece of scurrilous gossip-mongering told me a lot about you, Kennis. Apart from the fact that you're a lousy writer. You don't begin every sentence in a paragraph with the word 'I', all right? I, I, I—I did this, I did that, I found this, I said that. It's boring. And it's all about you. A man's career was ruined, a fine police department was thrown into scandal, but all we get to read about is Henry Kennis, the hero of the story, the white knight in shining armor. And you're still out-maneuvered and outsmarted at every turn by a junior FBI agent—some little girl, basically a *trainee*, as far as I can understand—who walked in out of nowhere and turned your whole case upside down. She made you look like a fool."

He was talking about Frances Tate, my old flame, now a powerful figure in the DHS. She had helped me solve a major bombing case on the island a few years before, but I knew at the time she'd never stick around to help me oversee the summer specials and process the parking tickets. Nantucket kills ambition and Frannie had more ambition than anyone I'd ever met, including me. For the record, Callahan was right about the Los Angeles murder case. Frannie solved it all by herself, though she wound up giving her boss the credit.

"Frances Tate was a full-grown woman, Mr. Callahan," I said. "She was a special agent, not a trainee. You should have read the paper a little more carefully."

"I was more interested in you. My take? An arrogant insecure headstrong insubordinate punk with father issues. Is that reading carefully enough for you?"

"Well…I had the arrogance beaten out of me, and insecure plus headstrong turns out to be a pretty good combination for police work. I don't worry about insubordination anymore, since I run the NPD. Having kids cured the punk problem, and I worked things out with my dad."

"So you're perfect now."

"I'm improving."

"Lucky us."

I stared him down. "Where were you yesterday afternoon?"

"We were out riding in the moors. We saw no one and no one saw us."

"Who takes care of your horses?"

"We do."

"No stable hands? No one to help you muck out or tack up?"

"These are Irish quarterhorses, Kennis. I brought them over from County Cork myself. I wouldn't let some ten-dollar-an-hour barn rat anywhere near them."

"So you have no way to verify your whereabouts?"

He grinned at me as if he had just taken my Queen for checkmate. "None at all."

"Neither of us killed anyone, Chief Kennis," Marge said. "We're not killers. I think you know that."

She was right, much as I would have liked her husband to

be guilty. But you can't pick your suspects. I decided to try a different tack. "Do either of you have any idea who might have killed Refn?"

This got Callahan's back up again. "Why would you ask us a question like that?"

I shrugged. "Most people are killed by someone they know. The faceless assassin, the anonymous hitman…that's mostly a fantasy. Outside of the movies."

"A killer who appears out of nowhere with no apparent motive or connection to the victim, does the deed and vanishes again," Callahan mused. "That guy would be almost impossible to find, unless you caught him in the act."

"True."

"So, in fact, any unsolved crime could be a hit."

"I suppose. But I'm going to make my best effort to solve this one before I give up and blame thugs—or the thugee."

He nodded at the reference. "Good thinking, since we're not living in nineteenth-century India."

"So? What do you think?"

Marge shook her head. "You never really know people."

"No suspicions? No one acting strange?"

'I worry about Bessie Kohl."

"Jesus Christ, Marge! She couldn't harm a fly! I mean that literally. She made her husband take back one of those sticky strips for killing flies he bought for a backyard barbecue."

"We've already spoken with the Kohls."

"Did she tell you what she was doing while someone was killing Refn? Binge-watching *Game of Thrones*, gobbling Ambien and Ativan. That's her version of AA! Refn destroyed her. She may never recover. She's a *husk*, Kennis."

"She's very, very angry," Marge said.

"And she'll hold it in until she gives herself a stroke. I think you should look at this Blair Hollister. The writer? He shows up with a murder mystery play and a month later the Artistic Director of the Theater Lab is dead. He has a grudge of some kind. He's a creep. He made some comment about life imitating art—"

"—more than art imitates life. It's a quote from Oscar Wilde."

"Fine, but Hollister's 'art' just happens to be about murder. He's a killer."

"Why broadcast it then?"

"That's what these psychos do, Kennis. You should know that. They brag, they strut. They think they're better than the police. They taunt the authorities. They hide in plain sight. 'How could I be a killer? Do you think I'd confess in a play and go public with it?' Well, that's exactly what I think. When he walked into this house, he looked around and said, 'I guess money can't buy taste.' Can you imagine? He's a troublemaker."

"This house is very tasteful,' Marge said. "Nantucket Interiors helped us. They're the best."

"And the most expensive," Callahan added.

"We'll look into Hollister," I offered. He was on my list anyway. I'd had my own run-in with him the week before and I was not impressed.

"Do that."

"And check out Judy Barsch also," Marge said.

"The president of the board?"

Marge crossed her arms and squeezed her ribs, "She's cold. A very cold person. We were driving with her the other day and we saw a deer in the road. It must have been hit by a truck. There was a lot of broken glass but the impact would have totaled a car. Anyway…it was horrible. The poor animal was still alive and sort of—twitching? Traffic was blocked and one of your officers arrived. He pulled out his gun to…you know…put the deer out of its misery. But he couldn't do it. Traffic was lining up in both directions. People were starting to honk. I realized the policeman was just a boy, really. No one knew what to do. Then Judy made this kind of snort of disgust, piled out of the car, took the boy's gun and shot the deer. She handed the gun back and said, 'Now do your job and get this thing off the road. There's good meat on the undamaged side.' Does that seem normal to you, Chief Kennis?"

"I suppose it depends on what part of the country she comes from. It certainly seems practical. At least she took some action. No one else was able to, including my officer."

"I suppose."

"Refn wasn't killed with a gun, Margie," Callahan pointed out.

"No, that's true."

"I'm going to have to talk to Ms. Barsch anyway," I said. "I'll keep what you told me in mind."

Judith Barsch owned a house in a new development off Hummock Pond Road called the Nanahumacke Preserve. The subdivision was marked by a giant stone with the name chiseled into it. I turned into the winding road thinking that there were too many of those on the island. They were everywhere. Did a boulder with your name on it make you feel more substantial? Maybe it was a question of status, a way of getting one up on your friends: "Nice wooden sign, guess you couldn't afford the boulder."

Like the couple in Madaket, who had their house redone with aeronautical paint, always handy if they happened to be flying their house six hundred miles-an-hour at forty thousand feet. But mere yacht paint, at a hundred and fifty dollars a gallon, wasn't exclusive enough anymore.

Barsch's house was set above what the brochure no doubt referred to as a "private lake"—in fact a sad little pond that reminded me alarmingly of a cesspool. A half-hearted fountain sent a plume of water up from the middle of the turbid surface. The big undistinguished mansion looked just like all the others around it—a cliff of gray shingles with a column-lined porch, dormers squinting from the second floor. I had heard that the Martha's Vineyard building codes allowed for more eccentric and even outrageous structures. Nantucketers sneered at their sister island for that architectural fiesta, but this was worse. The homes on this new road had all the cheer and excitement of the identical SUVs lined up at the Don Allen Ford dealership.

There were quite a few of them lined up at the curb here as well, along with Fred Hamburger's big van, with its eye-staring-out-of-the-Nantucket-map logo. He had started running real estate promos on his little TV station. Were people trying to unload some of these houses? I doubted a thirty-second video would help much. Fred was what Jane Stiles called a "major avoid"—someone she'd back out of the Fast Forward parking lot to dodge. These weren't people she disliked, necessarily. "Catching up" with acquaintances was a dreaded ordeal for her, and Fred made me understand what she meant. Short and wiry with a totally bald head and a dense tightly trimmed black beard, he had a relentless canine energy and always wanted to involve me in some harebrained media project that never came to fruition—a ride-along with my detectives, a program where I'd recite my poems.

My ex-wife, Miranda, was at the party where Fred made that suggestion, and her eye-rolling look of dismayed contempt brought back the worst of our marriage. Her head shake, with a swipe of her finger across her throat, made me smile, though. I knew she wanted to spare me an embarrassing moment. Fred's fulsome praise and fawning demeanor could make Dylan Thomas look like a pompous drunk. I stood no chance with him.

Seeing Fred meant ducking one more idea—would I narrate a history of the NPD, judge police recruits on a local reality show, wear his brand-new body camera for a week?—so I glanced around quickly when I climbed out of my cruiser. The street was empty.

I crossed over to Barsch's house, stepped across the porch and saw the door was open. I took a tentative step inside. "Hello?"

No answer. I moved through the mansion, all glossy bead-board walls, pickled oak floors, and pale expensive furniture. It looked like the Callahans', right down to the ubiquitous ship models and wooden herons. Maybe she used the Callahans' very expensive decorator—I wondered if they also designed high-end hotel suites. At least Barsch had books. There was a wall of shelves across from the big wall of French doors that overlooked the rear patio and the pond.

I found her in the garden, deadheading flowers while Fred Hamburger's three-man video crew tilted reflectors, swiveled the boom mike, and adjusted the camera. Her black pit bull lounged on the sun-warmed fieldstone.

Barsch was a short, squat fireplug of a woman in expensive sweats, her dense helmet of graying blond hair tightly cropped to her jawline. The jaw was still sharp. She either had great genes or the best face work that money could buy. She could certainly afford it.

"…so really it's my garden that keeps me sane," she was saying.

I stepped back into the house and let them finish. I strolled the big sunny rooms looking for some clue to Barsch's past or her personality, but the place was purely generic. The paintings on the walls showed lighthouses and rose-covered cottages, whaling ships and cranberry bogs. There were no family photographs. No quirky collectibles. The end tables featured cut flowers and bowls of fruit, lamps, and coasters with real estate logos. It struck me that the house might be rented. The library had a rental feel to it—Nantucket history and picture books, the usual Elin Hildebrand, Nancy Thayer, and Nathaniel Philbrick tomes, along with the standard best sellers and thrillers. I noted several of Jane's Madeline Clark cozy mysteries among them. I gave the owners points for that. The shelves looked impeccably dusted, the volumes lined up as evenly as row houses on a city street. Barsch was either compulsively neat or she just didn't read.

I was reaching for one of Jane's books when she strode into the room. "Sorry to keep you waiting, Chief. You should have called ahead."

I smiled into her inquiring glare. "I like surprising people."

The dog trotted up to me, tail wagging. I patted the blunt head gingerly.

"Don't be afraid, Chief. I read your editorial against profiling. It applies to dogs as well as humans. Corky's perfectly friendly. Pit bulls are the sweetest dogs on Earth…or should I say, American Staffordshire terriers are? Isn't that so, Corky?" The dog's ears lifted at the sound of her name, then she went back to licking my hand.

"This one's adorable," I said.

"Indeed. Well, your timing is good at least. Fred is just finishing up for the day."

Hamburger and the crew trooped in. He said, "It's part of my *Open House* series, Chief. An intimate look at the homes of Nantucket's most important people. We should do your house! Aren't you living in the old Fraker place on Darling Street? Two writers, three kids, and a dog! It's a natural."

"I don't think so."

"Come on. I promise to stay out of your closets."

"We spent an hour in mine," Barsch said. "It's a nice little walk-in—"

"Little? It's huge! I could move in there!"

"Now, really, I don't think—"

"She's got more shoes than Imelda Marcos—no offense, and racks for her bracelets and rings, and this teak stand that holds all her glasses and her sunglasses, plus the hats! She has this silo of hatboxes, and drawers full of cashmere sweaters, not to mention the—"

"Fred."

He stopped, pulled up short like a man at a curb facing heavy traffic. The city bus of Barsch's disapproving frown roared past an inch from his face, and the wind of it seemed to knock him back a step.

"Uh, sorry—"

"You make me sound like some grasping old parvenu dowager." She turned to me. "My money goes back three generations. For your information."

"I was just saying," Fred attempted.

"Don't bother. Chief Kennis can see your little film, when it's done. Then he'll know all the details. Don't spoil it for him. We'll finish up tomorrow."

"She's going to let me shoot while she cooks dinner."

"I'm quite an accomplished chef," she added. "If I do say so myself."

When the filmmakers were gone we walked outside and sat down at the wrought-iron table on her terrace, under a wide umbrella. Below us a gentle breeze troubled the fountain and carried a waft of standing water.

She passed a proprietary hand across the vista. "So what do you think of the place?"

I shrugged. "Not my style. And I'm tired of all these made-up Indian-sounding names for Nantucket subdivisons."

"Made-up? Really? Nanahumacke was a real person, Chief. What they called a 'petty sachem'—a figure of great social standing within the community. He owned all this land, including Hummock Pond, which is in fact a bastardization of his name. You should study your history before you make silly, off-the-cuff comments. You're something of a petty sachem yourself, you know."

"Thanks for that. I can't help wondering what old Nanahumacke would think of all this."

The blunt face hardened in the afternoon light. "I don't think it matters. His kind lost their say a long time ago."

"And I'm sure some of your ancestors supplied the smallpox blankets."

"Superior races conquer inferior ones. It's always been that way. No need to get sentimental about it."

"Arrogance and better weapons don't make you superior."

Her smile was icy. "Yet here we are. And Nanahumacke is a name on a rock."

Time to put the needle down. "So where were you on the afternoon Refn was killed?"

"I was walking Corky."

"All afternoon?"

"On occasion, yes, I do walk her all afternoon. On this particular afternoon, she ran away. She caught the scent of a deer and she was gone. I stayed out until sunset calling for her. She finally came back just as I was giving up. Her beautiful tartan jacket was shredded. She must have been running through the brambles all day."

"Did anyone see you?"

"I have no idea. I didn't see anyone, if that's what you mean."

"So you have no way to prove your whereabouts?"

"Well, I called the dog officer. They log those calls, I assume."

"But you could have made that call from anywhere."

"Carmen saw us leave the house, and she was here when we came home four hours later, with Corky much the worse for wear."

"But in between…"

"No. Does that make me a suspect?"

"At the moment, everyone's a suspect."

She raised her eyebrows minutely in brusque professorial chastisement. "Focus, Chief Kennis. Focus."

"How did you feel about Refn? Did you like him?"

"I adored him. You might say I came here for him. I was sick of the Midwest, my husband had passed, and I was looking for a vibrant East Coast small town, someplace where I could dig in and make a difference, some place where the arts mattered and I could matter to the arts. So I did what I always do. I studied the problem and I made my decision. Ultimately, it came down to Martha's Vineyard or Nantucket, and Horst Refn was the deciding factor. He was making real theater here and I knew I could help. It was a wonderful experience until—well, until this horrible incident."

"The murder."

"I detest that word. I don't see how it could have happened. Who could have done it? Who could hate Horst so much?"

"Quite a few people, apparently."

"It's all gossip. I don't believe a word of it. My grandfather was an Oklahoma oil man. He was accused of murdering Osage Indians to steal their mineral rights, just because he was friends with Willie Hale! A great man, by the way. Unjustly persecuted, forgotten by history. Tragic story—look him up, see for yourself. My father and my two brothers have been accused of causing earthquakes with their fracking operations! What's next? Will they blame us for tornadoes and hailstorms? It's despicable. If I could move the Earth so easily, I'd have knocked California into the sea a long time ago.

"In any case…I'm well inured to innuendo and guilt by association. I'm just sorry to see it all happening here. People aren't always killed because they're bad, Chief Kennis. In fact, that rarely happens. The bad people prosper and thrive! No one knows why these crimes take place. They're irrational. Trying to blame the victim just makes you look lazy and mean-spirited. Dig deeper, that's my advice."

"Any suggestions?"

"It's not my place."

"I think it is. You know all these people. I don't. You've been present at the board meetings, you socialize with the board members. You've seen things. You've heard things. Maybe something struck an odd note but you dismissed it at the time. But now everything's different. A man's been murdered and his killer is probably someone you know. Like the lipstick you might find among your husband's ChapSticks in the bathroom drawer. You ignore it until you find out he's a cross-dresser. Then it suddenly makes sense."

"This happened?"

"A long time ago. A case in Los Angeles. I'm just making a point."

She picked a fake lemon from the bowl of them on the table, rolled it between her fingers. "Now that you mention it…"

"Tell me."

"It's probably nothing. Just…it did strike me as odd. At the time. And that's the sort of thing you're looking for."

"Yes."

"Well…I was talking to the playwright, Blair Hollister? He wrote the play *Who Dun It*, which the Theater Lab is mounting this summer. Handsome boy, very bright, very talented, very charming. Hardly anyone's ideal suspect for such…for a thing like this."

"But?"

"He said the most peculiar thing the other day. Out of nowhere, at the Kohls' cocktail party. He said, 'I know you have my back.' I said, 'Excuse me?' I was standing alone on the Kohls' little strip of beach facing the harbor, and he startled me. 'Is this about the play? Are they trying to make you change your play?' He laughed at that idea. 'They can't make me change a word. And they wouldn't.' I said, 'Then what are you talking about?' He was quiet. The harbor lights looked like a stage set at that moment. Finally, he said, 'Sometimes you have to lie to tell the truth. And sometimes you have to trust the truth even when it sounds like a lie.' It was my turn to laugh. I said, 'That sounds like your philosophy of playwriting.' But he was serious, deadly serious. 'Everything will be okay as long as you trust me.' What do you think he could have meant by that?"

"I have no idea."

"Well, I didn't either. But I started thinking, Who is this man? Why did he come here? What does he really want? He writes a play about a murder, and a murder happens. Is that a coincidence?"

I was getting tired of that trope. "Probably."

"I looked into the matter and I made some disturbing discoveries. You must know Victor Galassi."

"The District Court judge."

"He's a twin."

"I'm not sure why that—"

"An identical twin."

"Okay."

"Just like the judge in Hollister's play."

"Who gets killed, I assume?"

"Poisoned."

I took a breath, let it out slowly. "No one has threatened Judge Galassi, Ms. Barsch. He would have reported it. He reported a break-in at his house two days ago, but no one was harmed and nothing was stolen. He's still alive and well. More to the point, Horst Refn is the murder victim. What's Hollister's connection to him?"

"It's your job to find out."

I was getting tired of rich people telling me how to do my job. I stood up. "We'll look into all this. Thanks for your time. I'll let myself out."

Outside in the freshening wind from the ocean, I checked my watch—just past two. Hollister's play was rehearsing at Bennett Hall. I decided to take a look.

Chapter Seven

The Rehearsal

Driving to the Congregational Church, I thought about my previous encounters with Hollister. I had seen him several times hiking in Dead Horse Valley—or Chicken Hill, as some people called the little patch of open land and wooded trails wedged between the old windmill, the hospital, and a new housing development under construction. On school snow days, it offered the best sledding in town and it was a favorite year-round spot for dog owners. I rarely saw an unaccompanied biped walking the trails, though, so Hollister stood out. He strode past us on both occasions, in his own world and in a hurry, grunting a minimal acknowledgement to me and ignoring Bailey. I never actually spoke to him until the parking lot incident.

It was a couple of weeks before Refn's death. Jane and I were getting lunch at Provisions, the little sandwich shop on Harbor Square at the base of Straight Wharf. We had parked in the Stop & Shop lot, using the locals' standard no-spaces-available tactic: Jane simply slotted her newly acquired dream car—a beautifully restored, sky blue 1970 Volkswagen Beetle—parallel to the slant-parking. It's a practical solution: one person runs in for the sandwiches while the other one stays behind the wheel, in case one of the blocked cars has to get out. By early August you can see as many as ten vehicles lined up this way, using the tag team system, some of them waiting to pick up friends from the Hy-Line, others grocery shopping or grabbing an ice cream cone. But in mid-June it was just us.

Jane parked near the top of the lot and I dashed in for the food, nodding to the two Summer Specials, Jim and Judy, I couldn't remember their last names, directing traffic as a baffled crowd of tourists trudged off the ferry. They took an extra second to recognize me—I wasn't in uniform that day, or the incident might never have happened.

I got our lunch, two Caprese sandwiches (tomato and mozzarella with pesto and a balsamic vinaigrette on ciabatta bread) plus two of the store's own mint iced teas with lemon. I was strolling back, past the crowded outdoor tables at the Tavern toward the parking lot, when I heard the altercation.

I broke into a trot.

A dark green Range Rover was idling next to Jane's Beetle and the driver had leaned over to shout from the open passenger side window. "What the hell's the matter with you? Can you speak English? Speka de inglese? Move the goddamn car! You're blocking the street!"

Jane seemed supernaturally calm, a long-suffering poltergeist tolerating irrational abuse for simply moving the armchairs to flank the couch and face the fireplace. The arrangement was obvious, she was just trying to help. But living people were scared of ghosts. Oh, well. "Your car is next to mine," she pointed out gently. "I can't be blocking it."

"Then how the hell am I gonna turn right up there?"

"It's left turn only."

I leaned into his window. "What's going on?"

He swiveled to face me. "This bitch won't move her car and no one can get by!"

Bitch? I let it go in the interest of civil polity. "Just keep driving, sir. I'm sure you'll have no problem."

"Jesus Christ, you fucking people! Shit."

He shoved the car door open and I stepped back as he lurched out onto the pavement. He pointed at Jim…McKitrick—that was his name! And she was Judy Toole. "I'm reporting this! I'm telling that cop!"

"I'm the Chief of Police."

"Bullshit. Get out of my way."

He pushed past me, strode away, and dragged Jim McKitrick back with him. Ironically, cars were now lining up behind his Range Rover.

"…so it's really not a problem," Jim was explaining. "It's kind of like an ad hoc solution? But it works pretty well and it actually keeps the traffic moving through the parking lot, which I mean, in August? You should see this place." He looked over and saw me. "Sorry, Chief."

"No problem, Jim, But you should be getting back."

"Right, yeah—sure. On my way!"

He scurried back to his corner, where a tourist bus had two wheels up on the sidewalk and someone's rolling suitcase had just tipped over among a tangle of poodles. Range Rover Guy turned back. He was a big blond surfer type with a scrappy blond beard, maybe an inch taller and twenty pounds heavier than me. He loomed a little, chest out, trying to leverage the difference. "You're actually the Police Chief? I don't believe this! Where's your uniform?"

Someone honked their horn. A few other drivers joined in, "I'm off duty. Now get back into your car and drive."

"This is anarchy!"

"Actually it's the opposite of anarchy. We work things out together. And things work out pretty well."

He glared at me. "What kind of goddamn policeman are you, anyway?"

"The polite and considerate kind. I don't yell at strange women and I don't block traffic while I yell at other people for blocking traffic. So move along."

"You haven't heard the last of this!!"

"Right."

He slammed back into his SUV and burned rubber pulling out. The other cars followed and the lot was clear a few seconds later. I handed Jane the sandwiches.

She smiled. "Strange women?"

"Well, you are sort of odd."

"That guy's the new glamor writer at the Theater Lab. He and Mark Toland are on the cover of *N Magazine* this month."

"Right, I saw that. I seem to recall he was smiling in that picture. No wonder I didn't recognize him."

So that was my introduction to Blair Hollister.

Nothing I saw at rehearsal that day improved my opinion.

I walked up the wide steps to the foot of the white, newly repainted Congregational Church, its spire rising above the clapboards to the cloudless blue sky. On the phone, Refn's assistant, Tim Hobbes—now temporarily promoted to acting-Artistic Director—told me they'd be rehearsing all day, and I thought it was sad—working on a play meant you had to stay inside in a dark theater on such a gorgeous afternoon.

Tim Hobbes seemed like a nice kid, overwhelmed by his new responsibilities and eager for the board to choose a replacement. He had flown back from New York the day after Refn's death. He'd gone to the city for his father's funeral. At the time of the murder, he had been delivering the eulogy, in front of roughly three hundred people. That was one of the first alibis Charlie Boyce checked out. So, a rough week for Tim Hobbes, and he was still in a state of shock. Reality hadn't closed in yet and the cascade of new responsibilities kept him too busy to brood, at least during the day. I had a feeling he wasn't getting much sleep, though.

Death was everywhere that summer, including on the stage at Bennett Hall. I arrived at the rehearsal just in time to witness an attempted murder, albeit a fictional one. The scene was being blocked meticulously by Mark Toland. I heard thumps and shouts as I crossed the lobby of the little theater attached to the church.

Inside, Toland was on stage with two of the actors. One of them crossed the set to a rolling drinks table placed under the window. "You have guesses and theories and delusions, my friend. But no proof."

"I don't care anymore," said the younger actor. "I'm beyond that now. And so are you."

"Is that a threat?"

"People only ask that question when they already know the answer."

"And people only threaten when they can't do anything else. When they're weak."

He reached for the carafe of wine, hesitated for a second, then pulled the stopper, and poured himself a glass. He lifted it in a toast to the younger man. "Here's to weakness."

"No," came Mark Toland's voice from the seats.

"What?" said the older man. "What's wrong?"

"Judge Galassi, have you ever known a witness was lying when they came before your court?"

"Occasionally."

"And how could you tell?"

"Well…there are many ways. But I always noticed a sort of tightness in the body. It freezes a little, stiffens—like when you know someone is taking your picture."

"Very good! Well, that's how I feel watching you pour that wine. You pick up that carafe like it was a drugged rattlesnake. You're safe if it doesn't wake up!"

"Well, yes, of course, what would you expect? I mean…it's poison."

"And you know that, Judge. But *your character* doesn't. He just wants a glass of cabernet. He's nervous, he wants to calm his nerves. Not you, though. You know the future, and you're planning it in your head and going over the blocking. It's kind of like the way you could almost hear Ryan Gosling counting out the beats to himself as he was trying to dance like Fred Astaire in that ludicrous musical movie. Kind of breaks the mood."

"So what should I do?"

"Live in the moment. Feel the need for the wine, feel the relief of turning your back on this kid. Feel the fear, because you are, in fact, afraid of him. He's angry and he has nothing to lose. Try to keep control of the situation. Keep your hands busy. Don't let him see them shaking, don't give anything away—to him or to us. Your life depends on it. Can you do that?"

"I guess. I can try."

"You don't see the blow that takes you down, Judge. People never do. You don't see this one coming, and neither will the audience. Unless you flinch."

"All right."

"Okay, Jon? Let's run the fight scene."

Jon and the judge set themselves into grappling stances and engaged, pulling and pushing at each other. "Line."

"Come on! Still?"

"I don't know what to tell you, Mark," Jon said. "I can't seem to talk and fight at the same time."

I couldn't help noticing that he bore more than a passing resemblance to Blair Hollister.

"Forget the line," Toland said. "We'll just work the physical beats for now."

"Bad idea."

The voice came from the dark rows of seats sloping up from the stage: Hollister, himself. "He's got to learn action and words together. You should have been off book two weeks ago."

"Yeah, I know, sorry. But it's just—I start pushing and shoving and my mind goes blank."

Hollister grunted. It might have been a laugh. "Yeah—everybody has a plan until they get hit. But you've gotta hold onto that plan, buddy. We need those words."

"Remember why you're fighting." Toland added. "Remember what this guy did to you."

"Okay."

"Let's take the whole scene again from the top."

The judge raised a hand. "Can we take a break first?"

"No." That was Hollister, from the seats.

Toland patted his shoulder. "Afterward. Let's get this done, okay, Victor? Then we can quit for the day and enjoy a little sunshine."

The judge gave him a pinched smile. "Thanks."

"I want to do the switch this time," Toland added. "We'll work out the lighting in tech but, Judge Galassi, figure you've got about twenty seconds in the dark to go go go. You too, Pete."

The judge groaned dramatically. "Dear God."

Toland laughed. "Tell me about it."

"If I could get up that quickly, I'd still be running marathons."

"Crawl, if you have to," Hollister added helpfully from the shadows.

"Fuck you, Blair."

"From the top?" Toland said. "Places, please."

I had no idea what any of them were talking about but I remembered watching TV as a child with my mother. To my pestering questions, "Who's that guy? Where are they going? What's in the box?" she would always answer serenely, "Let it unfold."

So I did.

Toland stepped off the stage and took a seat while Jon faded into the wings. Judge Galassi took the armchair in front of the painted plywood fireplace.

"It's pouring rain outside. Do we have sound yet, Jenny?"

"Hold on," a voice from backstage called out. "Yeah."

"Thunder, too?"

"The whole package."

"Run it."

The hall was filled with the muted sounds of wind and rain.

"Okay," Toland said. "Let's go."

Jon entered. "Good evening, sir."

Galassi twisted in his seat, authentically startled and afraid. "What are you doing here? How did you get in? What do you—?"

"You turn your alarm off when you get home. That's a common mistake. So is a having a glass-panel front door. But you can afford to get it repaired."

"You broke into my home—"

"I hate that word—home. My home. Welcome to my lovely home. So bourgeois. Show some class, sir. This is your house. And a very nice house it is, too. Very expensive. Location, location, location, am I right? You can't beat those water views. And the koi pond! Nice touch. Bet it draws the mosquitoes in the summer, though. Blood-sucking, disease-spreading parasites—your soul mates."

"Wait, stop—this is crazy! Who are you?"

"Shut up. There's no point trying to fake it. I did my homework. I was going to hire a private detective, but I thought, screw that. I have an Internet connection. I can google people. Detectives are as obsolete as travel agents. It's a DIY world."

"It—I…what are you talking about?

"DIY—Do it Yourself. Learn the lingo, sir. It's the twenty-first century."

"I don't understand this. I don't understand any of this. What on Earth do you think you—?"

"Fine. I'll explain it, so you know that we both understand. A man goes on trial for fraud, misrepresentation, grand larceny, and second-degree murder. It's a bench trial—no jury. That often happens when a case is so complicated or abstruse that a random group of twelve people might not be able to understand what the hell's going on. It's efficient, it's quick. But in this case there was just one problem."

"Wait! Please. I see now. You're making a terrible mistake. Let me just—"

"Shut up! Or I'll hold you in contempt. Oh, too late. I already do."

He reached into his overcoat pocket and came out with very real-looking Beretta Brigadier 92 combat pistol. I flinched a little, as if I'd just noticed that sleeping rattlesnake. I had observed firsthand the impact of the nine-millimeter Parabellum rounds from one of those guns, and I never wanted to see it again.

No one else seemed alarmed—except Galassi, of course, who was fully committed to the scene and staring into the barrel of the prop weapon.

Jon kept talking. "Seriously, though. Not another word. As I was saying. The problem, the problem. Oh, right. The problem! The problem for the man whose mother was deceived, robbed, and driven to penury and suicide by the defendant? Well, his problem was that the judge presiding over the case was actually in business with the defendant! Oh, yes. They had their own little criminal enterprise going, selling fake jewelry to credulous geezers, repairing settings by replacing the real diamonds with paste, selling the real stones on the international market, and using the cash to finance their heroin start-up. It turns out, for people who can't afford prescription opioids, heroin is the new hillbilly heroin! Lots of money there, it's a volume business, am I right? And the jewelry business makes a perfect little money-laundering set-up for the profits. Full circle. So the judge was a crook. That was the plaintiff's problem. But the judge had a problem, too."

"Please, whoever you are—"

"You know exactly who I am."

"If you would just give me one minute to explain—just sixty seconds! That's all I need. Thirty seconds! I can clarify this whole crazy—"

Jon lifted the gun again. "Shhhhhhhh."

"But I—"

"I'm warning you..."

"I'm not who you think I am!"

"Right. You're just misunderstood. Now let me finish or I will blow your fucking brains out. Pardon my French. No, I tell a lie. The French would be *Je vais souffler tes putains de cervelle*. But you wind up dead either way. So—your problem. Right. Your problem is the crazy accomplice who can't keep away from the older women or give up his dirty little con games. He's turning into a liability. Then he gets caught. Not necessarily a bad thing, at least for you. You make sure he gets tried in your courtroom. How am I doing so far? The rest is easy—you make a deal. He gets off—and he goes away, for good."

"No, no, no—I never—you can't—"

"Oops. You talked. If it makes you feel better, I was going to kill you anyway."

Galassi catapulted himself out of the chair, an unexpected utterly feral leap—an old cat pouncing on a cocky mouse. He hit Jon and knocked the gun out of his hand. Both men staggered backward. Jon tripped over a coffee table and went down hard, with the judge right on top of him.

Jon pushed him aside. "What the hell? I'm supposed to grab him!"

"I changed the blocking," Toland said.

"Without telling me?"

"It worked."

"What do you mean, it worked? What worked? What are you—?"

"You looked alive for a second there. Something unexpected happened. You were in the moment. I actually believed you were scared and surprised."

"Because I was!"

Toland shrugged. "Okay, so it's not acting, but it's the next best thing. Just remember how it felt. And be prepared. Because it could happen again any time. I'm going to ambush you into giving a real performance, even if it kills both of us. Judge, back in the chair. Take it from the jump."

The old man leapt again, the two went down again, swinging inept punches. Toland's trick had worked. The scene snapped with a new intensity. Maybe too much intensity. Jon lost the text again, in the jumble of action.

"Are you crazy, old man? Do want me to—shit! Line."

"Just keep going," Toland ordered.

"Do you really want me to beat you to death?" Jenny called out from the wings.

"Do you really want me to beat you to death?" Jon struck a glancing blow off Galassi's shoulder and knocked him backward. Galassi hit the floor on his back, and the impact seemed to knock the wind out of him. Jon scrambled on top of him, locked his hands around the older man's neck and started strangling him. Galassi thrashed and flailed but he couldn't break Jon's grip. Thunder pealed from the sound system.

"And the lights go out!" Toland shouted. "Go! Go go go!"

The judge heaved himself to his feet and stumbled off-stage, as Pete slipped past him to take his place on the floor.

"Okay, hold it," said Toland. "I'm hearing the shoes. Can't he be wearing just socks? Or slippers, at least? He's at home for the night. Those footsteps ruin everything."

"Slippers," invisible Jenny said from off-stage. "I'm on it."

"How will I ever have time for the costume change?" Galassi asked.

"Velcro," Jenny snapped back.

"Okay. Let's run it again."

They ran the switch six more times, with lots of grumbling, creaking knees, jokes, and cursing. I started timing the move. The third time around, Galassi was off-stage and Pete was lying down on the carpet in fourteen seconds. Not bad.

"Sweet," Toland said. "Let's take it from there. You ready, Judge?"

"All set."

"Whenever you like."

Galassi ran on stage, shouting, "Stop!"

Jon wrenched himself sideways to see the intruder—the man he'd just been strangling to death. I had to admit it was an effective bit of stage business, if they could pull it off every night—light cues, shuffling actors, costume change, and all.

Pete croaked out, "David! Help me!"

Jon looked authentically stunned. "David?"

"Stop him! He's trying to kill me! He thinks I'm you!"

Galassi stared down at them. "Jesus Christ—John Fenwick!"

"David...David LaFrance... Judge David LaFrance..."

Galassi pointed down at Pete. "His twin brother."

"Oh, my God, I almost—"

Galassi spotted the gun on the floor and leapt for it. Jon went after it, too, but tripped on Pete's body. Galassi picked up the gun, aimed it down at Jon. "This solves all our problems."

He thumbed the hammer back but Jon managed to grab his ankle and yank him off his feet. Galassi broke his fall with one hand, yelping in pain. It sounded like real pain to me. Jon seized the moment, pushing to his feet and sprinting out the door at the left side of the stage.

Galassi got himself vertical somehow. "Stop!"

He started shooting—two shots, three, four, five—until the gun was empty. I was pleased to hear the sound of blanks—a rubber snake. Chalk it up to PTSD. But even the rehearsal of this outlandish melodrama worked the theater's mysterious effect on me. You don't suspend your disbelief—it floats away on its own.

"Breaking-glass sound," Toland said.

Jenny's voice: "Working on it."

Galassi tottered to the door, panting. He stared into the darkness for a long moment, then turned back to Pete.

"Fenwick's gone. He got away."

Pete nodded solemnly. "And now he knows everything."

"Lights to black. And that's our second act curtain, people! Nice work."

Everyone, including Jenny, short and dark and anorexic, in ripped jeans and an Adele concert t-shirt, came out onto the stage.

"That was much better," Toland said. "Jon and Victor—you're going to have to work the fight together on your own. I want real punches. Both of you are too feeble to hurt each other anyway. And start binding the line to the fight itself—match the action to the word, as Shakespeare put it. That's actually the problem with getting off book too soon. I like actors to learn the text as they learn the blocking. That's why I tricked Jon today. Pete, I need more of a nasal sound in your voice. And pitch it a little higher. You're trying to sound like Victor. You do a fantastic Johnny Carson, a classic Chris Walken. This is your next great challenge. Seriously. It's got to be perfect if we're going to sell the switch. Jenny, let's organize that costume change and the breaking-glass effect." After a few more notes, he turned to me. "Any thoughts, Chief?"

I had plenty, and not just about the play. "Well…"

"Come on, speak your mind, we're all friends here, and I'd love to hear what someone in law enforcement—with a show business background!—thinks about the play."

"Show business?" Hollister said.

"Are you kidding, Blair? His father wrote *Airport Time* and *The Virgins of West Fourth Street*."

"And the book for that *Clue* musical," I added.

"There was a *Clue* musical?"

"It closed after ten performances. Frank Rich said he would have preferred a show based on *Parcheesi*. John Simon said, 'David Kennis, in the Belasco Theater, with a typewriter.' Not exactly a career highlight."

"So how do we stack up?" Hollister said.

"Pretty well. I did have one question, though. If Fenwick googled Judge David LaFrance, why didn't he find out that the judge had a twin brother?"

"That's obvious," Hollister said. "The whole…it's—I…" The bluster dwindled to silence.

"We should think about that one, Blair."

"I—yeah, I guess…"

The cast and the stage manager seemed inordinately pleased by Hollister's embarrassment. I guessed he wasn't caught speechless too often.

I reached over and clapped his shoulder. "I'm sure you'll be able to figure it out. My girlfriend writes mysteries and she says... well, it's like this—in a literary novel a character determines the plot. But in a mystery, the plot determines the character. Like with your play. If Fenwick googled the judge he'd find out too much information. So...make him a Luddite. He hates computers! He never even learned to e-mail. He thinks "google" is something that Cookie Monster does with his eyes. Maybe he still uses a rotary dial phone and an eight-track tape deck. See? That's an odd quirk. He's eccentric! It makes Fenwick more interesting—and it just happens to be extremely convenient for you—since it explains why he never googled the judge."

"Who's this girlfriend of yours?"

"Her name is Jane Stiles. She writes the Madeline Clark mysteries?"

Hollister coughed out a snide little laugh. "The ones with the blowhard douchebag Police Chief?"

"That's them."

"Well, she's smart. And that's good advice."

Toland opened his arms and flipped his hands in a "voila!" gesture. "There you go. A little artful exposition in dialogue—and pouf! Problem solved."

"'Pouf' for you. I have to sit down and write the stuff."

I pushed on. "Anyway...you know how your detective says he doesn't believe in coincidences?"

"It's a cop thing. Cops always say that. You're a cop, so I mean—you know, right?"

"Well, I believe in them. I just don't trust them. But they keep cropping up. Like, for instance, your play is about a judge with a twin brother, and we have one, right here on Nantucket, where you came all the way from Hollywood to mount a production. And he seems to be starring in it."

Hollister grinned. "And he's playing the judge! It's perfect. I just wish we could have gotten his brother, too, but the guy's a surgeon in Cleveland or somewhere. No interest, too busy saving lives or some shit. But the judge is pretty good, don't you think?"

"He's getting there."

Toland pulled a pamphlet-sized booklet from his pocket. It featured a cast photograph. All of them posed in costume on the set. "We just got the playbills. Take a look."

Hollister took one, opened it and stopped short. "Shit. Hold on." He patted his pockets, touched his head. "Crap. Where did I put my glasses? Did I have them with me today, Mark?'"

"Toland shrugged. "Yeah, probably—I don't know. I didn't really notice."

Hollister turned back to me. "That's his laser-like focus. Anyway, I always carry a spare." He pulled a pair of red-framed glasses from his carry-all, slipped them on, and handed me the playbill. "Anyway, fuck it, see for yourself. The bios are right in front."

I took the pamphlet, leafed through it until I found the Cast Notes. Galassi had spent twenty years as a prosecuting attorney for San Diego County, five years as the district attorney, and ten years as a Superior Court judge. Since his move to Nantucket three years before, he had played Big Daddy in *Cat on a Hot Tin Roof*, Scrooge in *A Christmas Carol*, Willy Clark in *The Sunshine Boys*, Wilfred in Ronald Harwood's *Quartet*, Pseudolus in *A Funny Thing Happened on the Way to the Forum*, and Quixote in *Man of La Mancha*.

I looked up from the page "He can sing?"

"Like an angel," Toland said. "With a bad head cold."

I nodded. "Dreaming the impossible dream."

"Something like that."

"You ever see him work, before this afternoon?' Hollister asked.

"I don't get out to the theater much. I guess I've been missing out."

"Victor does voice-overs, too. And commercials. And he's the old guy who's scraping his windshield with his American Express card in that Visa ad."

Toland jumped in with a good impression of Galassi's grumpy old man act, brandishing an imaginary AmEx card. "Finally! Some use for this damn thing!"

"Right," I said, "I saw that one."

"Everybody did. He probably retired on the residuals."

Toland nodded. "A national ad! Where you get to say a line of dialogue! That's the actor's Holy Grail, Chief."

I handed back the playbill. "So, did Judge Galassi ever dabble in the stolen jewelry trade before he retired?"

Hollister snorted. "Come on. I made that up."

"Good to hear. So he has no dark criminal secrets in his past?"

"Not to my knowledge. But we all have our secrets. I wouldn't presume."

Silence settled in. We watched Jenny straighten up the set. I decided to close in. "So, Blair—where were you on Tuesday afternoon?"

"Tuesday afternoon? That's when Horst—hold on a second. I'm a suspect now?"

"You were always a suspect. I'm just getting around to you now."

"Do I need a lawyer?"

"That's your call. I'd certainly consider it."

"This is bullshit! It's nuts. I'm a writer! If I could actually kill people I wouldn't need to write about it."

I quoted: "Because I don't know enough about killing to kill him."

"*The Sting*. Thank you! Exactly. I'm just like Johnny Hooker."

"A con man?"

"I guess. In a way. We're both looking for that willing suspension of disbelief."

"So why would you kill want to kill Victor Galassi?"

"I wouldn't!"

"Or Horst Refn?"

"I'm telling you—I wouldn't! I wouldn't kill anyone. I don't want to get away with murder. I just want to write about it and win a Tony."

"So...just for the record—where were you on Tuesday afternoon?"

"Come on, man! Oh, I get it. You think I'm the bad guy because of that thing, that stupid argument in the parking lot."

"It wasn't your finest hour."

"Hey, I was stressed out. I was on the phone and I looked up and I almost rear-ended your—oh. That was Jane Stiles."

"Yeah. And you can expect to see that scene in her next book. I saw her taking notes. 'Nice intro for my next villain.' Her exact words."

"I yelled at your girlfriend. That makes me some kind of homicidal maniac?"

"We're working on that. Where were you Tuesday afternoon?"

"Jesus! Fine. I was visiting Judith Barsch, okay?"

"She wasn't home."

"I know that! I was getting to that."

"Sorry. Go on."

"Well, I went there to discuss...it was a money thing. We're using a couple of Equity actors in the show and they're not happy with the—you know, the accommodations. The Lab has an actors' housing set-up out in Tom Nevers, but it's like a college dorm and Celia Dunbar, from *General Hospital*? She's been trying to get the kids to clean up and they're driving her crazy. She and Ted—Ted Brownell, he played the furry ninja guitar hero in those *Galaxy* movies...Great guy, he has kids of his own, but he hit the roof when someone spilled an order of takeout chili in his bed and just left it there. Anyway, I was hoping Judy might kick in a couple of grand to put them up in someplace a little nicer."

Toland added, "I suggested one of the guest houses on North Water Street. They wanted to be in town, so..."

"Judy was all for it," Hollister pushed on. "You know, she was like, come to the house and we'll talk it over. We made an appointment and I kept it. But, like you say, she wasn't home, and her maid gave me carfare so I could grab a cab back to town."

Toland jumped in. "Blair doesn't have a car on island and he's too cheap to rent one."

"And the Theater Lab is too cheap to rent one for me!"

"So how did you get there? She lives way out, off Hummock Pond Road."

"I took the bus—the Wave. It was fine. I get good ideas riding on busses. I wrote my first play riding down to L.A. from Fresno."

"So people saw you. On the bus."

"I guess. Probably."

"And the maid can verify you were there."

"Sure."

"Plus the cab driver who took you back to town."

"Oh, yeah—yeah! Definitely."

I could see he was cheering up as his alibi came together. "Do you remember the cab company?"

"Uh...no, I mean, I wasn't really paying that much attention. But Judy's maid might know—Carmen Delgado? She talked to them. Ask her."

"We will."

"Great. He was a funny little guy, the cab driver. We did some *Who's on First* together. He was good! We really got into it." Hollister launched into both parts. "'You know the fellows' names? Yes. Well, then who's playing first? Yes. I mean the fellow's name on first base. Who. The fellow playin' first base. Who. The guy on first base. Who is on first. Well, what are you askin' me for?' I love that shit."

"Funny stuff."

"But you don't laugh."

"It's a family thing. My dad wrote comedy for a living and he thought it was unprofessional to laugh at jokes. Like a chef belching. It drove his comedian friends crazy. 'You never laugh,' I remember one of them yelled at him one time. He said, 'But my eyes are twinkling merrily.'"

"He sounds like a dick, no offense."

"He was a dick. But funny makes up for a lot. And he always made me laugh. Listen. Can I have a minute or two with Mark?"

"Sure, right, no problem."

"Alone."

"Oh, yeah, right—sorry. I'm outta here."

When he had climbed the side stairs to the lobby and we heard the big doors close, Mark said, "He's a nervous wreck now."

"I like him that way."

"Me too. And by the way, we were rehearsing all afternoon on Tuesday and my actors would probably cover for me, but I wasn't here. They just ran lines with the stage manager."

"So where were you?"

"It's—I'd rather not say. Unless you put me under arrest or something and I have to. It wasn't exactly a triumph. I will tell you…it had to do with that…that item I outbid you for at the auction."

"Oh."

"Kind of an expensive mistake."

"So it didn't work out?"

"It was a crazy stupid plan. I was just—I guess, when you live in your own head as much as I do, you forget that other people have real lives outside of it. Your dreams are not their goals. They have their own plans. Anyway. I'd love to just leave it at that, for now."

"No problem."

"If you really think I'm a killer, talk to Jane. She'll set you straight. She's known me forever."

I nodded. "You grew up here, right?"

"Part of the time. Enough of the time."

"For what?"

"To know this island pretty well, Chief. And to be glad to get the *H. E. double hockey sticks* out of here. That's what we used to say at NHS. Small-town kids who thought you'd get in trouble if you said 'Hell.' Good old Nantucket High School. Not that we were angels, or anything. Far from it. Some weird stuff went down here, back in the day. Shit I'm not proud of. But we all grow up right? At least I hope we do."

"Did this stuff you're talking about involve Haden Krakauer?"

"It's—I...why would you say that?"

"Last summer, when you were scouting movie locations near where Andrew Thayer's cottage burned down, you came into the station for questioning, and as I recall you were desperate to avoid Haden. It struck me as a little odd."

"It was odd. It still is. So, call me a gutless worm. Though the other gutless worms might protest. "Hey, give us a break, we're not totally gutless, like that little punk."

"You're pretty hard on yourself."

"Well, I deserve it."

"So what happened back then?

"Ask your girlfriend. She knows the whole story. Hell, she was the whole story. It might be tough to pry out of her, though. I notice she's never written about it. The Nantucket in her books is way too warm and fuzzy."

We sat silently for a while. I realized that Jane hardly ever talked about her childhood on the island. "Why come back?" I asked finally.

He blew out a breath. "What can I say? I missed the place. It's the only spot on Earth that ever felt like home to me. The steamboat whistle for the six-thirty ferry woke me up yesterday morning. It went through me like...I don't know. It really got to me. It's the sound of my childhood. It made me feel like an exile. That's why I throw a penny off the side of the boat when it clears the breakwater, just like everybody else."

"To make sure you'll come back."

"Yeah."

Jenny called from the stage, "I'm gonna take off, if that's okay?"

"Thanks. Tomorrow at nine?"

"Oh, yeah."

She disappeared into the wings.

I turned back to Toland. "So how did you hook up with Hollister?"

"His agent called me. I guess Blair read that profile in the *Hollywood Reporter* when *Acid Reign* came out. I talked about Nantucket, and how I missed it and how I wanted to direct a play. Well, that lit up the board for him. Blair had been reading about the island for years and he had the perfect play for me. He wanted to try it out in secret—some small-town company where he wouldn't have to worry about New York critics lurking in the wings. The Nantucket Theater Lab seemed perfect. I know that's kind of a backhanded compliment...but anyway, I liked the play, the actors were free, the Lab had a slot open...so everything kind of aligned perfectly, and here we are. Trying to get a community theater diva to talk and fight at the same time. Not exactly the Old Vic."

"Does Hollister seem off to you in any way?"

"I don't know. What way?"

"Moody. Angry. Quiet. Drinking by himself."

"Nope. Just the opposite. Even-tempered, patient, chatty, buying rounds for the bar. I don't see a problem there."

"And the judge playing a judge?"

"Typecasting?"

"How about Galassi, himself?"

"Sweet old man. Loves the theater. Started acting when he finally put his wife into a nursing home. Alzheimer's. Terrible business. But he came out the other side and kind of took wing, you know? It's a nice story. I don't see him as some kind of jewel thief con man dude. That doesn't fit."

"How about Refn?"

"I only met him a few times. Parties and fundraisers. We talked on the phone mostly. He was here for the first day of rehearsals. That's it."

"Any thoughts?"

"He was a creep. That's my thought. A nasty little creep with a phony smile. Calling you a genius while he stabs you in the back. And with an ice pick, not a knife. He was an ice pick-kind-of-guy, though I heard he hated the cold."

"And yet…winters get chilly here."

"Refn never stayed for the winter. He always flew south when the last show opened. He spent his winters in the Caribbean somewhere. That's what I heard."

"Any idea who might have wanted to kill him?"

"Gee, I don't know, Chief. Pretty much everybody who ever had to deal with him? Except the Theater Lab board. They bought his bullshit down to the last shovel-load. But as far as I can see, none of them know a thing about how the theater actually works. They just like cocktail parties and swanning around as patrons of the arts. It's the same way everywhere. Nonprofits are notorious—nothing but overpaid idiots at the top."

I stood. "Thanks for your time, Mark. If you think of anything else, or notice anything odd—give me a call at the station."

We shook hands. "Will do. And you're comped for the show, Chief. You and Jane."

"Thanks. Maybe we'll come opening night."

"I'll be looking for you."

In fact I wasn't sure I wanted to take him up on the offer. I certainly didn't expect to be making my theatrical debut that night, and I had no idea that Hollister's creaky, contrivance-ridden production would turn into a deadly true-crime drama before the first curtain call, but as Oscar Wilde pointed out, art imitates life.

And life gets even.

Part Three:
Washashores

Chapter Eight
Otto's Story

Karen Gifford fired her first five rounds, all grouped around the fifteen-yard target bull's-eye, and popped the magazine.

"Cover!"

"Covering," I shouted back.

She rammed the second magazine home and locked the slide back. "Ready!"

"Okay!"

She holstered her Glock.

"Issue the verbal challenge. We can do this dry first if you want."

She shook her head. "Halt!"

"All right, advance!"

She pivoted to the left, still in the Weaver stance, moved to the ten-yard line and shot twice. She was still grouped in the bull's-eye. She walked back, called out the same warning, performed the same maneuver, but pivoting right, and a third time, walking backward. All the shots looked good. All the commands felt real.

She'd obviously been practicing.

We worked the same procedure to five yards, and then to three. "ECQB," I said.

That's Extreme Close Quarters Battle, the final stage of the handgun qualification exam. Karen ran through a set of elbow and palm-heel strikes, kicks, and punches against her phantom perpetrator, with solid snap and focus. She changed out the magazine again.

"Every round counts at this stage," I reminded her.

"Got it." She discharged five rounds, reloaded, fired five more, left and right, stepping backward for the final shots. The paper targets were shredded and useless by this time, but I had set up another scoring target for her.

She pulled the trigger for the last time, and turned to me. Despite the earplugs, both our heads were ringing.

"Do I pass?"

"Flying colors," I said.

"You were a little sloppy at the seven-yard mark," Billy Delavane said, walking up to us. He'd been practicing at the range when we arrived, fine-tuning the sights on his hunting rifle and working some new rounds through a used Beretta he'd picked up on a surfing trip to South Carolina.

Billy pointed. "You can see—four shots went a little wide, outside the grouping. You have to get your feet back set parallel every time."

Karen glanced over at me. I nodded. Billy was an expert shot, and I suspected he'd bagged quite a few deer out of season with that Mossberg Patriot of his.

"Here, let me show you."

He already had his arms around her shoulders, straightening her outstretched elbow with one hand and nudging her feet apart with his hiking boot.

Karen smiled. "This is cozy."

"He's ten years older than you," I blurted. It was embarrassing, but I'd seen Billy at work before. He just smiled. He knew I was a Quaker at heart.

"I don't think that matters much, once you pass the age of thirty," Karen said. "I've actually had a boyfriend or two, Chief.

And the ones my age were idiots. More like big dogs than grown men. I like pets, but…"

"You'll love Dervish," Billy said. "He's a pug."

"The biggest little dog I've ever seen," I added.

Billy nodded, resettling Karen's left hand around the butt of the Glock. "Dervish may actually have too much personality for his size."

"But we love him."

Billy nodded. "Everyone loves Dervish. One time when he ran away…or not exactly ran away, he's kind of a dog-about-town, but he's always home for dinner…but one time I drove into town looking for him and some little girl was carrying him down Main Street.

"'We're calling him Nemo!' she said. 'Because we found him!' I had to nip that one in the bud. There you go. A little higher." Billy had nudged Karen's arms up. "You'll get much better recoil control now."

"Can I borrow my officer for a moment?"

"Sure, sorry."

I took Karen aside. "I have to submit the paperwork, but you're officially handgun-qualified as of this morning," I told her. "Nice work."

She flashed her sunrise smile. "Thanks, Chief."

Normally, I would have let Charlie Boyce or Kyle Donnelly run her through the exam, but I wanted to talk to her away from the station. "I know you feel like you should be breaking down doors now, and dropping fleeing perpetrators in their tracks, but I have another research job for you."

"Chief—"

"It's important. Something's going on in this case, between Hollister and Refn and Judge Galassi, and I need to know what it is. I want a complete rundown on all three of them—go back at least ten years. Education, employment status, marriages, divorces, debt problems, lawsuits, criminal histories. Everything.

We know Refn—whoever he really was—used a stolen identity. The real Refn vanished. He's probably dead, and our boy probably killed him. You need to track him back to the identity change and figure out who he was before that. God knows when the print identification is going to come back. It could take another week and I need a complete rundown on this guy now. He was a predator. He came to Nantucket because it was a good hunting ground for the kind of people he liked to use. I think his path crossed with Hollister somewhere along the line. That's a good place to start."

She was nodding as I spoke, instantly committed to the job on hand. She had a pad and pencil in her pocket but she didn't take them out. She reminded me bizarrely of the old waiters in my father's favorite L.A. restaurants like Musso & Frank, Romanoff's, Dan Tana's. They were seasoned pros—not secret writers or movie star-wannabes—who never wrote down an order, even for a party of ten, because they didn't need to. They remembered. They'd been doing this job for thirty years and they were good at it. Karen had the same poised quiet expertise, the same lack of vanity. She could take a compliment, but she didn't need one. I didn't give her one now.

I just said, "Get back to me as soon as you can. We need to untangle this."

She glanced over at Billy with a regretful shrug and followed me back to my cruiser.

Otto Didrickson was in the backseat, with a hand jammed into the pocket of an old Burberry raincoat. I noticed what looked like a Marine Corps pin on the lapel. I didn't see him as a soldier; maybe he'd stolen that, too.

"I have a gun," he said. "Lose the girl, get in and drive."

Karen laughed. "He does not have a gun! And he wouldn't know how to shoot it if he did."

Otto squinted up out the car window. "Karen Gifford?"

"Hi, Otto. Take your hand out of your coat pocket before you get yourself in trouble."

"Karen Gifford on the NPD. I would have guessed—corporate lawyer?"

"But I don't like lawyers."

"Me, neither. Same with brokers. That's why I never got into real estate."

"Also you couldn't pass the broker's exam."

A sheepish shoulder lift. "Yeah, that too. So, you like cops?"

"Some of them."

I stepped up to the car. "I'll take a ride with him, Karen. Billy can give you a lift home."

"Yeah?"

"Go on, finish your lesson."

"Thanks, Chief."

She jogged back to the range and I climbed into my cruiser. "Get in the front with me, Otto."

When we were settled and seatbelted I pulled out onto Madequecham Valley Road. The dirt had been graded for the rich people but recent rains had reduced it to the usual rutted moonscape. We undulated over the potholes and washboards.

"I didn't kill Refn," Otto said.

"But he was blackmailing you about the Tarrant engagement ring."

"I told your detective—I got the ring at an auction. Years ago."

"Rafael Osona has no record of it."

"It was a Jim Kirkpatrick auction."

"He doesn't sell estate jewelry." I was guessing there, but I clearly guessed right. Otto folded.

"So are you going to arrest me?"

"I'm going to warn you. Losing our premier Ghost Walk guide would disrupt the summer season. But stop. No more grave-robbing, Otto. Seriously."

"Grave-robbing! It sounds crazy even saying it. Like—who would rob a grave in this day and age? Am I right?"

"Otto."

"No more grave-robbing."

"Thank you."

"I went to his house, though. Refn's."

"When was this?"

"About a week before the murder. We had a fight. I was inside searching the place when he came home. He clocked me good! Right in the kisser."

I thought of the blood on the chair pillow. This could be an alternate explanation. "How did you get in?"

"The door was *open?*"

I recognized that interrogative upswing in his voice—you hear it when liars are trying out a new lie, as if they were asking for your approval.

He didn't get mine. "Come on, Otto. Refn was paranoid. He kept that place locked up tight."

Otto surprised me with a toothy grin. "But on the other hand, he lived in Naushop, where the houses are built cheap and the locks are garbage."

"Now I have you for breaking-and-entering as well as assault."

"He assaulted me!"

"He was justified. Technically, it was a home invasion."

"Jeez. I'm trying to help you out around here."

"Feel free to start."

We had turned onto the tarmac of New South Road and were waiting for a line of cars to pass on Milestone Road. Everyone slowed down for the police cruiser.   .

"I found something in his house. A couple of things, actually."

"And you took them."

"They could be evidence."

I made the turn and we started back to town. "You're pushing it, Otto."

He pulled a folded piece of paper and two bills out of his pocket. I eased over onto the grass by the side of the road, and he handed me the money. They were hundred-dollar bills.

"A bribe?"

"Just look at them, Chief. Take a long hard look." I unfolded the bills, turned them over. "Look at them side by side. Like they were twins."

I thought of my dad's friend Lee Pozniak, a brilliant production designer, whose impeccable eye for detail had created the look and the atmosphere of dozens of great films, stretching back to the seventies. He had been like a second father to me, as arrogant, charming, and funny as my real father, and I had always been able to tell him apart from Carter Pozniak, his identical twin brother—also a production designer, and quite a good one, though not quite in Lee's class. Minute, fractal differences set them apart, nuances of expression, hand gestures, a shared squint that looked intent and curious on Lee but suspicious and calculating on his brother. My dad said I had an "odd small genius for spotting discrepancies."

Was Otto asking me to do that now? I spread the two bills flat, one on each knee, and really looked at them.

"Anything?"

"Not yet."

"See the vertical strip? That should fluoresce in this light." He leaned over to work a yellow pencil and blue bar-light out of his pocket. The vertical line stayed dull under the illumination. "That's one way to tell," he said. "But you don't need the high-tech stuff. Joe Shop-Owner uses this." He handed me the pencil. "Draw on it. Wrong paper, the yellow goes black." I scribbled an X—it stayed yellow. "That means they either got some paper mill—probably in Europe somewhere—to make the perfect linen-cotton mix paper. Or, more likely, they bleached a one-dollar bill and printed over it. Hold it up to the light, see if you find see the ghost image."

It was faint, smoke on fog, but I picked it out. "Wow."

He grinned. "You're ready for the Secret Service now, Chief!"

"You found this at Refn's house?"

"Yeah."

"And thoughtfully seized it as potential evidence in your role as an upstanding member of the Commonwealth's citizen-constabulary?"

"Naaah. I just stole it."

"But then you realized it was fake."

"Oh, yeah."

"How did you know what to look for?"

"Fake is my business, Chief. It's what I do. I find this shit fascinating, always have. Art forgeries, those small-town facades they put up at movie studios for street scenes? Masks, human doubles, the plastic food in Japanese restaurant windows, you name it. One of my best friends back in the day did faux painting—you know what that is? This guy could make anything look like anything. He could paint mahogany to look like knotty pine and vice versa. He took all the steel door handles in this guy's house and painted them to look like burled oak so they'd match the floor. Crazy shit.

"When they moved the organ in his church, it cracked a couple of big marble slabs on the floor. This stuff was irreplaceable, I mean, it came from some quarry in Romania or something that closed down in the fifties. So Tucker, that's his name, Tucker Brand, he painted new faux marble squares right on the floor—cement base, fifteen layers of glaze, the whole schmagoo. And nobody can tell the difference. The guy's a genius, but according to him, it's his brother who's got the real brains. Go figure.

"Anyway, Tucker's the one who got me into the counterfeit money thing. I think he was considering it, you know, as a sideline, but he couldn't afford the equipment."

"That's comforting."

"It's a real problem. We're talking paper, engraving plates, printing presses, ink—oh, yeah, they have a special ink that changes color in different lights. You can get it on the black market but that's a whole other crime and you're dealing with, you know…"

"Criminals."

"Bad ones. There's great counterfeit money coming out of Columbia right now, but that's a whole other level. This stuff looks strictly American grade to me."

I handed back the money. "So you found this in Refn's house."

He nodded. "What do you think it means?"

"It could be nothing—some counterfeit bills are circulating, and Refn wound up with one of them. I can check with the Statics and the FBI, see if they've heard anything."

"But it could be more than that."

"It could be. Refn could have been the counterfeiter, or had dealings with them. The bill could be a trophy, or part of a bigger stash."

And the thought occurred to me—it ran parallel to Hollister's play—fake money, fake jewels.

"Could it be a message?"

"Or a warning. Someone knows about him. Someone knows what he did."

"Big-time. Check this out."

He gave me the sheet of paper—expensive stationery with initials engraved on the top of the page.

I carefully unfolded it and read:

jFl

Horst:

Do you ever think about justice? The real meaning of justice? I do. I ask myself, would justice mean you both being arrested and going to jail? Would that satisfy me? Because that's the real question of justice: how to satisfy the victim.

I've imagined it many times. The quiet courtroom, crowded with reporters and the public. Everyone waiting for the verdict. The foreman standing, clearing his throat. Watching your faces as he reads the words: guilty as charged. Then watching you both crumple, sobbing and broken, shambling out in chains, doomed to languish in jail for decades. Would that be enough for me?

No. Indeed not. Not even close.

Some people make quite an opportunity out of a jail sentence. They run whole criminal enterprises from a prison cell. They become Lord of that sordid domain. I could easily imagine you monsters wringing such a wicked victory out of defeat.

No, the only true justice is death, and more than that, the fear of death, the dread of its approach. Not hitting the pavement, but the long fall from the parapet, the long rushing contemplation of the impact.

Justice lies in the ticking clock of those few seconds. The problem is how to make them last. This letter is my solution to that problem.

I'm coming for you.

You're dead men.

Think about that. Think about it every day. Think about it every night, all night long. Don't worry about losing your sleep.

You'll catch up with it soon.

I read it twice. No date, no signature. It was produced on a standard laser printer. The writer was obviously educated and clearly deranged.

"Did you find an envelope?"

He shrugged a no. The postmark might have helped, but I had the strong feeling that this note had been hand-delivered. There was obviously another one of these letters, sent to Refn's partner in crime. But the odds were, whoever received it, burned it instantly. Any way to trace that? Ash? Long gone. Trash? Needle in a pin cushion. So why didn't Refn get rid of his letter? He thought he was invulnerable? He liked keeping mementos of his exploits, like that hundred-dollar bill? A dozen pathologies could explain the security lapse, but Refn was no longer around to clarify things.

The partner might have already fled the island, either after getting the letter, or more likely after Refn's death. A date on the letter would have helped. Still, it would be worthwhile checking the airline manifests for one-way tickets, and the Steamship Authority computers for vehicles with short notice reservations and open returns. Still, for the moment, for practical purposes, I had to assume the person was still on island, and in jeopardy.

It sounded like they probably deserved whatever was going to happen to them, but that wasn't my call.

Calls—we needed to check Refn's phone records. There could have been a flurry of panic phone calls between the two partners.

That left the monogram at the top of the page: J.F.L. It was a giant clue, but whoever sent this letter must have assumed Refn would destroy it. Anticipating Refn's first sight of those initials must have been worth the risk.

J.F.L. Joseph Frederick Little.

The man who had summoned Donald Harcourt to the crime scene, whose wife was being blackmailed by the newly deceased Artistic Director.

It felt like a fourth-quarter third down and inches on the

other team's goal line. One quick rushing play and the game was over. The case was solved, another life (however unworthy) was saved, and I may as well admit it, sitting there staring down at the letter, I began to feel like the hero.

I would remember this moment the next time Lonnie Fraker blundered into a false solution and came strutting into my office bragging. I teased our local State Police Captain, but Lonnie wasn't the only one who could be tricked by the sly trifecta of eagerness, arrogance, and ignorance into making a complete fool of himself.

As Jane said to me later: "Welcome to the club."

Chapter Nine

Sanctuary City

I caught up to Joe Little at the new golf course in 'Sconset.

"He and his friends have their boys' club out there," Laura told me when I called the house. "It's not even exercise—they ride those ridiculous carts. But it gets him out of the house and he's always in a good mood when he gets home. So I'd be crazy to complain."

I found them on the eighth hole—Little, Don Harcourt, and Howard Kohl. I was the last person any of them wanted to see, but I took advantage of the moment—"one stop shopping," as Chuck Obremski used to call it. I needed to talk to Kohl, also—his wife was another blackmail victim.

Kohl cut an elegant figure between his two hefty friends—six-three, barely one-eighty, by my estimate. With his aggressive beak and close-set eyes, he reminded me of the red-tailed hawks circling above the manicured, pool-table lawns of the golf course.

He was glad to clear himself. "I was in Bonn, West Germany, until last night," he told me. "Business trip." He pulled a flask out and took a swig. "Wheatgrass smoothie—from The Green. World's best jet lag cure."

"I'll give it a try, next time I get out of this time zone," I said.

He put an arm around my shoulders and led me away from

the others. "Do me a favor, Chief. Leave my wife alone. She had nothing to do with this—this incident. She's right on the edge. She couldn't hurt a deer tick…which is the closest insect equivalent to Refn. Don't look at me that way! Of course I hated the guy. So what? Your bona fide killer, that's a rare animal in this world, Chief. Cops forget that. They see murder all the time and they start to think it's normal. My dad was a highway patrolman in New Jersey. Listening to him, you'd think it was some kind of demolition derby out there. Road rage and drunk drivers and drug mules. It never occurred to him that ninety-nine percent of drivers were regular boring people just trying to get home. He dealt with the worst element and it warped his mind."

"I deal with lots of regular people here," I said.

"But you come from Los Angeles. And your brother is that sex crimes FBI guy. I can't imagine what he must think about the world!" He caught my surprised look. "Hey, I googled you—and your brother. That Phil Kennis is really something! He must lord it over you, doing this nothing job."

"I like this job. And I don't talk to Phil much these days. Just birthdays and Christmas, mostly." Time to pivot. "Tell me about Bess."

"There's nothing to tell. She spends all day in her bed, drugged up with the TV on. She's so full of anger and hate…I think she'd confess to the murder just so she could take credit for it. But who'd believe her? Don't waste your time on Bessie. That's my job."

We walked back. Kohl's friends were waiting for him, and another foursome lingered on hole behind. I was disrupting the game, slowing things down.

I spoke to Joe Little while Kohl teed up for his drive. "What else did Refn do to you?"

"Excuse me?"

"What was the crime exactly? It had to be more than blackmail."

"That was enough."

"To justify murder?"

He stepped away from me. "What the hell are you talking about?"

"I have your letter. Refn never got rid of it."

His look was authentically blank. "I never wrote Refn a letter."

"So you're saying someone stole your stationery?"

"I don't use personal stationery. I have letterhead paper for my business. Laura has some kind of pink notecards with a lighthouse and scallop shells. Sound familiar? No? Didn't think so. It's not exactly appropriate for death threats."

We stared at each other. There was nothing more to say. I reached into my pocket and handed him the letter.

He skimmed it and handed it back. "Someone's pissed off. I suggest you find them."

"I just did. Or do you know anyone else with the initials J.F.L.?"

He laughed, a short smirking snob's laugh, as if I'd used the dessert fork for the salad or referred to a sofa as a couch. "These initials are J.L.F. The last name goes in the middle in a monogram. Ask your girlfriend about it. She comes from a good family. And double-check your facts before you bother people next time."

"It's true," Jane said later. "I thought everyone knew that."

I sighed. "Almost everyone."

We were standing in the cemetery, inspecting her grandmother's grave. It looked good. She had finished cutting back the big juniper tree. With the new grass and the gravestone lifted and resettled and scrubbed of lichen, the area had a civilized, cared-for look.

"All it needs is some mulch," Jane noted. "Want to go to the dump? I have two barrels in my truck."

The town set piles of mulch and compost at the entrance to the landfill; all you needed was a container and a shovel. "Absolutely."

But I lingered for a moment by the iris and santolina. Set

between a triangle of busy roads, Prospect Hill felt like an entirely separate world. Sound carried differently and time itself seemed to slow down. You looked out at the busy cars and felt invisible, at one with the generations below your feet.

Jane studied my face. "The millions."

"What?"

"The millions—that's what Thornton Wilder called them in *Our Town*. All the ancestors up here."

I nodded. "You can feel them."

She took my arm. "You are a much finer specimen than Chief Blote."

Blote was the pinhead Police Chief in Jane's cozy mysteries. "You set the bar low," I said.

She stood on tiptoes to kiss my cheek. "Don't trip over it."

I filled her in on the case as we drove out to the dump. The moors rolled down to Hummock Pond in the mild air. I knew what Jane was thinking as she drove, she'd said it to me before: the island was still beautiful, despite everything, this stretch of it at least. She could still see the Nantucket of her childhood out here, where she'd spent the long summer days on her bike, roaming with her friends, a bag of lunch in the handlebar basket, not straggling home until dusk.

Today she drove quietly and let me talk. When I was done I said, "So who is J.L.F.? That's the question."

"Well, the first thought that comes to mind is Joe's sister Jenny. She divorced Aaron Feldman five years ago. Switched sides, if you know what I mean. She's quite a strident member of the LGBTQ community now. Aaron runs Feldman Properties. It was his dad's business, he's one of those second-generation Nantucket stuck-ons. He'll never leave the island. And he's kind of a rat. If anyone could turn a heterosexual girl into a lesbian…"

"Jennifer Little Feldman. That works. Wait—J-Feld? the disc jockey on ACK radio?"

"Right. She could have taken the law into her own hands.

Jenny always was a vindictive little bitch. They say she poisoned Lonnie Fraker's dog just because it growled at her once. No one could prove it."

I smiled. "So she's Caroline Cressman in *The View from Altar Rock*."

She patted my knee. "You've completed all your reading assignments! You are an 'A' student, Henry Kennis. But kind of a suck up. Are you trying to be the teacher's pet?"

"Always. So what did Jennifer think about that portrait in your book? The 'she should thank me. Ugly girls are better off dead' vixen?"

Jane laughed, short and emphatic. "She didn't recognize it. Most people have zero self-awareness, thank God. Jenny thought she was the nicest girl in school."

As we were shoveling mulch into the big plastic garbage can a few minutes later, Jane said, "I don't think Jenny's your killer. That letterhead looked so—I don't know. Businesslike and blocky? Like a man's monogram. Jenny was always kind of a girly-girl, even after she came out. Pink skirts and pedicures. She was the first person I knew who got a perm. I would have bet she'd have flowers on her stationery. Or at least flowery lettering."

I speared the shovel into the pile and caught my breath. "Besides, she was broadcasting when the murder went down."

My phone rang as we were hefting the big barrel into the back of the Ford Ranger Jane used for her landscaping business. I checked the screen: the main number at the station. That had to be Barnaby Toll, at the front desk.

I poked the connection open. "Yeah, Barney."

"You gotta get down here, Chief. They're trying to take Hector's dad."

"What? Who is? And what's he doing there anyway?"

"He came down to bail out his brother and they got into an argument about the cockfighting and it turned into a shoving match and pretty soon they were rolling around on the floor, punching and kicking. Anyway, they both wound up back in jail, public nuisance, disturbing the peace, assaulting a police officer—"

"Assaulting a police officer?"

"The brother took a swing at Ham Tyler. You know Ham, he went nuts. He clocked one brother, then the other brother jumped in, and Charlie Boyce and I pulled them apart, but—"

"Which brother punched Ham?"

"Who knows? Who can tell them apart? They're practically twins, seriously."

I knew it; I had made the same mistake myself just two days ago. It had been Hector's uncle, not his father, at the cockfight.

Jane opened her mouth in a silent grimace—"What?" I held up one finger, the new universal "wait until I'm off the phone" gesture. I had to organize this news. "Okay. You have both brothers in lockup. Who's trying to take them away?"

"ICE, Chief! Three guys from ICE. They have the jackets and the earpieces and everything."

"Who told them that the Cruz brothers were even in custody?"

"I don't know. Ham Tyler, maybe? He hates Mexicans. He calls them 'spics,' Chief. I've heard him."

"I'm on my way. Don't do anything until I get there."

"But these guys want to—"

"Stall them, Barney. Ask for the paperwork."

I put my phone away. Jane said, "I'll drive you back to your car."

We jumped in the cab, and I slammed my door as Jane cranked a perfect two-point turn. We roared out of the dump and back up Madaket Road. "Hamilton Tyler," I said as we passed the Ram Pasture parking lot, crowded with cars, as usual. "That punk has no business on the force."

"So what's he doing there?"

"He was hired long before I showed up, He's like, grandfathered in."

"You can't fire him?"

"It would be tricky. He'd have to do something a lot worse than getting rough with two undocumented aliens in the booking room."

"Can you suspend him?"

"The Selectmen wouldn't like it. He's Dan Taylor's cousin or something."

She nodded. "The Taylors and the Tylers. Ham was always a nightmare. I remember he dropped a load in someone's lunch bag one time."

"Dropped a load? You mean—?"

She pulled her mouth down, shook her head, as if to deny the memory. "Yeah. But who was it? Billy Delavane would know. He stood up for the kid and Ham laid off. Billy was great, he did it quietly, nobody knew but me and Haden Krakauer." She tapped the steering wheel with her fist. "Right. It was Lonnie Fraker's half brother, Doug. Ham made that kid's life a living hell until Billy stepped in. Douggie everyone called him. He left the island and never came back."

We were slipping off-topic. "I'll deal with Ham Tyler later. Right now I have to think about Immigration and Customs Enforcement."

"Don't let them take Sebastian."

"How do I swing that?"

She shrugged. "Just say 'No'?"

"Nancy Reagan would approve."

"I think even Ronald Reagan would approve."

I mulled it over. "I can make Nantucket into a Sanctuary City."

"They'll take all your federal funding away."

"What federal funding? We spent all our bailout money. I think we repaved every road on the island. The new middle school is up and running, the hospital money is all in place and most of that was private donations, anyway. How much more can we spend?"

She smiled. "Nantucket can always spend more."

"I guess."

We drove along. Jane turned off onto Millbrook Road, a dirt track cut-through between Madaket Road and Hummock Pond Road. It was early summer; the rich people had returned for the season, so once again there was a good chance that the lane had been graded recently, maybe even since the last rainstorm. Millbrook Road was always a gamble, but it paid off this time. It reminded me of a poem I'd written at the end of my marriage, when all the temporary fixes had failed, when we could no longer count on the counselors, and our new experimental "open marriage" had broken apart. The short-term solution to Nantucket's dirt road problem, filling the ruts with sand and gravel, had struck me as peculiarly apposite.

"No longer graded, but paved," I said.

Jane chimed in: "No longer rescued, but saved."

That spun me around. "What?"

She offered a bland helpful face. "Excuse me?"

"How do you know that poem?"

She swerved to avoid a rabbit. "Well, Chief Kennis, that happens to be one of the only poems you ever actually published. *Mulch Magazine*, issue number forty-five, Autumn 2008."

"You googled me."

"I did."

"Yikes."

"I found another one, from some defunct magazine called *Tesseract*. 'Because a true poem is always a four-dimensional construction.'"

"Please."

"It's such a sad poem."

"*Mid-Life Crisis*?"

"That's the one. Want to hear it?"

"God, no."

She grinned. "Tough. I have an excellent memory."

Then she launched:

> *"Turning forty*
> *Asleep by ten*
> *Yearning for different things*
> *Than other men —*
> *Not craving cars or travel*
> *Drugs or one-night stands or Zen.*
> *Just wondering about if and when*
> *Thinking about now and then—*
> *Scraping at this single longing*
> *With a pen:*
> *I want you to fall in love with me*
> *Again."*

"That packs a lot of sad into fifty-four words."

"But who's counting?"

"Well, me."

"The really sad thing is what happened when I gave it to Miranda for Valentine's Day."

"She didn't like it?"

"She hated it. She said she was the one who felt unloved. And if I wanted her to fall in love again I should try doing the dishes or folding the laundry once in a while. 'More prose, less poetry.'"

"Ouch."

"She had a point, actually."

Jane let that one alone, as she turned onto Hummock Pond Road.

I went on: "It reminds me of something Sebastian Cruz said to me a couple of weeks ago. I was dropping off Carrie at the house and he was working in the yard. His wife called out the kitchen window, 'Do you have your gardening gloves on? You should be wearing your gloves!' He shouted, 'Got them!' and pulled them out of his back pocket. He put them on, looking kind of sheepish. He said, 'I used to argue with Mirabel, but it turned out she was always right. Now I just follow orders.'"

"He's a good guy."

I nodded. "He really is. I would call him…a keeper."

"So let's keep him."

"I'll do my best."

The three ICE agents were waiting for me in the booking room with Charlie Boyce. They reminded me of Lonnie Fraker's State Police storm troopers: same crew cuts, same attitude of toxic authoritarian swagger. They wore windbreakers with the word POLICE on the back.

I was glad to see they'd made that mistake.

They introduced themselves with swift bone-crushing hand-shakes: Grimes, Shaw, and Hardesty. Over their shoulders I saw the two Cruz bothers in the main holding cell. Ramon was sitting on the bench with his elbows on his knees and his head in his hands. Sebastian was pacing. He had too much energy to sit still, even in jail.

"Nice to meet you all," I said, when we finished with the introductions. "Detective Boyce will walk you out to your car."

Charlie shifted from foot to foot. "Uh, Chief…I'm not sure if we should—"

Grimes made a brusque wiping gesture with his open palm. "Relax, son. This isn't your problem." He swung back to me. "Just turn over the prisoners and we'll be on our way."

"That's going to be a problem, Agent Grimes. These men aren't prisoners."

"They're under arrest."

"They were."

"Wait a second—"

"They were initially charged with misdemeanor disturbing the peace, but—"

Grimes pointed into the cell. "That man attacked a police officer!"

"It was an accident. Officer Tyler found himself in the middle of a family dispute. There are no hard feelings and no one's pressing charges."

"Oh, yes they are!"

Charlie stepped toward me. "Uh, Ham said he was determined to—"

"Ham's not doing anything. He's in enough trouble as it is. I'll talk to him later." I faced Grimes—faced him off. "It was a misunderstanding, Agent Grimes. The charges will be dropped by this afternoon."

He shook his head. "Doesn't matter. Until that happens, we're legally empowered to take custody."

"No, you're not."

"Really? Are you familiar with the Priority Enforcement Procedure?"

"What used to be called S-Comm? Yeah, I am."

"Then you understand the guidelines. It clearly mandates—"

"—that you can detain convicted felons and or individuals who pose an immediate danger to the community to ICE custody. Neither of these men is a convicted felon. And neither of them poses any danger to anyone…except possibly each other."

"That's for us to decide."

"Not yet, it isn't. You're not law enforcement on this island, and by the way—until you are, never show up here again with the word 'Police' on the back of your windbreakers. That's impersonating a police officer. You pull that shit and people sue the town, not the federal government. You have your fun, and we have to pay the damages. People win those suits because in this country, the police are supposed to handle public safety—not the immigration system. Get the distinction?"

"As a matter of fact, I don't. And I see no reason to stand around listen to some local yokel lecturing me on—"

"You wouldn't need the lecture, if you'd paid attention in civics class. But okay, I'll cut it short and make it simple. When you use the immigration system to enforce criminal law, you create a double standard where nothing matters but a person's immigration status. That's the problem, Grimes. Because in

America, we still guarantee due process and equal protection for everyone. Even immigrants.'

"Nicely put. But the fact remains. You are in violation of a forty-eight-hour hold order legally issued by ICE to this jurisdiction."

"I never saw it. And I don't have to acknowledge it."

"I can arrest you if you don't."

"Sure. Then the case will go to the State Attorney General, he'll file charges against ICE, and you'll get fired."

"You don't know Dave Carmichael. He's tough on immigration."

"Actually, I do know him. He's tough but he's fair."

"He'd never file on us."

"Try him. Try it, right now. Or get out of my house." Then came the staring contest. What Grimes didn't understand was that by entering it he had already lost. He wasn't going to get me to back down. He had to pull three pairs of handcuffs or walk away. Procrastinating only made him look weaker.

He finally figured that out. He tried the traditional stymied villain's fallback line. "This isn't over."

"What is over, Grimes? What is ever over? I got divorced six years ago and I'm still putting my ex-wife's sticky bun dough in the refrigerator to rise at five a.m., every Christmas morning. On the other hand, I don't have to come home to her every night. That's another important distinction for you to think about. Things don't have to be over to be done. And we're done."

I tipped my head toward the door and Charlie herded them outside.

Sebastian was grinning when I opened the cell door. "For a candy-ass liberal who never throws a punch, you are fucking badass, *pandejo*. You mess with the Feds—and then you bitch-slap their stinking clichés, too! Next thing, I thought you were going to tell him his shoes came from the two-for-one table at Payless."

"The shoes were bad. But that's a line I won't cross. And

speaking of clichés? The only bitch you know is your dog Daisy and you'd never slap her. So don't call women bitches. And don't insult men by calling them women. You have a reputation as a revolutionary populist playwright to maintain, *hombre*. You'll mess that up, talking like a sexist thug."

"Hey, man—"

"Don't worry about it. Word to the wise. I'm a little on edge right now."

With good reason—the expected call from Dave Carmichael came as I was driving the brothers home. We had just dropped off Ramon and we were sitting in his weedy driveway off Fairgrounds Road.

"What the hell do you think you're doing, you goddamn crazy, dumb-ass fuck-up? You're killing me out here!"

"Hi, Dave."

"You stand down three guys from ICE using my name? To keep a pair of wetback deadbeats in the country? I'm the guy who wants a wall! Remember? A ninety-foot wall that ruins all the wetlands and bird habitats and bankrupts your snowflake school lunch program and gives you ulcers every time you open the fucking newspaper!"

"But you know these guys aren't deadbeats or wetbacks."

"Really? And how do I know that? Do I take their word for that?"

"No, Dave. You take my word for that."

A short tight silence. Then: "Shit."

"These guys are hard-working immigrants, just like your great grandparents and my great grandparents. Here's a funny story. Miranda took the kids to New York last Thanksgiving, and they checked out the new interactive exhibits on Ellis Island. There's a big computer screen where you can look up anyone's name and Miranda found Abraham Kenisovsky."

"So that's your real name! I always thought Kennis sounded fake."

"They picked it, not us. Anyway, my daughter, Carrie, was staring at the name and she said, 'That's daddy's ancestor! And I give Miranda credit—without missing a beat she said, 'That's your ancestor, too.' It was a revelation for my daughter. I wish I could have seen her face at that moment."

"Okay, I get it—starving huddled masses yearning to breathe free. But Grimes tells me one of these guys you boosted is a murder suspect. That right?"

Grimes must have talked to Charlie Boyce while they were waiting for me. "I have lots of murder suspects right now."

"And this piece of wretched refuse from the teeming shores is one of them."

"Yeah."

"I do not believe this. I may be running for Governor in a couple of years!"

"And you'll win because you stand by your principles."

"No. I'll win because I have the best attack ads. Now listen to me, my friend. You're telling me—you honestly believe this guy is innocent?"

"Absolutely."

"Then prove it, before the story hits the papers. Clear his name. You have twenty-four hours. After that I'll come out there and drag his hard-working immigrant ass back to Guadalajara myself!"

He ended the call.

I turned to Sebastian. "We have to talk."

Chapter Ten

A Layer of Dust

The bitch I'd mentioned to Sebastian earlier met us at the door, in a barking, body-twisting seizure of delight. Daisy was a two-year-old springer spaniel, so pretty much par for the course. Sebastian grabbed her and manhandled her to the floor, rubbing her chest as she jack-knifed in circles on the linoleum. "Who's my girl? Who's my best girl?"

Daisy was no savant, but she knew the answer to that one.

Five minutes later we were all settled on the sagging couch in the messy living room, the humans with cups of coffee—the remains of the morning's dark roast, microwaved—and the dog with the tattered stuffed rabbit, her constant companion. She shook it hard and occasionally let go, sending it flying. Then she'd bound off the couch, retrieve it, and start again.

Sebastian grinned with pride. "You see? She plays fetch all by herself. All I have to do is watch."

We watched Daisy rip into her hapless friend for a few seconds, then I began. "I'm not sure how much you got from that phone call."

He frowned in thought. "Let me see. Your family arrived at Ellis Island with a different name. The State Attorney General has political ambitions, and you have many murder suspects.

Since at the end of the call you told me we need to talk, I must now assume I'm one of them."

"Good listening. But there's more. I have to clear you by this time tomorrow or he's going to let those three stooges from ICE walk in here and take you away."

He shook his head sadly. "I live on this island more than a decade. I raise my boy here, start a business, good business, I employ fourteen people, and yet…I could be gone tomorrow, like I was never here at all. Like a beer can on the beach. You see those clean-up crew people? Rich do-gooders?"

"They do some good. This place needs a lot of clean-up."

"You see how they spike the cans with those poles they have? Jab, lift, into the trash bag and gone. That's me. When do you feel like you really live here, man? Like you're part of the life here?"

"I don't know, Sebastian. I'm a washashore, too."

"So not yet?"

"Not yet."

We sat silently for a while, Daisy watching us for some sign that a new game was going to begin. Time to get practical. I edged forward on the couch. "Right now? I want to focus on keeping you here as long as I can. That means I need something for Dave Carmichael."

"To prove I'm innocent. That's not good for me, *Padrone*. I have lots of motive for this killing, and probably opportunity, too, if I set my mind to it. But no alibi."

"Are you sure about that?"

"I don't know, I don't know. How do people even remember exactly where they were at such-and-such a time? That seems suspicious to me right there."

"It can be. But people aren't usually that sneaky. Or that smart."

"And I am both?"

"I know you're smart."

He sighed. "It feels like a lottery, like the scratch cards at

Lucky Express. If you happen to remember where you were at the time of the murder, if someone happened to see you, if they happen to remember, if they noticed you, and most people notice nothing. They're too busy worrying about people noticing them. 'The suspect says he was at the car wash Saturday afternoon. Did you see him?' 'I don't know—did he say anything about my car? It was so dirty I was embarrassed to drive it!'"

Cars had come to his mind first thing. That could be useful. "Were you driving?"

"I don't know. I guess I could have been."

"The Red Sox game was on. Were you watching it?"

"I was listening to it. On the radio—yes! In my car. So I was driving. Does that help?"

"It depends. Do you remember the Sandoval home run?"

"Everybody remembers the Sandoval home run."

"Were you driving when it happened?"

"Yeah. I hurt my hand, banging it on the steering wheel. Is that an alibi?"

"It depends. Was anyone with you?"

"No. I was driving out to Shimmo to check on a job."

"Where did you start from? Could someone have seen you getting into the car?"

"I was in town, I had just gotten a late lunch from Walter's."

"So they'd remember you."

"Probably not. I didn't know the girl behind the counter. Some Nepalese girl, she spoke just enough English to take my order and she never even looked up at me. I was one of a thousand Hispanic men in work clothes ordering a New Yorker sub and a bag of chips."

I brightened. "Did you pay with a credit card?"

"Cash."

"You're not making this easy, Sebastian."

"I like to pay cash and get paid in cash. It protects me from the government. That's why no cell phone. See over there?" He twisted his head toward the cluttered desk that served as his home office. "I have a landline with an old-fashioned answering machine. One of those micro cassettes. The sound is always off on both of them. You call, you leave a message. Every day at four I check the machine."

"That's it?"

"That's it. You should try it sometime, lower your blood pressure."

"But what if one of your guys has an emergency?"

"They take care of themselves. Like Daisy."

"What if a customer needs to talk to you?"

"They wait."

"Wow. How do your customers feel about that?"

"Fuck my customers. I'm the best and they know it."

He was one of the best, it was true, installing the elaborate gardens that Paula Monaghan sneered at, mowing lawns, putting in hedges and even stands of trees, laying down crushed-shell driveways, building stone walls, and laying brick walkways and flagstone patios. Jane had mentioned him. In her day job, she worked as a humble grass-cutting landscaper, occasionally deadheading a flower patch or picking the weeds out of a bluestone driveway. She couldn't compete with giant crews like Sebastian's and she didn't even try. "Hey," she told me once, "they can't write clever dialogue."

Of course in Sebastian's case that wasn't quite true, either. Most of his dialogue was strident and dogmatic but I recalled a moment from his Columbine-on-Nantucket play, *Thinning the Herd*, where a kid much like Hector is talking to his crush, trying to reassure her about the unlikeliness of being attacked by crazy kids with guns:

I don't know, for me, talking to girls is the scariest thing. I've had a monster under my bed since I was three years old and he's never done shit to me. I think he has a crush on the monster in my closet. No, really—it's a girl monster in there. The monster under my bed can't talk to girls, either.

The girl takes his arm and says, "You're doing okay tonight."

It was a lovely moment of calm before the bloodbath. If writing about murder made you a potential killer, as so many people seemed to think, he and Jane had that in common also. But the idea was absurd. Sebastian was no killer. We just had to prove it.

We had a good start. He was driving at the TOD. "We need some external anchor to place you on the street at that time. Do you remember anything?"

"No, man, I was working, I wasn't paying attention to anything—not even the ballgame until Sandoval. I'm lucky I didn't run somebody over."

"I'm not sure I understand. You were working? On what?"

"My new play, man. Kind of a *Prince and the Pauper* thing, set on Nantucket. Except in my version the little prince wakes up."

I thought of Jackson Blum, the classic Nantucket Scrooge, now living an extraordinarily generous and open-hearted post-*A Christmas Carol* life. It could happen, but it wasn't a typical Sebastian Cruz development. "Are you getting mellow in your old age?"

"My middle age, *amigo*. Yeah, maybe, I don't know. Somebody got to learn something sometime."

"How were you writing in the car?"

"I use a little dictaphone."

"More micro cassettes?"

"I work it old school."

"Old school would be dictating to your wife, like Nabokov."

He snorted. "Maribel would never go for that shit."

I pushed forward. "So the tape was on while you were driving?"

"Yeah, sure, had to be."

"Can we listen to it?"

"Oh, I see. Yeah, why not? But you're not gonna find anything but me talking."

"You never know."

"Okay, hold on."

He levered himself off the soft pillows and Daisy used the opportunity to snuggle up to me with her head in my lap. I scratched her behind the ears and her tail thumped the couch. Sebastian picked the little tape player off his desk and fiddled with it as he sat down—little bursts of high-pitched word-scramble, then a moment of his voice, then more fast-forward noise.

"Okay," he said finally. "Here we are. I remember I was working on this 'money can't buy happiness' thing between the father and the son, just fooling around." He pressed *play*. I could hear the car engine and the low mutter of the baseball color commentary under the tinny version of Sebastian's voice:

"Money can't buy happiness. No—it's a barter system. No, but you think you can lease something just as good. No, Dad, or you wouldn't be so fucking miserable."

"I was just riffing here."

"If money could buy happiness, you'd still be waiting for that half-off sale," he said from the tape. "You'd have cornered the market by now. You'd be manufacturing it in China."

"I was closing in on it, here," Sebastian offered.

Then I heard the dogs barking.

"Stop the tape." He did. "Play it back." He did. "What's that? Do you remember that?'"

"I don't know. Wait a second. Oh, yeah—there was a big dogfight on Main Street—some little mutt and this huge bull mastiff."

"Great! We can verify that."

"I don't know. It could have been any dogfight anywhere."

"Maybe. Keep going."

He pressed *play*. More "money can't buy happiness" jokes: "You'd make sure there was five-hundred-page user's agreement and a no-returns policy. You'd be cutting it with cheerful, and selling it on the street. You'd be scalping it to the clinically depressed."

I heard the roar of the crowd—that had to be the home run.

Then the announcer started shouting and his voice broke up into static. Sebastian stopped the tape. "I remember now. I couldn't hear shit after that until I got past Fast Forward. Those fucking powerlines, man. There's no reception on Orange Street, not in town. Not for AM radio, anyway."

I reached over to turn off the tape. I remembered my conversation with Joe Stiles, when Jane and I were picking up Max at his house a few days before. Joe told us he'd mapped the bad radio reception areas in town. In any case, just driving under those powerlines with the radio tuned to WFAN would be proof enough, plus I had the dogfight to define the chronology. How many bull mastiffs could there be on the island? And, anyway, the fight would be memorable. All we had to do was canvass the store owners; tracking down the dog people was just a matter of footwork and phone calls. The MSPCA would have vaccination records.

I had Sebastian pinpointed at an exact place and an exact time at the moment the murder went down.

He was in the clear, with twenty-three hours to spare.

I made a mental note to call Dave Carmichael after lunch. For the moment Sebastian and I had other things to talk about.

"This is perfect," I said. "At the exact moment of Refn's death, I can place you within a hundred feet, more than two miles from the crime scene."

Sebastian let out a long breath. "Bad radio reception and a dogfight. Amazing. So we're done?"

"Not quite."

He nodded. "Of course. The sexting."

"I'm afraid so."

"My Hector had nothing to do with that."

"Yeah, but we still have to prove it."

"Then find the person who took his phone!"

"It's a big school, Sebastian. Hector's a popular kid. People misplace their phones all the time. And whoever did this only needed the phone for a few minutes. Does Hector have any idea who it could have been?"

"Many ideas and none. It could have been anyone, so it might as well be no one."

"But the boy is interested in Carrie."

"Probably."

"And jealous of Hector."

"Yes."

"And he knows Carrie well enough to know she'd hate getting...a picture like this on her phone."

"So he wants to break them up?"

I nodded. "That's my reading of it. It's someone who knows both of them, I'd guess a teammate on the Whalers, someone who's talked about Carrie, and probably gotten rejected by her, someone who's done crazy stuff like this before. A person who doesn't mind lying and cheating to get what he wants. That narrows it down a little. Talk to Hector. He may know someone who fits the profile."

He was studying me as I spoke. Then he made his decision. "You still suspect my son."

"Sebastian—"

"I heard the speech you gave at The Rotary Club last year. You were talking about all the crime scene technology available today—the lasers and electron microscopes and all of that. All the toys, you called them. You said you preferred to work old school—like me and my cassette tapes, yes? You said one smart, observant investigator could trick information out of a crime scene or a suspect's apartment better than any fancy, high-priced gizmo. I remember you used the word 'gizmo.' It made me laugh."

"What's your point?"

"Come upstairs with me. Look at Hector's room. Study it. Be smart and observant like the ideal investigator in your lecture. You will see the home of an innocent boy. A good boy. A boy incapable of such...obscenities."

"Listen, Sebastian, I'm running late and I really should—"

"Put yourself to the test!"

"I—"

"See what I see every day! Then you'll know the truth about my son."

I stood. "Okay. Let's give it a try."

Sebastian led me upstairs, with Daisy right behind us, stuffed rabbit clamped in her jaws. Someone might want to throw it, or have a tug of war with it, at least. I admired her unfailing optimism.

Sebastian nudged the bedroom door open. "I'll leave you alone. Don't move things around. Hector's very particular about his things."

"Okay."

I stepped inside, scanned the set-up: neatly made bed under the big double hung window, posters on the wall—Joy Huerta featured on a Jesse and Joy concert one-sheet, pictures of Kiko Alonso and Blake Martinez, suited up and ready for the next pass rush or tackle. The was a travel poster for a place called Sumidero Canyon, in Chiapas—immense vertical walls rising out of the dark blue river against the pale blue sky.

The other wall was taken up with bookshelves—planks resting on metal brackets. Poetry—Marquez, Lorca, and Neruda, along with younger poets like Juan Felipe Herrera and Mirtha Michelle Castro Marmol, who had branched out into acting, public speaking, and podcasts, with a huge following for her Instagram account. Maybe that was the way to make poetry work these days. I muttered aloud, "Beats scribbling doggerel between the budget proposals."

Daisy nosed into the room and cocked her head at me as if she took the "doggerel" slur personally. I gave her head an apologetic pat and went back to Hector's books: Harry Potter, *Hunger Games*, the *Passage* trilogy, *Milagro Beanfield War*. I pulled a paperback copy of *A Hundred Years of Solitude*. The spine was well-creased, the margins marked up. On a blank page after the end, I read this:

Note for paper. The book is all fireworks. One beautiful explosion after another. But at the end you're standing on a cold beach. You gather up your stuff and walk home. You're already forgetting it, except for a couple of the best ones. The galleon in the trees, the blood that flows home and detours around the rug. But is it enough? Not for me. Admiration, not love.

I set the book back on the shelf carefully, remembering that I wasn't supposed to touch anything, thinking Hector had a point about Marquez. Smart kid. Maybe a little bit of a smart ass. But I liked that about him.

What else? A framed Boy Scout certificate of merit, trophies for football and swimming. The desk held his computer, pictures of him and Carrie, a group shot of the Whalers. An empty bag of potato chips humanized the tidiness, along with a t-shirt on the floor and a Coke can on one of the shelves. He was measurably neater than Carrie—maybe he'd be a good influence. Jane would like that.

Sebastian stepped into the room, and stood behind me, looking past my shoulder to the travel poster. "Hector wants to visit Sumidero Canyon someday. I told him maybe we could take a boat trip down the Rio Grijalva. He said…'After we're all deported!' He was making a joke. It's not so funny right now."

"But still, kind of funny."

"Yes, he is a clever little man. So, did you see anything significant in here, Chief?"

"I think I did. I'm just not sure what."

I meant it: some detail was fractionally askew. I thought of those "What's Wrong With This Picture" puzzles featured in the doctor's office *Highlights* magazines I read as a kid, waiting for checkups and allergy shots. Something was definitely wrong with this picture.

Years before I had walked into a big house in Pacific Palisades with Chuck Obremski. The place belonged to a big-time real estate developer who had scammed his clients and disappeared with their money. Chuck was sure the wife had gotten ripped off also, but she was adamantly denying anything had happened. Her famous social graces had frozen into a rictus smile and a bizarre robotic hospitality, "Can I offer you juice or coffee, officers?" It was two in the afternoon. Chuck said juice would be fine, just to get her out of the room.

"She's in total denial, Hank," he whispered to me. "She's flat broke and scared shitless."

I remember looking round the lavishly appointed space. "How do you know?"

He grinned. "Pop quiz, buddy. You tell me." I took some lame guesses—had she sold her original art and replaced it with reproductions? Had he noticed a "for sale" tag on some expensive piece of furniture?—but I was stumped. "She had to fire the maid, dude. I would say about three days ago, from the dust levels."

Then I saw it, on the coffee tables and the grand piano, the burled arms of the chairs, the front edge of the bookshelves—everywhere. The glitch in Hector's room was something as subtle as that film of dust, something you'd always see once you noticed it, like the arrow in the FedEx logo.

But that didn't make seeing it any easier the first time.

I took a few pictures of Hector's room with my phone before I left, hoping I'd catch something when I could study them. Still, I noted the sardonic question on Sebastian's face as I turned for the door. Was I the smart, observant detective I praised in my Rotary Club lecture, or just one more Luddite gasbag blowing smoke? Wait and see, Sebastian.

Time will tell.

Chapter Eleven

The Swift Rock Road Irregulars

Halfway back to the station, I found out Lonnie Fraker had solved the murder.

The text didn't spike an adrenaline rush—Lonnie and I had been through this before. And of course I'd just pulled a classic "Lonnie" myself the day before. To say Fraker tended to "jump the gun" in his eagerness to close cases didn't quite cover it. He'd launch from the starting blocks if he heard a cough from the grandstand. But no one was wrong every time. This could be Lonnie's moment of triumph. I had joined the club, and I was rooting for both of us.

Lonnie was waiting for me in his office, bulging like the boa constrictor who swallowed the bobcat.

"It's the magic of technology, Henry."

I sat down in the chair facing his cluttered desk. "I'm not sure exactly—"

"We all make butt calls. I solve cases with them!"

"So this was an accident?"

"I'd call it fate."

I jammed my eyes shut for a second. Lonnie was still there when I opened them, oversized and tiny-voiced—"a talking bear on helium," as Jane liked to say.

I sat forward. "Tell me."

"So yesterday Gary Posner accidentally called me—the architect? He's turning half our garage into a workshop for my carpentry projects. You know Gary—he runs Nantucket Engineering, Remodeling and Design." Lonnie tilted sideways to pull his wallet from his hip pocket, fingered through it for a second, and pulled out a card, He handed it across the desk.

I smiled as I passed it back. "NERD?"

"He thinks it's funny. He wasn't exactly a football star in high school."

"Anyway, he butt-called you?"

"Listen up. He has a young daughter by his third marriage, cute little girl named Gemma. She's twelve years old and she's doing that kids' play at the Theater Lab."

I could tell what was coming. "Refn made a move on her?"

"He walked in when she was changing and made her try on different costumes. There was no screen to stand behind, it's just an open room with a clothes rack."

"Did he touch her?"

"Apparently."

"Jesus Christ."

"The girl wouldn't let Gary say a word about it."

"He's in the play they're doing."

"I know. He quit, and wrote some kind of letter and never sent it, and then when Refn died, a couple of board members, Judy Barsch, and Joe Little, they bought him a drink at the Club Car and apologized and asked him to come back."

"They couldn't recast the part?"

"It's pretty short notice. And Gary's a big donor to the theater. They didn't want to lose him. One of those money guys goes— who knows how many of his pals are going to follow him, you know what I mean? Also they're doing some high-brow English play next summer, with a big part for a little girl. And they more or less promised him that Gemma would get the role. Total bribery, right? But they were on the same page anyway. I mean the two of them hate Refn, they don't care how good he's been for the theater, so the next round of drinks it turned into kind of a 'Ding Dong the Witch is Dead' Munchkin dance party."

"So, you're telling me…Gary killed Refn?"

"I don't have to tell you a thing. Let Gary tell you himself."

He had his phone hooked up to a little wireless speaker box on the desk, but the sound was still muffled and smudged by traffic noise and the car's ventilation system—not to mention the fact that the phone itself was stuck in Gary Posner's hip pocket.

You could make out the conversation, though:

"You can't be serious."

"I'm telling you, leave me out of it."

"After what he did to you?"

"I'm moving on."

"Moving on? Where? Where can you move to? The moon?"

"It's not worth it, man. Okay?"

"I don't believe this."

"Two wrongs don't make a right."

"Yeah, they do! You bet your ass, they do. When people say 'Do the math,' they really mean 'do the addition,' and this is what they're talking about. Two wrongs totally make a right! One cancels out the other, don't you get that? The second one clears the books. It fixes things."

"And what about the person who does the fixing?"

"What about him?"

"Well…in this case, HE COMMITS MURDER! And probably spends the rest of his life in jail for it."

"So you're going to turn me in?"

"What? No, of course not, what are you talking about?"

"I'm saying—you don't turn me in, you're going to jail anyway. We talked about it, that's conspiracy, man. You're a—whaddyacallit… an accessory. Accessory before the crime. You're gonna do the time anyway. You might as well do the crime. At least you'll get some fun out of it."

Lonnie turned off the recording. "Enough for you?"

"Not quite. Keep playing it."

"The guy confessed!"

"Lonnie, when did you get this butt call?"

"This morning!"

"So, he's talking his friend into committing a crime that already happened."

"Maybe Refn was just the first. You ever think of that?"

I had another theory. "Play the rest of it."

Lonnie pushed the button.

"I'm not like you, I don't have the heart for this stuff."

"It's not about heart, it's—what is it?"

"Jesus Christ, Jono! How could you blank on that? It's the most obvious—"

"Hey, anyone can blank on anything anytime! All right? I blanked on my wife's name when we did Virginia Woolf! *Martha! George and Martha! Who forgets that?"*

I reached over and turned off the recording.

"Jon Favreau?"

Lonnie pounced. "Jon L. Favreau!"

That made sense. He must have added the initial when he got his SAG card. They can't have two Jon Favreaus on the rolls. "J.L.F.," I said. "Like the monogram on the letter."

"Yes! That's it! Haden faxed me a copy. I put it together and—boom!"

My heart sank. I hated to cancel his ticker-tape parade. But at least I could soften the blow. "It's okay—I made the exact same mistake, Lonnie. But with a different name."

"What mistake? There's no mistake."

"Yeah, uh, sorry…but stationery monograms put the last name in the middle. We're looking for a last name 'L' not 'F.' Besides, I saw this Favreau guy rehearsing yesterday. So in the car, on your butt call…he was just running lines from the play.

Blair Hollister's play—*Who Dun It*. He even flubbed a line. Right at the end there."

"So…what are you saying? He didn't kill this Virginia Woolf woman?"

I kept my face neutral, but how the hell could he not know who Virginia Woolf was? Or Edward Albee? What did they teach these kids at Nantucket High School? I sighed. "It's the title of another play, Lonnie. *Who's Afraid of Virginia Woolf?* They're actors, not killers."

"There's a play called *Who's Afraid of Virginia Woolf?*" I nodded. "Shit. Really?" I nodded again. "Goddamn. Fuck! Who writes a play called *Who's Afraid of Virginia Woolf?*" I shrugged. We stared at each other. "This stays between us?"

I nodded one last time. "Sure, Lonnie. No problem."

"Thanks, man. So, then…I mean…now what?"

I stood up. "Now we get back to work."

Lonnie would have appreciated my next piece of work. There were so many different mistakes you could make in the course of an investigation, so many details that could trip you up.

My mother worked briefly for Electric Boat in Groton Connecticut, after a late-life graduation from Harvard's graduate School of Education. I went to my mother's Harvard graduation—few people can make that claim. Anyway, her job for the nuclear submarine-builder was fixing the communication problems between managers and workers. One of the first things she noticed at the plant were signs with the word "mistakes" written in the middle of a red circle with a red line cut through it.

Seriously: no mistakes.

With human error forbidden by company policy, people chose not to report their oversights and blunders. Months later when the finished submarines were X-rayed and the bad welds were discovered, the company had to spend millions of dollars in extra work, at taxpayer expense. Mom made the radical suggestion that workers report mistakes promptly, and even get rewarded for it.

They tried out this quirky new policy and over the next couple of years, she saved the government so much money, no one in our family should have ever have to pay taxes again.

Mistakes in police work were less costly in dollar terms, but they were just as mortifying and potentially dangerous. More importantly, they impelled the same urge to cover up. No one likes looking foolish.

But I certainly felt that way as I drove past the Lily Pond parking lot on North Liberty Street that afternoon. I had WACK on the radio, and I was listening to JFeld rhapsodizing about a group called The National when I saw the woman herself lifting two dachshunds into her beat-up old Bronco. Jane had missed it, too, which was some consolation—Jennifer Little Feldman taped her radio show. That was obvious now.

She had the right initials for the monogram, and she wasn't in the control booth when Refn was killed.

So where was she?

I checked the rearview mirror and saw her pulling out of the parking area, heading the opposite direction, toward Cliff Road. The street was empty for the moment—I cranked a three-point turn and started to follow her.

But someone else was following me.

Two big guys in a dirty white Ford Taurus. They tracked me as I tracked JFeld, up North Liberty Street past the State Police HQ. For a second I thought of turning in there, to see if they'd follow me, but a chilling thought cancelled that idea. What if they were following Jennifer Feldman, not me? It was classic surveillance trade craft—putting another vehicle between you and the subject, especially on small, uncrowded streets where you were more likely to be spotted. I drove on.

We caravanned all the way to Madaket Road and then took the quick right onto Eel Point Road, still in an ever-more-obvious procession until we reached Swift Rock Road and the Taurus ran me off the street onto the bike path.

So they weren't chasing Jennifer Feldman. That was one bright spot in the situation. With the grimy sedan parked across my headlights, I watched her Bronco disappear in a trailing swirl of dust.

The Bulgarian brothers, Dimo and Boiko, rolled out of the car and you could see it lift on its suspension with their combined bulk taken off the axles. They weighed more than a quarter of a ton together, but Boiko looked almost normal next to his brother, who lifted his arm and curled a finger at me in a charmless "come hither" gesture that said "Get out of the car."

There was no point in procrastination. I knew what was coming. I strolled over to them. Dimo was leaning against the car and for a second I thought he was going to lift it up and beat me over the head with it, like a kid with a plastic yard toy. I set the image aside. "Let me guess. Whoever you work for, and they don't want you to know exactly who they are, so you can't tell me or anyone else…they want me to back off the Refn murder case."

"Uh…"

"And if I don't, you're going to kick the living crap out of me and make me regret I ever became a cop. Or something like that."

Dimo rallied. "Yah! Something exactly like that."

He pushed off from the car and his brother eased toward me from the other side. I noticed with a mixture of alarm and amusement that Boiko had slipped on a set of brass knuckles. These were black steel, with spikes on the circles. Used properly they were a killing weapon, and not particularly well-regulated. The only law I knew of about them in Massachusetts said you had to be over eighteen to own a set. But using them was a different matter. I had high hopes that these were just for show.

"You need to think about this," I said.

"Grab him, Boiko."

Not the best use of brass knuckles, but I felt no obligation to point that out. Boiko wrestled my arms behind back. I didn't struggle. There was no point. He could have dislocated both my shoulders like a kid snapping a glow-stick.

"Seriously," I said, "you're used to roughing up store owners, people who owe your bosses money, even the occasional private detective poking around on a missing persons case. Am I right? These people can't hurt you. They can't retaliate. You're looking at zero consequences."

"Unless they don't look bad enough when we finish!" Dimo added with a loud grunt that was probably some kind of laugh. Not the nice kind, though.

"Right. But I'm the Chief of Police, Dimo. You fuck with me and you've got nothing but consequences, especially on an island this small, where everyone knows you and there's nowhere you can hide. Felony assault on a police officer, resisting arrest, possession of contraband weapons, conspiracy—there are two of you and you must have talked about this first—"

"That's only if you can tell anyone afterward."

"Dimo, I'll be able to communicate in some form afterward, even if all I can do is hold a pencil in my teeth and poke at the 'yes' and 'no' buttons. You'll have to kill me to shut me up, and we both know it. That's murder one, and you're looking at life in jail, maximum security, most of it in segregated restrictive housing—if they don't just deport you back to Bulgaria. I'm sure the cops there would love to see you again."

That jab hit the mark. So he was more afraid of the Bulgarian police than two American decades in solitary confinement? Those boys knew something we didn't. But that was probably a good thing. America wasn't a police state yet.

Dimo was squinting at me. "So what are you say, Mr. Police?"

"I was remembering something you said to me when we first met. That I shouldn't make you feel unwelcome. But how could I really embrace you as a new member of our island community? That was the question. Well, I think I just figured out the answer."

"What is this? What are you do?"

"I'm offering you a position, Dimo. You and Boiko."

"What is this mean, this—position?"

"You'd work for me."

"Doing what?"

"Spying. Sound good?"

"He grinned, showing giant teeth. "Sounds extreme of good.""

"Think you can handle it?"

"With easily."

"Sounds like this is turning into a job interview. So let go of my arms, Boiko. You don't have to prove anything that way—I don't need your muscles. I need your ears. And your brains."

"You hear that, Boiko? He thinks you have brains."

"Fuck you! I have big brains."

"So what we do?"

I shook my arms. They had started to go numb. "First of all, you tell me who hired you."

He offered his wrists, as if I was going to handcuff him. "I wish I knew."

"What was your arrangement?"

"Boss sends text. Leaves money for us outside in plastic bag."

"Where?"

"At the windmill park. There is bench with little metal sign for man who walked his dog there. 'In all weathers' it say. All weathers! Let's see if he walk that dog in all Bulgarian weather! February in Varna! That would make him think twice."

"So the money is on the bench?"

"Taped under it. We text back when job is done, he tell us when to get money."

"How long does that take?"

"Sometimes one hour, sometimes one day. Sometimes is there before."

"This boss must trust you."

"Yah—or maybe not. Maybe boss not want to meet there. Very tricky. Not to predict."

"So when you text back today, the payment could be there already?"

"Could be."

"And when the boss finds out I'm still working the case?"

"We get fired! But, okay, we work for you now!"

"They're going to want the money back."

He shook his head, pondering this bizarre idea. "Hard to get money back from Dimo."

"I bet." I thought for a second. "Let me see your phone—scroll to the last text you got."

Dimo dug in to his pocket, poked the screen, skimmed his finger over it and handed it to me. The text came from 508-280-2294. I closed my eyes for a second, committing it to memory: five-oh-eight, two-eight-oh, two two nine four. Could it really be that easy? Probably not, but I had to try.

I was done with the boys for now. "Listen up. You do odd jobs for a lot of rich people. Someone was murdered here three days ago, and I think one of your clients—or more than one of them—might have been involved with the killing. They won't talk to me, but they talk around you because…well—"

Dimo pressed a fist to his teeth. "I know what you say. I like that you don't want to be say it. We are nothing to these people, yes? Like the animals. Who keeps a secret from his dog?"

"They don't even know we are speak English," Boiko added.

"We may not talk good, but we understand good enough."

"That's right. That's what I'm trying to say. And that's what I want you to do. Listen to them. And report back to me."

He peered at me with sudden suspicion. "You pay?"

"If the information is good."

"American money? Like the boss?"

"No, Dimo, I'll pay you in Lev—the exchange rate's about sixty cents on the dollar these days. Good deal for me!"

"You kid with Dimo."

"Yes."

"And you know Bulgarian money."

"I know a lot of things."

"You know how to get out of big beating, that's for sure!"

"So we have a deal?" I stuck out my hand.

He shook it. "I am hire?"

"Both of you. And I'll pay you off the books—so no taxes."

"Taxes? What is…taxes?"

"You're sounding more American all the time, Dimo. Now get to work. And wash your car! You're an employee of the Nantucket Police Department. Show a little pride."

I watched my new Swift Rock Road Irregulars driving away back toward town and considered my next move. First, I checked the number from Dimo's phone: Joseph Little again. Or whoever cloned his cell. The theory had seemed far-fetched when he floated it, but I had just made a small, probably trivial, perhaps irrelevant connection that gave the idea some traction.

Dimo said the payoff money was left under the bench in Dead Horse Valley. I'd seen Blair Hollister walking there a couple of weeks ago. It wasn't exactly a common stamping ground for tourists who didn't know the island. And he'd been in a rush. He had also been at Ventuno the day Little's phone disappeared, standing by the table when the drink spilled and Joe Little got sick.

The coincidences were piling up. I thought of my kids when they were little, building towers out of the single-serving containers of Smucker's jam at The Downyflake. You could always tell when one more packet would send the whole flimsy structure tumbling to the table.

Hollister was teetering. One more scrap of evidence and he was going to fall. But I didn't want to bring him in yet. I'd put someone on him, see where he went and what he did. If he had in fact stolen Jennifer Feldman's stationery and written the letter, that meant he was still hunting Refn's partner and his killing work was unfinished. I turned it over in my mind. Blair Hollister, cold-blooded assassin? I couldn't quite buy that concept. And I didn't have enough to charge him with, anyway—not yet.

Meanwhile, I still had to deal with Jennifer Feldman. I looked up the empty strip of asphalt. She could be anywhere by now in the snarl of paved and unpaved lanes that twisted off Eel Point Road. I could have called in a description of her car or staked out her house, but I wasn't sure I even wanted to arrest her yet, and I'd made enough mistakes for one day. Besides, I had a better idea. Her girlfriend worked at The Nantucket Theater Lab, and could probably tell me everything I needed to know.

I climbed into my cruiser and headed back to town.

Chapter Twelve

The Smell of Marshmallows

Kelly Ramos was re-painting the walls of the set when I got to the theater, turning the judge's den from a cheerful off-white to a somber forest-green. I walked down the steep steps between rows of seats, caught in the seductive thrall of empty theaters, the night's illusions still under construction, the mundane and the mysterious side by side.

I watched Kelly work for a minute or two, a tall, strikingly pretty girl with a crew cut, wearing paint-spattered overalls and a white t-shirt, barefoot on the drop cloth. She was pushing expertly into the cut-in, making big Xs with the loaded roller, and spreading the latex up and down from there. Finally, she sensed my presence and peered up into the shadows.

"Hello," I called out. "Looking good."

"It's going to take two coats to cover and I'm almost out. We don't have another gallon in the budget, so I'm gonna wind up buying it myself. Out of my generous eight-dollars-an-hour salary."

"Sounds familiar."

"Yeah, right?"

"Do you have time to talk?"

"Chief Kennis?"

"You recognized my voice?"

"Anyone who's been to a movie at the Dreamland would recognize your voice, Chief. From that don't-litter-the-beaches, leave-only-footprints public service announcement."

"Right."

"Leave only footprints? That's kind of corny."

"I didn't write it. It's not strict enough for me. I don't think people should even leave footprints. Make them sweep behind themselves with a broom!"

She laughed. "Good idea. And they could pick up their dog poop while they're at it."

I climbed onto the stage, as she set the roller in the pan and her brush in the working pot. I felt the backdrop surrounding me—the bookshelves and the fireplace, the worn leather chairs and the big couch, the paintings in their heavy frames, the dark windows—the judge's den, the alternate world.

"It's quite a set."

"It's the last one, with Marcia and Harry gone. It's all going to be 'black box' now. 'Conceptual' stage dressing. That's what Refn calls it. I love that. He wants nothing on stage, that's his concept—nothing." She caught herself. "*Was* his concept, I mean. Sorry. They say don't speak ill of the dead."

"I think they'll make an exception in Refn's case. Whoever 'they' are."

She smiled. "I've always wondered that myself. Anyway, Tim might be different, if they let him stay on. Tim Hobbes? He's the Acting Artistic Director."

"I met him."

We stood quietly for a moment or two. "So...is this about the murder?"

"I'm actually trying to find Jennifer Feldman."

"She'll be at work in an hour. Just go to the station."

"I may not have to. You told my officers you were at Squam Beach with some friends at the time of the murder. Was Jennifer one of them?"

"Fortunately. I mean—that lets her off the hook, right? The rest of us, too—unless…we all did it together, and we're all covering for each other."

"Sounds far-fetched."

"You don't know how Refn treated us."

"I've heard about the sexual harassment."

She frowned. "I wouldn't call it that. Sexual harassment—that's, I don't know—weird flirting? Or long hugs and playing grab-ass, or at worst, using your position to force people. Like they'll get fired if they don't do…you know. Whatever creepy thing you want them to do."

"And Refn didn't do that?"

"No, he did. But not with me. That would have been too easy. He enjoyed his mind games too much for that."

"Mind games? What kind of mind games?"

"He'd get to know you, figure you out, and then use things against you. He was a smart guy, I'll give him that. He could have been a shrink." She must have read my puzzled look. "Okay, here's an example. He knows I'm gay and he sensed or found out somehow that I'd been bisexual for a long time, really until Jenny. And he knew she was paranoid about it, like I could go back any time."

"How did he know all this?"

"I have no idea. He sniffed around, he got people talking, he may have gotten Jenny talking. It's not too hard after she's had a few beers, and she came to all the Theater Lab parties. Anyway… so Refn called me into his office one afternoon and told me to undress, and said—get this, this is how twisted he was—if I did it, he'd make sure it stayed our secret, but if I didn't do it, he'd tell Jenny that I did. That I seduced him. Can you follow that? 'She'd believe me,' he said. 'And you know it.' And I did know it. That's what I mean by mind games."

"So you did it?"

She nodded. "I had plenty of motivation to kill that miserable prick."

"But you didn't."

"And neither did Jenny. She still doesn't know what happened, by the way. He kept his word."

"So, he could do it again whenever he wanted."

"Yeah."

"Well, now you have a lovely anecdote to share at Refn's memorial service."

That tricked a small laugh out of her. "Sounds like fun. But I think I'll skip it."

An awkward silence settled between us. I broke it. "Do you mind if we sit down for a few minutes?"

"No problem."

I wasn't particularly tired, in fact I was feeling restless, but settling into the darkened front row would commit Kelly to our conversation, and—just as importantly—give her the option of not looking at me head-on as we spoke; the formalized impersonal intimacy of the confessional booth. I was no priest, I wasn't even a Catholic, but I was onto something. Kelly physically uncoiled a little once we joined the phantom audience, stretching her legs out and sliding down to rest her head against the seat-back.

"I've been here since five in the morning," she admitted.

"It's a lot of work."

We studied the half-painted set, a haunted house waiting for its ghosts to return—Hollister's ghosts. "You must see a lot, being here so much."

"My home away from home."

"Isn't the landlord supposed to repaint?"

"Yeah, and I'm supposed choose the colors. But this is the Theater Lab. So I just do what I'm told."

"This isn't your first season, is it?"

"It's my fifth."

"So you know how the place works, the rhythm of it, the routines."

"Yeah—mess and chaos and panic, right until the lights go

down opening night. There's a song Marcia Stoddard used to sing…'Three weeks, you rehearse and rehearse, two weeks and it couldn't be worse.' Something like that."

"'Another Opening, Another Show.' Cole Porter. From *Kiss Me Kate*."

"I know, Marcia told me. She was pissed off that I'd never seen it."

"All theater people should see it. They should do it at the Theater Lab."

"Yeah, well."

We looked quietly into the set. Marcia's rolling stick, which she had propped against the mantelpiece, started sliding. It moved slowly at first, then faster until it slipped off and clattered to the floor. The roller sleeve bounced a little but no paint spilled.

Still, Kelly squeaked in alarm. "Jesus! This place is haunted. I swear."

That caught my interest, and not because I believe in ghosts. "So—odd things have been happening lately?"

"Yeah, we should get the Ghost Walk dude in here."

"What kind of things?"

"I don't know…like stuff disappearing from the fridge all the time, and there's this one pair of shoes that supposedly belonged to Eugene O'Neill. Howard Anderwald brought them with him from New London, years ago. The story is, ever since they did *Long Day's Journey* back in the nineties, the shoes keep disappearing. They vanish, they turn up. They vanish again. The last time anyone saw them was 2012. Just before my time, before Refn—they were doing *Summer and Smoke*. I guess the shoes approved of Tennessee Williams. It's probably bullshit. I've never seen them myself."

"That's wild."

"Yeah."

"Anything else?"

"Well, there was one thing. Just the other day."

I stayed still and looked straight ahead. "What was that?"

"Well, there's an office in the theater for the visiting hot shots—directors mostly. Or writers, if there's some visiting author who wants to use it. The Lab put it in when the church did that big renovation a couple of years ago. It's no big deal—two desks and an old armchair someone scrounged from the thrift shop. A wireless modem, a Mister Coffee. That's about it."

"And something went missing from there?"

"Almost no one ever uses it. I don't think Mark Toland has spent fifteen minutes in there the whole time he's been here. There's a window with a fan, so people use it for smoking. It's kind of a clubhouse for the interns. I clean it up every day. Well, I mean, I clean this whole place every day, you can't believe the mess people leave."

"And something went missing recently?"

"Something appeared recently. And then disappeared, like O'Neill's shoes, and nobody has any idea what happened."

"Tell me."

"This sounds dumb. But anything could be important, right?"

"Absolutely."

"Well, there was this can of computer keyboard cleaner? On one of the desks. Not Mark's, the other one, the smaller one. Have you ever seen this cleaner stuff? It's a big spray can for blowing the dust off the keys. I noticed it was there one day and then, like, two days later it was gone."

"And that struck you as strange?"

"Kind of. Since Mark never brings his computer here, and Blair uses an iPad. No keyboard."

I thought about it for a few seconds. "Probably some well-meaning staff member bought it and then when they realized no one needed it, they threw it away, or dropped it off at take-it-or-leave-it."

"I thought of that. I asked everyone. Even Homer Boyce— the fabric store guy? He volunteers part-time now. Sort of like caretaker, handyman, whatever. He helped me clean up after the last cast party. The toilets overflowed, it was gross. But Homer's been in such a good mood since he got his store back and stopped drinking. It's almost scary. Anyway…I asked him about the keyboard cleaner—it's the kind of thing he might pick up at the office supply store. Kind of a super nerd's impulse buy. But he knew nothing about it. Neither did the Reverend or his wife. I even talked to Pat Folger—his crew did the renovations, he's been around doing punch list things since then. Nothing. He looked at me like I was crazy."

"That's just Pat."

"I checked with the garbage man—Sam Trikilis? He's a big snoop. He didn't remember anything either. He would have, too. He would have been pissed off. That stuff doesn't belong with the regular trash. You try to burn those aerosol cans and they explode. That's what he told me. After that, I was stumped."

"So…ghosts?"

"Why not?"

"Well…it's not the go-to solution in most criminal investigations."

"Yeah, but there's nothing criminal about a can of keyboard cleaner." Her face lit up with a new idea and I thought of those cartoon light bulbs popping on over animated characters' heads. "Unless…what if someone was using it to get rid of fingerprints?"

"Now you're thinking."

"The ransom note was typed on Hollister's computer!"

"But there was no ransom note. And Hollister uses an iPad, you said."

"Oh, yeah, right, sure. That was dumb."

"Not at all. You have to go through the bad ideas to get to the good ones."

She brightened. "That's what Mark says about rehearsing a play. He lets actors come up with anything they want, their interpretations or whatever? And eventually they start saying smart stuff. It never fails."

"Makes sense to me."

We settled back, inspecting the stage.

"There was something else," she said finally.

"What?"

"It's a little weird."

"That's okay."

"The morning I noticed the keyboard cleaner was gone, there was this—smell. In the theater. Backstage."

"What kind of smell?"

"It was...it smelled like—marshmallows."

"Marshmallows?"

"I know, crazy, right? No one eats them, there's none in the kitchen, there was no kids' thing happening at the church, so..."

"But you smelled them anyway."

"Maybe it was the ghost of a Boy Scout troop leader!"

"Ghosts making s'mores. I'll have to tell Otto about that one."

"He'd love it. I don't think he's ever used a smell on his tour before." She thought for a second. "The weirdest part was, Ted Brownell—he's one of the New York actors? He stopped by a few minutes later and I asked him about it, but neither of us could smell anything. He thought I was high. But I wasn't, I swear. The smell was just gone."

We sat quietly, then. I had no more questions and it sounded like Kelly was done. I pushed myself upright. "Thanks, Kelly. You've given me a lot to think about."

"And Jenny's not a suspect?"

"She never should have been. I have bad ideas too, sometimes."

I climbed the stairs, crossed the musty lobby and stepped out into the clear June sunshine. I was thinking of packing it in for the day when I got a jubilant call from Lonnie Fraker.

He had arrested Mike Henderson for the murder.

Chapter Thirteen

Needles and Pins

"Jesus Christ, Lonnie, what the hell are you talking about? You're losing it. You've finally gone crazy."

He chuckled. "Crazy like a fox, Chief. Crazy like a fox."

"I've never understood that phrase. It assumes foxes are smart. Are foxes really smart? They're wild animals. They live by instinct."

"Well, my instincts have been telling me that sleazy house-painter pal of yours is guilty of something for years."

"You thought he was robbing from the houses he worked on last summer. It turned out to be Sheriff Bulmer. You thought he was walking away from the LoGran Corporate residence with blood on his hands two years ago. It turned out to be paint. You were sure he killed Preston Lomax—"

"He had no alibi!"

"He didn't need one. He didn't do it."

"Well, he sure as hell did something."

"I don't have time for this, Lonnie."

"He cheated on his SATs! How about that?"

"There's no way to cheat on the SATs."

"He found a way! How else do you explain those scores? And then he goes into the building trades? Come on."

"He went into his father's business. Just like Billy Delavane."

"But Billy didn't get any 1600 on the SATs. Trust me on that one."

I drove along for a while, letting Lonnie stew.

"You still with me, Chief?"

"Hanging in. You've decided Mike Henderson killed Horst Refn."

"I didn't decide anything! I investigated the crime. I found suspects, I formed theories. And now I have proof."

I blew out an exasperated breath. "How was Mike even a suspect?"

"He was working two houses down from Refn in Naushop that day. He was right there. Then he was gone! And his wife has a big-time grudge about Refn. It's clear as day."

"What kind of grudge?"

"They were doing some play a couple of years ago. Cindy had to quit because Refn made a pass at her or something."

"And years later that's reason enough for Mike to kill him?"

"He painted the inside of the theater last year. Refn stiffed him on the last payment."

"You mean the Theater Lab board stiffed him."

"Yeah, well, Refn signs the checks and apparently there was quite a little tiff about it. No love lost there, my friend. We're talking about a big-time long-running feud based on sex and money that finally erupted into murder. We're talking about an unstable guy with a serious grudge who took a job virtually next door to his victim for next to no money just so he could have total access and seize the right moment to do the deed. Which he did! The neighbors heard someone crashing through the hedges. There was a ladder up against the first one. A painter's ladder."

I shook my head in the privacy of my car. "I don't buy it."

"Then check this out. The blood work came back on that couch pillow you gave Monica Terwilliger."

"And she called you about it? I told her—"

"Hey, calm down, Chief. Yeah, she called me first. Of course she did. I've known Mon since she was the prettiest girl in my senior class. That's twenty-two years and sixty-five pounds ago, buddy. We go way back. She was the prom queen. She broke my brother's heart."

"I hear a lot of people broke his heart."

A grunt. "Including Jane. Yeah, I always said Douggie aimed high for a kid who hated rejection."

I pulled into the police station parking lot, killed the engine. Time for Lonnie to deliver his knock-out punch. I stoically tilted my chin up to receive it. "Okay, Lonnie. So what did Monica tell you?"

"The blood work came back diabetic, type two diabetes. They did a whole insulin panel, just to make sure. And guess who just strolled into the Firehouse with two containers full of diabetes syringes yesterday? Mike Henderson."

"Are you kidding?"

"It's open and shut, Chief."

"What does Mike have to say about all this?"

"Don't know—he won't talk to anyone but you. Which I gotta say, sounds a little suspicious all by itself. I don't think law enforcement personnel should be that cozy with perpetrators."

"Alleged perpetrators."

"Whatever you want to call them. When they'd rather talk to a cop than their own lawyer? Something screwy is going on. That's my professional opinion."

I chose not to comment on that. "Where is Mike right now?"

"Holding cell two, right there at the Nantucket Police station."

"Thanks, Lonnie. We'll talk later."

I climbed out of my cruiser, trotted across the parking lot and into the building. The first person I saw crossing the lobby was Hamilton Tyler, just coming off duty.

Mike Henderson could wait another few minutes. He was used to spending time in jail on trumped-up charges. "Ham!"

He turned at the door. "Hey, Chief. I was just taking off. My girlfriend's—"

I had noticed Chloe Peterson's Jeep Renegade idling near the front of the station. Nice girl—she taught English at the high school, she'd brought Jane into work with her creative writing class. What she saw in Hamilton Tyler, I had no idea. "Chloe can wait. This won't take long."

"Is there a problem?"

I pointed a slow finger at him where he stood as if I was taking aim with rifle. "Never contact any other agency on behalf of this department again. If ICE or the FBI or the NSA or even the Veterans Administration or the goddamn Boy Scouts of America contact you, do nothing."

"I can't even say—"

"Here's what you say. 'I don't know. You'll have to talk to Chief Kennis about that.' Got it?"

"Okay, but I mean—"

"Let's try it. This is Bob Bullyboy from Immigration and Customs Enforcement: 'Is it true that you have several undocumented aliens currently incarcerated at your Fairgrounds Road facility?'" I was pleased with my use of bureaucratic jargon. I sounded just like Agent Grimes.

"Ah…I—you'll have to ask Chief Kennis about that."

"And certain officers are putting in for unused overtime allowances; can you verify that, Officer Tyler?"

"Ah, no…I mean…you'll have to ask Chief Kennis about that."

"That's better."

"Sorry, Chief, you're right, I know. It's true, that was stupid. I shouldn't have called ICE, but those guys were—it was just… Listen, it won't happen again. But these people—"

"'*These* people'? Really? 'These people'? If we hadn't stolen their land 'these people' would still be living in what we call Texas right now. So how does that make them inferior to you?"

Because they lost, that would be Ham's answer, though he didn't dare say it. He stared at me and I thought of Judith Barsch

sneering, "Here we are. And Nanahumacke is a name on a rock."
Ham Tyler was no different.

"Get going," I said to him. "And Ham—as of today, I'm
looking for an excuse to fire you. Try not to give me one."

He scurried out the door.

Mike Henderson was waiting for me when I got downstairs, in
the same cell where I'd found the Cruz brothers earlier that day.

I signaled Drew Pollack to release the cell door and stepped
inside as the low shriek sounded.

"Hey, Mike."

"Hey."

"Kill anybody lately?"

A glum little smile. "Everybody needs a hobby."

I sat down on the hard cot next to him, scootched back to
lean against the cinderblock wall—about as close to comfortable
as these Spartan furnishings got. Outside the cell, the booking
room was quiet. Drew had NPR on the radio—some call-in
show about cancer or aging or money or all three: extending
your retirement benefits to cover your loved one's hospice care.
I preferred the fundraising.

"So what happened?" I asked.

"The day Refn got killed? I saw someone leaving the house in
a hurry and chased them. But I didn't get a good look at them
and they were over the first hedge before I got down off my
ladder. So much for my citizen's arrest."

"Hey, you tried."

"I didn't know anybody got killed. I thought it was a burglar."

"And the diabetes was a nasty coincidence."

He laughed. "I don't have diabetes! My dog does. Check with
Sherry Holt. She's been taking care of Gus since he was a puppy."
I remembered Mike's old collie. He must be twelve or fifteen years
old by this time. "Sherry told me not to feed him treats between
meals. She didn't tell me it would get me arrested for murder."

"Sorry, Mike."

"It was kind of funny, actually. The guys at the firehouse were like, hey, tough luck buddy. Time to fix that diet! And I was like—it's my dog! And they were like, yeah sure, whatever, rolling their eyes. And as I left, one of them picked up the phone really fast, just like in the movies. You know that scene in every dumb movie when the bad guy ominously picks up the phone right after the good guy leaves his office? Just like that. Next thing I know, two of Lonnie Fraker's goons are snapping on the handcuffs."

"Jesus."

"Most of the diabetics I know have a pin or something— maybe a card in their wallet—in case they faint or have a seizure. Of course the Staties never checked. You ever see those pins?"

The delayed recognition struck me like a slap. "Yeah, Mike. As a matter of fact, I have."

Otto Didrickson was wearing one of those pins when he tried to kidnap me at the gun range. I had thought it was a Marine Corps button, but now I identified its medical insignia—the snake curled around the stake.

Otto was a diabetic.

It was his blood on Refn's couch pillow.

Neither of them was the killer, but that didn't help me much. "So," I said, pushing to my feet. "Are you planning to sue us for false arrest?"

He stood also. "Naah. Maybe next time."

"I admire your fatalism."

"It's the only proper response to fate. And false arrest seems to be my fate around here."

As we walked out into the parking lot a few minutes later, I put a hand on his arm to stop him. "Do I need to talk to Cindy? Lonnie says she had problems with Refn, too."

"I never let her kill anyone without me there to chaperone. She makes such a mess."

"I'm serious."

He stared me down. "No, you're not. You can't possibly be."

"I guess not. But I still have to talk to her, check the box. And I don't want to delegate that job."

"Thanks, Chief. Listen, she's home right now. Give me a lift and you can talk to her, get it over with."

I dropped him off, and wound up taking a drive with Cindy. She told me just enough to get herself off the suspects list. The police officer in me was satisfied with the redacted version of her story. The poet in me—and I might as well admit it, the small-town gossip—wanted to hear every detail. But that was none of my business. The truth of what happened that afternoon was her secret and she deserved to keep it. Only one relatively trivial aspect of her illicit romance affected me personally, and I wouldn't understand why until much later.

Chapter Fourteen

Harebrained Ideas

So, Mike and Cindy Henderson, Mark Toland, Jennifer Feldman and her girlfriend Kelly, were all cleared, along with Jane Stiles and her ex-husband. Lingering suspicions about Donald Harcourt and Joseph Little had faded. Other Theater Lab board members with no obvious alibis looked less and less plausible as cold-blooded murderers. That left me with the unhappy supposition that Blair Hollister was the perpetrator, the "unsub," as my brother Phil liked to call the ever-changing, eternal quarry in his FBI investigations.

Random bits of evidence pointed at Hollister, but arresting him would mean I belicved a man would, with no apparent motive, write a play about the very killing he planned to commit and then come to the killing ground to see it produced. It sounded more like Hollister's next production than any actual scenario you could use to secure an indictment from a real life district attorney.

In any case, whoever had been giving Dimo and Boiko orders from Joe Little's cloned cell phone was still keeping them busy, and they helped me solve one crime that week, though there was nothing I could do about it, because they were the criminals. I had more or less given them immunity, especially for a small

offense like this one, more of a misdemeanor, really, with no
evident purpose and no apparent victim.

At that point, though, I was happy to close any case, no
matter how small.

They weren't going to make it easy for me. I could tell by the
jovial look on Dimo's wide shovel face that he had some little
game in mind.

We met on the flight of steps that ran down the hill from
Gardners Court to Main Street, just above the old wrought-iron
gate that led to the little alley beside Met on Main. Beyond it,
we could see people passing on the sidewalk but no one glanced
our way. Nantucket had many pockets of privacy like this, in the
middle of its public spaces.

A UPS truck clattered up the cobblestones as Dimo said, "We
broke into judge's house—Judge Galassi."

I recalled the incident report. "That was last week, right after
Refn was killed. But you didn't take anything."

"You think?"

"Judge Galassi didn't report anything stolen."

"He not notice! He not look. Judge should be able to look.
Devil is with the detail, yes?"

"Yes."

"Today we break in again, through bulkyhead door we use
last time."

"Bulkhead," Boiko corrected him.

"Right! Bulkhead. He never even lock it after! Judge should
worry more about crime. Door to basement steps close with—
what is it?"

Boiko jumped in: "Hook and eye."

"Right! Excellent Boiko! His English very good. He knows
all the idiots."

"Idioms."

"Right, right. So you take your knife, you slip blade between
door, then one flick—" He snapped his wrist up. "Hook pops
out of eye, and you walk right in."

He looked at me, grinning, a big dog waiting for his treat. I shrugged and gave it to him. "Nice work, Dimo. But why the second break-in?"

"To put back what we didn't take last time!"

They both thought this was hilarious.

"Which was what?"

"That you have to guess! We play *Match Wits with Inspector Kennis*."

He was referring to a column David Trezize ran in the *Nantucket Shoals* for a year or so after I took over as Chief of Police. People would send in puzzles and locked room mysteries and old crime stories cobbled together from moldering Agatha Christie books they scavenged from the take-it-or-leave it pile at the dump. I had until the next issue of the paper to come up with my solution. If they stumped me, they got a free cup of soup from Bartlett's Farm. I had forgotten this, but Jane was one of the only people to trick me, with an elaborate plot (taken from her current work in progress), where a man framed himself for murder with all the clues built to point back his old rival, when examined closely. She deviously exploited and reversed the fundamental law of her mystery stories—that the culprit is never the first person you suspect. I was thinking like one of her readers and fell right into her trap. Soul mates! I should have called her up for a date that very afternoon—a little chowder at Bartlett's Farm?—but I was in the middle of a nasty divorce and the thought never occurred to me.

Anyway, *Match Wits with Inspector Kennis* was a nice way to introduce me to the community, but David's name for the column still occasionally came back to haunt me.

Like right now.

I set my mind to the task. "It was something your boss only needed for a little while, something Judge Galassi probably wouldn't miss while it was gone."

"Good, good!"

"So, something small."

"Yes. You are warming."

"A credit card?"

"No, no—town too small for a fake credit card."

"I use Jane's sometimes."

"Yes—at grocery store or gas station. This would have to be big purchase. People would check. Ask for ID."

"Okay. Good point. How about the alternate head for one of those sonic care toothbrushes?"

"Why steal that?"

"DNA sample?"

"You think we steal DNA sample? Besides, you could get from a hair on his hairbrush, or tissue in trash. No need to steal anything."

"Right, right. How about a tie clip?"

"Crazy."

"No, it would be a perfect place to install a bug, if you wanted to wire him for sound."

"You would need duplicate, in case he sees."

"He probably wears a Yacht Club tie pin. That wouldn't be hard to find."

"Very good. This is possible. But sorry, not true."

"How about jewelry? Steal a brooch or a necklace, replace it with a fake later."

He barked out a laugh. "Yah! And all you have to do is find great jewelry fake-maker on island of Nantucket, where even the real jewelry is bad. But you are warming again."

I had to cut this short. It occurred to me that the three of us, two hulking immigrants and a middle-aged man in jeans and a long-sleeved Eddie Bauer t-shirt, huddled off the street together, looked like nothing so much as a drug deal in progress. In any case, the less we were all seen together, the better. I could have bullied Dimo into giving up the information, but that was a last resort.

I wanted to win the game.

I inventoried the small, interchangeable useful household items, items you'd find in drawers, closets, pockets. I actually thought, "The key is figuring out why, not what."

And that was my answer, from an accidental term of art struck off a stray thought.

"It's a key," I said.

Dimo clapped me on the shoulder. "Yes! Genius!" His eyes narrowed. "But what kind of key?"

House key? It was impossible to distinguish one from the other on a ring. Car key? The mileage would give you away if you took the vehicle for a joyride, and a missing car was a hell of a lot more noticeable than a missing key. Padlock key? Where did you still see padlocks? Storage lockers—did they want to take something from Sun Island? But those facilities had surveillance cameras running twenty-four/seven. I left it as a possibility. But there was a much more likely one.

"It was a safe-deposit key."

Dimo looked glum. "Damn it. No soup for me today."

Boiko laughed. "Match with Inspector Kennis? You lose!"

"So what did you take out of the judge's box?"

"We take nothing! We leave key. We come back. Key in envelope with money for us. We go back, replace key, talk to you."

"End of story," Boiko added.

"We don't even spend money."

"We send back to Bulgaria. We are buying property. One apartment building and two laundry-mats. Big profits in the laundry-mats. People don't realize."

"Now you have cash for us?"

I gave them each a hundred-dollar bill—a Nantucket sawbuck, as the rich locals called them. Sawbuck was old school slang for a ten-dollar bill, and the idea was that a hundred dollars bought you ten dollars' worth of stuff on rip-off island. Rich people loved to complain about how expensive everything was.

The Tabachev brothers were a bargain, and they were happy to take the cash. As they pushed the hinged cast-iron gate open on its squealing hinges and started down the narrow cement corridor that led to Main Street, I said, "Boys, just one thing. Next time someone asks you to commit a crime while you're on my payroll, talk to me first."

Dimo looked chastened—or was he just faking it for his own amusement? "Yes, boss," he said.

"No more unauthorized breakings and enterings!" Boiko added.

"That's what I like to hear. Now get out of my sight and prove you're worth the trouble."

When I was alone I called Judge Galassi and asked him to meet me at the bank.

"I'll miss my tee time," he complained.

For a crazy second I conjured an image of silver trays and Darjeeling, cream and sugar in matching salvers, little sandwiches with the crusts off—and the judge, tipping a cup to his lips with an extended pinky. But it was golf, obviously. I was tired of rich people and their golf games.

"I'll make it as quick as I can. Someone may have robbed your safe-deposit box."

The tone changed instantly. "Ten minutes."

Daryl Swain, Vice President of Customer Relations at the bank's downtown branch, met us on the circular steps that looked down the length of cobblestoned Main Street. "Paradise," he said expansively taking the whole vista—the giant cars inching their way along, hunting the precious slant parking spaces slotted against the curb beside the packed sidewalks—tourists window-shopping, inevitable ice cream cones in hand, kids tangling their legs in the leashes of a dozen different breeds of dog taking their afternoon constitutionals. Conversations took place into cell phones or Bluetooth units—packs of twenty-something kids organizing the next trip to the Brewery, businessmen snapping orders to city-bound minions. A sharp-eyed observer could pick out a couple of B-list network newspeople strutting along, trying to ignore the stares ("Wow, he's much shorter than he looks on TV"), or pretending to. The usual crowd surrounded the Bartlett's Farm truck, though neither the first corn nor the first tomatoes of the season had ripened yet. I saw a few people reading actual printed books on the benches and someone working a busy book-signing at a table set out in front of Mitchell's.

All in all, a typical summer afternoon on the Grey Lady, at ease under a peerless blue sky, posing the same old question: why aren't these people at the beach? I would have been, but I was working. And my job, for this moment at least, was striding up the cobblestones toward me. He was short and solid and furry, with thick graying hair, a dense silver-flecked beard, bushy eyebrows and coarse bristle that started at his knuckles and no doubt sleeved his arms all the way to the elbow. He resembled an Ewok, with all their superficial cuddly charm and merciless guerilla warfare skills. I suppose that made me an Imperial Storm Trooper, a role I hadn't played since I left Los Angeles.

"Judge Galassi!" Swain called out, almost tripping over his own feet, and scampering down to greet his prized customer.

Galassi stumped up the steps, ignoring him. "What's going on, Kennis?"

"I'd like you to take a look in your safe-deposit box, and let me know if anything's missing."

He stared at me. "How could anything be missing?"

"I think someone may have stolen your box key, used it, and replaced it."

"The two break-ins."

"That's right."

"And how did you arrive at this theory?"

"Process of elimination?"

"Really. And what exactly did you eliminate?"

"Every other small inconspicuous item you might possess, that someone might find useful for a very short period of time."

"Don't you have any real work to do? A murder was committed on this island last week."

I took a breath and ignored his tone. "This may be related to our investigation."

"How?"

"We'll know more when we find out what's missing from your box."

He shuddered out a sigh of impatient disgust. "Fine. Let's get this over with."

Swain led us inside and we waited while the judge went into the safe-deposit area and checked his box.

"I hope there's nothing to worry about," Swain fussed at me. Galassi was out again before I had to answer.

"It's fine."

"Nothing missing?"

"Not a thing."

"You're sure?"

"I think I know the contents of my own safe-deposit box."

That was meant to be the end of our talk, but I couldn't quite let it go. "Nothing tampered with?"

I saw a swift twist of concern contract his features. "Tampered with how?"

"You tell me." We stood staring. Who would blink first? He obviously wasn't going to tell me anything. These games were much more fun with Dimo Tabachev. "If you have papers, someone could have replaced them with similar-looking pages."

"How would anyone know what pages in my box look like?"

A rhetorical question, clearly. "Or forged documents?"

"It's not that easy to forge documents, Kennis. And downright impossible standing in a bank with no tools or equipment and less than five minutes to get the job done. I mean, seriously."

"How about sealed files? Someone could have opened and resealed them."

"I think I'd notice."

"Maybe someone was counting on that."

"This is absurd. My box and its contents are intact. Thank you for your concern. Now, if you'll excuse me—"

But he didn't wait to be excused. He pushed past me and strode across the lobby, and out the door.

I turned to Swain. "Could you let me know if he comes back to check his box again in the next twenty-four hours?"

Swain's nose and mouth pinched together, as if there was a bad smell in the air. "Not really, Chief Kennis. Our customers are entitled to their privacy."

"How about a list of all the people who rent boxes here? If someone tampered with Galassi's box—"

"But he just assured us—"

"—they'd need to have access to the safe-deposit room. And that means a box holder."

"Ummm, perhaps, but that would be quite problematical. We're not allowed to give out that kind of information, unless you could procure a warrant. But as no crime has been committed, and Judge Galassi has lodged no complaint, I'm not sure how you could arrange that. Besides, confidentially? A list like that wouldn't help you much. You might as well just check out the *Foggy Sheet*. It's a who's who of Nantucket society. Anyone who's anyone has a box here."

"And no one who's no one?"

He gave me a formal little laugh. "Oh, we have plenty of 'no ones,' too, Chief Kennis. We don't discriminate at the Bank of America."

I thanked him and left. By the time I was out on the street again I had the station on the phone. When Haden Krakauer came on the line I told him to find someone who knew Judge Galassi by sight and assign them to stake out the bank for the next day or two, in plainclothes.

"Ham Tyler pulled the judge over for a DUI last year," Haden said.

"Good, he can redeem himself. Tell him to bring a bag lunch. No slipping away for takeout. He can sit on the bench in front of the bookstore, and have eyes on both entrances from eight-thirty to three-thirty, solid."

"Yes, boss. Shall I have someone watching Ham, to be sure?"

"No, but let him know we'll be checking up on him. Scare him a little."

"Will do."

I slipped the phone in my pocket as I started strolling down Main Street to my cruiser. I knew what Ham Tyler would report. Galassi would be back. I had poked him with that comment about tampering, and he curled up like a snake. He'd be checking his box as soon as he knew he could do it without the Chief of Police waiting for him. I'd interrogated, interviewed, and even just chatted with thousands of suspects and witnesses and persons of interest in my career and I could generally tell when they had something to hide. The overplayed unwavering stare, the sincere smile whose spark never quite ignited the eyes, the trembling hands—and the shuffling feet, as if they were trying to tell the rest of the body to run. Judge Galassi had presented the full inventory of tells and twitches. But the question remained—what was he hiding, and what did it have to do with Refn's murder? I'd know so much more if I could find out who had opened his box. I thought of the security cameras, but once again I'd need a warrant and the request itself might alert my suspect. It was a small town and the *Foggy Sheet* crowd stuck together. Besides, there was no camera on the side door to the bank, which led into a private entrance for the safe-deposit room. The bank surveillance was prioritized for the hoi polloi. The cameras would show me nothing.

Best to wait, for now. I wasn't absolutely sure the key burglary was related to the Refn case. If Hollister was in fact the killer, what could he possibly want in Galassi's safe-deposit box? Did he have one of his own? Was it worth trying to force the bank to give me that information? The whole mental construction seemed flimsier and more unlikely by the second.

I was still working the problem later that day, frustrated and distracted, seeing suspects behind the wheel of every over-priced SUV—including, as Tim gleefully pointed out, a Maserati Levante and a Cadillac Escalade ESV—when I drove my kids to Stop & Shop, and they pulled me into another game of Grocery Gumshoes.

It started with cart shots, as we called them—snap guesses based on a quick glimpse as people passed us in the aisles. Carrie caught a sad bachelor (frozen burritos, Hungry Man TV dinners, quarts of juice and milk, single-serving chicken pot pies, microwave popcorn, and breakfast sandwiches), then a sleep-over cookout and pajama party (giant bags of chips and jugs of soda, packs of hot dogs and buns, cake mix, and a jug of frosting). There were two people on line ahead of us at the register. Tim nailed a healthy foodie family (tofu, bagged vegetables including the big hairy brown ones none of us recognized, fruits, boneless chicken, bags of dry black beans and chickpeas) with one lonely holdout (small frozen pizza).

And then I noticed, right in front of us but buried in her cell phone, NTL board member Judith Barsch. I was surprised, but I have to admit I liked her a little for doing her own shopping. Most of her crowd left chores like that to the servants.

That being said, she was buying an odd load of stuff: dried soup and powdered milk, shrimp cocktail pre-mixed with the sauce, plain yogurt, unsweetened Jello, a twelve-pack of Fresca, and a plastic tub of fresh chicken livers. Before the kids could start to speculate on this austere catalogue, she requested a plastic spoon and was told there were bags of them in aisle three. But she only wanted one. The pleasant Jamaican woman shrugged at the impossibility—and probably at the absurdity—of the request, and that got Barsch going.

"You're supposed to have all the ingredients. That's the Stop & Shop slogan. That's your claim to fame."

"Excuse me…I—is a spoon an ingredient?"

"I'm not talking about spoons! There's no gherkin juice in the pickle section and no pork spleens anywhere. You can get them fresh at any real market in the city."

"Pork spleens, ma'am? What do you use them for?"

Carrie jumped in. "They used them for balloons in *Little House on the Prairie*."

Barsch turned to her. They stood exactly eye-to-eye. "A little girl who reads!"

"I read too," Tim said. "I just finished *The Sun Also Rises*."

This seemed to amuse her. "Really! And do you have any idea what it was about?"

"Sure. Cool stuff, like—sitting around in French cafés and drinking Pernod, and fishing in the mountains with your cool friends and…other stuff. Bullfights, and sending off cables from your office and being in love with Lady Brett Ashley. Stuff like that."

Barsch favored him with a faint smile. "'Oh, Jake, we could have had such a damned good time together.' But it didn't really work out, did it?"

"Uh…no…not really."

"And do you have any idea why?"

"I, uh…the war?"

"World War One! Close enough. You'll read it again. That's all that matters."

Later, as we were packing our own grocery bags into the car, the lead gumshoe gave her verdict. "That lady was weird!"

"I thought she was nice," Tim protested.

"Are you kidding? She wanted that spoon so she could eat raw liver in her car!"

"Maybe she wanted to eat the yogurt. Did you ever think of that?"

"Who eats plain yogurt? In their car?"

"Impatient people," I said. "Hungry people who like healthy food. And don't care how it tastes."

"Well, she eats pork spleens, and there's nothing you can say about that."

Halfway home, after chastising Tim for his ongoing lack of courage in the surf ("Billy says you can't hesitate and back-off, and that's exactly what Debbie hates about you"), Carrie asked me what I was doing to solve Hector's case.

"There's not much I can do, right now," I admitted.

That wasn't good enough. "Do you even believe us?"

"Of course I do. Just give me a little time. I'll figure it out."

"You promise?"

"I promise."

"Mom says you should never promise if you're not sure."

"I'm sure."

But of course I wasn't. I felt sure Hector could help me, but so far he was refusing. The other path, figuring out who had lifted his device, came with its own complications. Carrie wanted me to put the situation to rest with complete secrecy, but that was hard when you were interrogating high school students about who stole their sacred cell phone.

I wondered if the thief had cloned it, like my adult unsub. It was possible, but unlikely—Hector could account for every other call and text on his phone and I couldn't see the point of taking the time for such a technically complicated trick for a one-off prank.

My interrogation of Hector himself hadn't gone well. He remained unhelpfully wedged into surly denial mode. When I'd made the awkward but obvious suggestion that he allow a private and confidential (law enforcement eyes only) photograph of the region in question, he had clamped down even harder. "Never," he said. "I'm sorry, Chief Kennis. But no way. There's got to be something else you can do."

Maybe there was, but I hadn't found it yet. After dinner that night, I scrolled through the pictures I had taken of Hector's room—something still snagged at me there. But I couldn't see it.

I felt the same way later that night, when Jane and I watched Fred Hamburger's video on NTV. Maybe it was the oddity of Judith Barsch's purchases at the grocery store, but I had started to suspect her of every unsolved crime in my career. (Had she spent time in Los Angeles when the "G.I Joe" veterans murders were going on? And how about those Ventura County dog-nappings? One of them was a pit bull!)

As Hamburger's video team tracked through the shiny modern opulence of Barsch's house, complete with sycophantic running commentary ("Did you study interior design or you just a natural?"), Jane, tucked into the crook of my arm on the bed, poked genial holes in my newest harebrained theory. Barsch had been one of Refn's biggest supporters, she had no motive, and since she had called the dog officer from the Pat Gardner Land Bank property as she hunted for her pit bull, she had a better alibi than the Callahans, for instance, who had basically bragged about the lack of witnesses to their supposed horseback ride on the afternoon of the murder.

"Do you see something odd about that closet?" I asked at one point.

"It's not a closet. It's a studio apartment for clothes. That's odd enough for me."

"No, I mean…" I rewound the video and watched the camera pan the rows of dresses and jackets, the regiments of shoes and racks of glasses. I gave up. "I don't know what I mean."

"Sorry about that 'harebrained' comment," she said later. "You're much smarter than the average rabbit."

"I've never intentionally run in front of a moving car, give me that much."

She rolled over on top of me for a kiss. "Absolutely. I couldn't have said it better myself."

By ten o'clock the next morning my concerns and theories didn't matter anymore. Karen Gifford walked into my office with her research completed. She had a cocky little smile on her face when she set the file folder down on my desk, and before I turned the first page I understood why.

Quietly, all by herself, using nothing but her cunning brain, our out-of-date computers, and the available law enforcement databases, she had broken the case wide open.

Part Four:
Open and Shut

Chapter Fifteen

Barry and Blair

I looked up from the file. "Barry Pomeroy?"

"That was his real name, Chief. I traced it back all the way to Providence Family Maternity Hospital, Portland, Oregon. There's a copy of the birth certificate in there. He spent K-12 in the Portland Public School TAG program—Talented and Gifted. Graduated from Benson Polytechnic in 2000, after a couple of speed bumps. An affair with a teacher. She got fired, he got a two-week suspension. Cheating allegations that no one could prove. Also he was supposedly dealing weed and Adderall, but they couldn't make a solid case against him. He never sold to a narc, and they had guys undercover at the school for more than two years."

"You're sure it's him?"

"Check out the yearbook picture. It's at the back of the file."

I lifted the pages, glanced at the photo. It was Refn, all right. Thinner, with glasses and longer hair, but definitely the same guy.

I closed the manila folder and pushed it to the side of my desk. "I'll use this for reference later. Right now I want you to tell me the story. How did you find him? Where did you start? Where does Hollister fit in?"

She took a deep breath, anchored her hands on her knees.

Her smile warmed the angles of her face like a wood fire in a Danish modern living room. This moment alone on stage in the glowing cone of the theatrical pin spot, was exactly what she needed and I was more than happy to oblige. I always found a little something extra in the way a person told their story—the moments of confidence or hesitation—that you couldn't glean from a report, no matter how well written.

"I started with Hollister," she said. "He had no police record, no prints on file, no military service, no hospitalizations. Kind of a clean slate. Or he would have been in the days before social media. I'm now his eight hundred and tenth follower on twitter. I like his tweets, by the way." She leaned over, pulled the file off my desk onto her lap, and sorted through a few pages. She lifted one, scanned it for a few seconds. "Here we are. 'Rain outside? No, just the kettle rumbling. Coffee time!' Or check this one out—'Norwalk California. Sun pounded stucco, fast food architecture, a broiling crapscape under an unblinking sky longing for the Chumash.' The Chumash were—"

"The Indian tribe who used to live there. I'm not sure what—"

"No, no, hold on, this last one set me on the track. 'Clearing out Mom's storage space. Letters, pictures, files: ephemera. But they persist and my mother is gone. Sad news. We're the ephemera.'"

"Okay, he's a good writer, but—"

"I checked the dates. His mom was born in 1967. Hollister was born in 1983. That makes her sixteen years old, a teenage mom. She kept the kid and raised him, apparently all by herself, though she ran through a series of part-time stepdad figures. Mom died in 2014. The tweet about the storage space was from two years ago. Hollister can't seem to let go. Which is a point worth remembering. It must have been tough—Claire Hollister was forty-seven years old when she died. That's young, Chief. I checked hospital records, Medicaid documents, insurance claims. As far as I could tell she was a healthy middle-aged woman. The strongest drug she ever took was Advil. No psychiatric records, or suicide attempt 911 calls. No nasty gossip. Friends say she was 'supernaturally' happy and upbeat. She volunteered at a food pantry, taught English as a second language to Mexican kids, played the bassoon, of all things. They had a little chamber group."

"Okay. So…?"

"So why did she go to Thompsons Guns & Ammo in September of 2014, sign the paperwork to accept the waiting period and the background checks, then pay cash for a brand new Beretta PX4 Storm compact 'G' model 9 mm autoloader, take it home, leave her son a note telling him to call 911 and not look behind the garage, and then go back there, sit down in her favorite lawn chair and blow her brains out with one shot to the temple? That's the best way to do it, by the way. She knew that because she did her homework. They pulled the search history off her computer during the discovery phase of the trial."

Now we were getting somewhere. "The trial?"

She nodded, shifting the papers in her folder. "Criminal action was brought against one Bartholomew James Pomeroy in Pierce County Superior Court, Tacoma, Washington, on July tenth, 2015. Charges included grand theft, extortion, fraud, mail fraud, racketeering, and second-degree murder."

"And the Complainant was Blair Hollister."

She nodded, still reading. "According to Hollister's testimony, Pomeroy seduced, blackmailed, cheated, and defrauded Claire Hollister, ultimately stealing every dime she had saved for her retirement, leaving her penniless, homeless, heartbroken, and suicidal. There was a co-complainant, Judy McAndless. Apparently, Pomeroy had worked the same con on her older sister, who wound up divorced with no custody of her three kids and quadriplegic when she totaled her car on the way to confront Pomeroy. She had an unlicensed gun in her purse and she blew .108 on the breathalyzer. So her life was wrecked, and Judy McAndless was just as angry as Hollister."

"How did he find her?"

"Well, he wound up hiring a detective, local guy named Robert Roman. Roman put them together, found a good criminal lawyer, did all the footwork, tracked down witnesses, helped with the depositions. The case looked like a slam dunk but the whole thing went south about halfway through."

"Let me guess. Judy dropped the charges."

Karen looked up from her papers, startled. "That's right. How did you—?"

I shrugged. "Refn—Pomeroy, whoever he was—got off and wound up here, so something strange must have happened. Probably a carrot and stick deal. Money and lots of it, if she backed off, and ending up like her sister if she didn't."

Karen turned a page, and then another one. "The biggest problem was Hollister opted for a bench trial. He wanted quick results, and he was afraid a jury would make mistakes, get the facts wrong, misunderstand some of the more arcane details… whatever. A lot of this was on his Facebook page. I downloaded his whole time line. But it didn't work out quite the way Hollister was hoping. The judge heard all the testimony on both sides, listened to the cross examinations, studied the evidence…then took ten minutes and acquitted Pomeroy on all charges. Closing arguments wrapped at eleven-fifteen, they were done by lunch. Hollister wanted to appeal the verdict, but…"

"Double jeopardy," I supplied.

"Yeah."

"Was the judge Victor Galassi?"

She stared at me. "Why do I bother? What's the point if you know everything in advance?"

"I don't! I make little leaps. You bring me the pieces, I snap them together like Legos. The question is, can we build anything with them?"

"I think we can. In fact, I think I already have. But let me take things in order. Like you said, Galassi was the presiding judge in the case—his last case before he retired. Hollister wanted to bring ethics charges, investigate him, get him disbarred, but that was never going to happen and everyone told him so—even Roman, the detective. Galassi was a country club guy, super popular, deacon of the church, on the board of every charity, big wheel in the local Democratic Party, huge fund-raiser, you name it. Thirty years of service and not a single blemish on his record. No one wanted a scandal and no one believed there was a scandal out there, anyway. All Hollister could do was turn himself into a pariah."

"So he gave up?"

"Not exactly. He hired Robert Roman to investigate the judge."

"Did he find anything?"

"Nothing he could take to court. He followed the guy for a few days, went through his trash, that kind of thing. Finally he 'let himself in' to the judge's house."

"How did he get past the alarm? There must have been an alarm."

"He waited until Galassi was home—in bed and sound asleep. Most people disarm their systems once they get inside."

I remembered Hollister's play. He had taken a least one detail from real life. "What did he find?"

"A home office in the basement. Bundles of counterfeit hundred-dollar bills, plus ledgers, tax information, and correspondence that linked Galassi to a small casino called the Double Down, outside of Spokane. The way Roman put it together, Galassi held a part ownership in this place and they were running counterfeit money through it, trading chips for real money, paying out in fake bills, and giving a skim to the counterfeiters. It's a win-win, and the bad currency spreads all over the country as people fly home with their winnings. Almost impossible to trace."

"And whose idea was this?"

I had a candidate in mind. The devious kink in the plan felt familiar—the kind of person who'd force a lesbian to undress by threatening to lie about it to her partner if she didn't. Karen smiled at me. "Don't mess with me, Chief. You know very well whose idea it was."

I lifted my hands palms up in genial surrender. "Okay, but I don't believe Refn had the skills to make good counterfeit money." And it was good, very good. Otto Didrickson said so.

"He was fronting for a group of Colombians. All the good counterfeit money comes from South America these days." If Otto was right about the Columbians, too, they weren't giving Refn their top product. Whatever works. The last person to inspect their cash is a casino winner.

We both sat back, letting the information settle on us like confetti. Ironic confetti—we had nothing to celebrate, just a lot of post-parade clean-up. I always felt bad for the sanitation crews after one of those giant celebrations.

Finally I said, "What did Roman do next?"

"He told Hollister, and that was about it. The information was gained illegally. They couldn't get a warrant, much less an indictment or a conviction. But at least Hollister knew why the judge had let Refn walk."

I nodded. "So this is where he takes the law into his own hands. He decides to kill Galassi, follows him home, not knowing that the judge has been having lunch with his twin brother, and he's following the wrong guy. He's about to blow poor Arthur Galassi away when Victor shows up at the door."

She just stared at me.

"I checked out Galassi and his twin brother. Everything else is straight out of Hollister's play. I swear! Seriously—he wrote it just like it happened. I went to a rehearsal, I saw them acting the whole thing out. Well, more or less—the Hollister character was a little tougher in the play. But the real question is—how did you figure this all out? Hollister would never admit to it."

"Roman told me. He was following Hollister that night. He was worried. He tracked Hollister to the house, saw the whole thing go down. He was about to intervene, when the brother showed up."

I stood and walked to the big window overlooking the parking lot and Fairgrounds Road. A lot of traffic, everyone headed out to the beach, at last. You can only spend so much time shopping. "So Hollister comes here, Refn gets killed and it looks like Judge Galassi could be next. What does your Robert Roman think about that?"

She smiled. "You can ask him yourself, Chief. He's sitting in your outer office right now."

"Jesus Christ, you brought him all the way from Seattle?"

"He wanted to come. He wanted to pursue this. And I could afford the ticket."

I shook my head. "Get him in here."

She got up a little awkwardly and hurried across the office and out the door. Ten seconds later she was back, leading a pudgy balding genial-looking middle-aged man in khakis, running shoes, and a Seahawks t-shirt.

He extended a hand. "Hey, Chief. Robert Roman, good to meet you."

He had a soft open friendly face with dog-like brown eyes. His grip was firm but not aggressive.

I dropped his hand, crossed my arms over my chest. "You know how police departments like mine feel about private detectives."

He shrugged. "Uncooperative private detectives. Information hogs. Investigation impeders. Justice obstructors. Pains in the ass."

"And that's not you."

His face seemed to expand. It wasn't quite a smile but he suddenly seemed absurdly, gratuitously friendly. "Cooperative, information-sharing. I never impede, I never obstruct. Maybe

I'm a pain in the ass sometimes. But I make my own donuts—yeast and cake, glazed and jelly. And I share. Seattle cops always liked that."

"Past tense?"

"I'm pretty much done with Seattle. Or Seattle is done with me."

"I have friends in the Seattle PD." This was a lie, but people always believe cops know each other, as if law enforcement was a fraternal society like the Elks or the Kiwanis. Maybe it is, but with almost eight hundred thousand of us nationwide it's a little hard to keep up. "Is there anything they could tell me about you?"

"Well…let's see. Assistant Chief Terry Oberfelder with the Special Operations Bureau would probably say to stick with yeast-risen cinnamon donuts. Very sad, since he doesn't even eat wheat or sugar anymore. And that's two out of the four main food groups. Cut out popcorn and coffee and he'll have to start eating vegetables or something."

"So what happened?"

He met my serious gaze. "Missing persons case. Rich husband, runaway wife. I found her, fell in love with her. She dumped both of us, took the divorce loot and joined the Peace Corps. Spousal abuse voided the pre-nup, lucky for her. Now she's setting up water purification systems or some shit in Namibia, and hubby got me blackballed with every other client in the Pacific Northwest who could afford my services. I'm seriously considering moving to Namibia, myself, I hear the food is great, when this lady here walks into my office talking Blair Hollister and Victor Galassi and Barry Pomeroy. Who, I understand, is recently deceased. And I thought…Nantucket? It's not Namibia, but it's on the way."

"So what's your take on Hollister?"

"As your murder suspect? I don't buy it. But then again, every serial killer has a flabbergasted neighbor or two. So what the hell do I know?"

"We'll have the answer soon."

"Yeah…well, anyway, my real interest was Pomeroy. He's been getting away with you-name-it for years. Money-laundering, blackmail, assault, felony trespass, confidence games. Then the counterfeit money deal blew up in his face—the Spokane PD busted the casino and those boys were cutting deals left and right. Galassi had kept himself clean. His stake in the club was buried under a half dozen nesting doll dummy corporations, and Pomeroy handled all the face-to-face meetings, all the daily stuff. No one could tie the great and mighty Judge Galassi to anything illegal. Not so much as a jaywalking ticket, and this guy never saw a red light he cared about. I'm serious, we're talking Mr. Magoo here.

"Well, anyway, Galassi denied everything and threw Pomeroy to the wolves. Or under the bus. Or maybe a bus full of wolves, whatever. Point is, Pomeroy disappeared. I heard the Columbians were after him, too—he must have had a ton of that counterfeit cash waiting to move through the casino, and he wasn't the kind of guy who gives back. The police showed up at his house with an arrest warrant, but nobody was home. The neighbor told them he'd split less than an hour before. They put out an APB on the car, but the neighbor never noticed that Pomeroy had switched license plates with him. I guess he switched cars a few times, too. The neighbor's plates finally turned up on some contractor's F-150 in Ojai, California."

"How long did the SPD look for him?"

"Couple of weeks, but Pomeroy was in the wind after the first few days. I spent a year trying to track that shit weasel down. Pardon my language. And I address that to the actual shit weasels—they get offended when you compare them to Pomeroy. And they don't even exist! Anyway, finally, I gave up. But it looks like you found him for me."

"Actually, he found us."

"Ojai," said Karen. "That's where the real Refn lived. And

died. Pomeroy was easy to track from there, once he had turned himself into Refn—a long trail of wrecked families and empty bank accounts. At some point as he worked his way east he got involved with local theater companies. He looked good and picked up the lingo. His resume was counterfeit, too. He sold himself as the breath of fresh air, the young new modern cool hip exciting genius who could revive their theater—while he was busily draining the operating fund and blackmailing the board members like he did here, picking the low-hanging fruit, and moving on. I spoke to one of the women. She had refused to press charges but she wanted me to hear her story. She said Refn told her once, "I love theater people. They need drama. I provide it."

Roman snorted. "What a prick."

Karen finished up. "My guess is Refn followed Galassi here. It's an ideal spot for Refn's kind of scam. He must have come to some arrangement with Galassi. Live and let live? They could certainly have hurt each other if they wanted to. They may have even been working together, but that's just speculation. There's no way to know for sure. Refn's dead and we have nothing solid on Galassi. Except, apparently, he's a really bad actor."

We were still standing in front of my desk, but there was no point in inviting them to sit down. We were done and I had work to do. I shook Roman's hand. "Thanks for making the trip, Rob. It's good to meet you."

"Ditto, Chief."

"Think you'll stick around?"

"I have a return flight Monday, but who knows? You have enough divorce up here to support a sleazy old parasite like me?"

"Oh, yeah. And we also have a long history of people coming for the weekend and staying forever. Word to the wise."

"I'll keep it in mind."

Karen said, "I'll show you out."

I stood alone in the office after they left, thinking hard. The information about Refn and Galassi was interesting—I like filling in the missing pieces, even if they were only bits of sky above the main image in that jigsaw puzzle picture. But ultimately, none of that mattered. What I cared about was our new playwright-in-residence. Suddenly, he had a motive, the most compelling motive imaginable, and if his alibi fell apart the way I felt sure it would, he'd had plenty of opportunity, as well. Karen Gifford had handed me my killer. All I needed was enough evidence to indict him, and I knew exactly where to look for it. The case was as good as closed. Blair Hollister had killed Horst Refn in cold blood.

And I was going to take him down for it.

Chapter Sixteen

The Interrogation

"Whoa, hold on there, Robo-cop. Take it easy."

Jane and I were eating dinner at Ventuno, celebrating the book contract for her latest Madeline Clark mystery novel. My kids were baby-sitting Sam, after a cold-blooded negotiation between warring siblings that gave Carrie sixty-five percent of their earnings. "I'm the oldest," she had announced, ending the dispute. "If anything happens I'll have to take the responsibility for both of you. I think your thirty-five percent is quite a generous offer."

Stingy people always think they're generous, and Carrie had inherited her mother's penny-pinching along with her temper. But Tim knew when he was beaten and soon they were all happily settled around the TV with microwave popcorn, watching a Harry Potter movie. Carrie had just hit the pause button to deride the rules of Quiddich as Jane and I slipped out the door.

Jane took another bite of lobster and let me mull her rebuke. The restaurant was jammed and noisy, with drinkers three-deep at the bar and waiters two-stepping and pirouetting between the tables. The NTL board lunch table was next to us. I studied it over Jane's shoulder as three couples conducted two conversations perfectly matched to place and gender. The women were dishing a mutual friend's imminent divorce; the men were mocking a rival's over-purchase of poplar trim stock for his over-budget spec house. I much preferred the women's topic and wondered idly if Rob Roman might wind up with a new client soon. I had a feeling he was on the Rock to stay.

Meanwhile, Jane was waiting for a response.

"I haven't arrested anyone yet."

She put on her gruff Western sheriff voice. "We'll give him a fair trial—before we hang him."

"So now I'm Judge Roy Bean?"

"The only law west of the Pecos. Open a saloon and build a scaffold."

I cleared my throat. "Just for the record, Bean wasn't much of a hanging judge. He only sentenced two people and one of them escaped."

"Details, details."

I tilted my chin up, the gesture like an underhand throw, gently tossing her attention toward the dining room behind us. "That's the table where the board members were having lunch when Hollister stole Galsssi's phone."

"If he stole Galassi's phone."

"If. But someone did. And this was the perfect opportunity, just as Joe Little got sick, and no one was paying attention to anything else."

"You're saying he poisoned Little's lunch?"

"Maybe. I want to check with the kitchen staff and the wait crew. But maybe it was just an inspired improvisation, like Marcus Mariota throwing a touchdown pass to himself in the playoffs."

"Or maybe you're barking up the wrong tree."

"Yeah. But dogs rarely do that. They pretty much know where the squirrel went, even if they can't catch it."

"That's why you have to be careful—Maddie Clark says it's like playing pick-up sticks. You want to lift each piece of evidence without disturbing the others."

"Oh, my God. I'm taking advice from a fictional detective."

"Which is more than Chief Bloat would ever do."

"So how do I proceed?"

"Well…Maddie would quietly check out each little twig of Hollister's alibi, and gently remove it, not disturbing the others. If the alibi checks out, fine. You move on. If not, you have the element of surprise in your favor. You're ready to go to the judge, get that search warrant, and pounce."

"Maddie Ckark never pounces."

"No, she gets Chief Bloat to pounce…and then lets him take the credit."

I toasted her with a forkful of dripping lobster. "Sounds like a plan."

I started the next day. It didn't take long.

The WAVE bus driver, Toby Vollans, on duty the day of the murder, had no recollection of Hollister. Chris Felleman, the funny actor/cab driver from Brant Point Taxi, ditto. He had met Hollister, though—at the auditions for *Who Dun It*. That was where they had run through their impromptu "Who's on First" routine.

I talked to Chris while he drove me out to 'Sconset in his cab. He did most of the talking and I was happy to listen.

"…oh, yeah, Hollister offered me a role in the play if I'd swear he drove me out to Cisco. And I never got the part! Can you believe that? Then it turns out somebody got killed that same day. Is Hollister a suspect? Man, I sure hope not. He said he was gonna find something for me later. He was talking about *True West*. Refn was planning some kind of Sam Shepherd tribute. Like anyone cares about the Theater Lab doing a tribute! But whatever. I've always wanted to play Lee in *True West*. With Refn gone, that's probably never going to happen. If it ever was. And Hollister's leaving the island when the show closes. Going back to Tinsel Town! Or to jail. Fucking Hollywood big shots. He thinks I'm nothing? Well, maybe I am, but I never killed nobody."

I asked him if he would be willing to come in after work and sign a formal statement. He agreed. Then, just as he dropped me off at the station, he added one more detail. "I did give Hollister a ride, though, about a week before the murder. Took him out to a house on Cliff Road—big old pile with a big hedge and a shell driveway. It was a real early call. I had just taken my brother to the boat. He jumped out of the cab, put something down on the table on their deck, like an iPod or one them metal wallets they used to advertise on TV? Then he jumped back in and I took him home. I figured he was returning something he borrowed, or maybe delivering something he found in the street. 'Cause, like, a wallet would have had a driver's license with the address. So, I don't know, but that's what happened, if it's any help."

It was a big help. Joe Little lived on Cliff Road. And now I had a witness to Hollister returning his cell phone.

The next stick to extricate from the pile: Judith Barsch's housekeeper, Carmen, who had supposedly greeted Hollister when he came to the house for his meeting, and called him a cab back to town.

"I never saw him," she told me. We were standing in Barsch's spacious kitchen while Carmen shredded pork for her signature chiles rellenos. "I remember so well because that was the day we almost lost our Corky." At the sound of his name, the pit bull lifted her head off her paws and let her tail thump the floor just once. Then she went back to guarding the kitchen and waiting for scraps.

We had nothing more to say. I told her I wished I could taste the finished meal, and she said, "Mrs. will invite you for dinner and I make special."

Lovely woman, and she had just destroyed the last vestiges of Hollister's alibi.

I had enough to get a warrant, and three hours later I was picking it up from Judge Perlman's office. I took Haden Krakauer, Charlie Boyce, and Karen Gifford with me to Hollister's Theater Lab residence.

The big ramshackle house on Rugged Road that the Theater Lab rented for staff and visiting actors was empty when we got there, everyone rehearsing or at the beach. The door was open and I had called ahead to Tim Hobbes to let him know we were coming.

The house had five bedrooms and we searched them all, on the assumption that Hollister might have concealed incriminating evidence among someone else's possessions, but we found nothing. The place was a mess, with the notable exception of the two upstairs rooms where the two SAG actors from New York, Ted Brownell and Celia Dunbar, took refuge from the post-adolescent squalor.

We saved Hollister's room for last.

Five minutes into the search I found ten hundred-dollar bills. I would have bet a real thousand that they were counterfeit. I was studying them, wishing for Otto's yellow pencil, when Karen Gifford emerged from the closet with the sim card-cloning hardware. She held it up and slightly away from her body, as if it were contaminated, like roadkill or a severed hand. For the first time it occurred to me that the netrile gloves we wore during these searches functioned as much to protect us as to preserve the crime scene. The air itself, dense with the scents of unwashed laundry, mildew, and burned coffee, felt tainted somehow, as if this were a plague house, not a killer's bedroom. I fought down the irrational desire for a face mask. There was nothing contagious here for healthy people

I took the blue plastic box with its single USB port from Karen's hands and turned it over. "Is this what I think it is?"

"Sorry. Hollister seemed like a nice guy."

"You met him?"

"I read the article in *N Magazine*. And he's had such a horrible time. His mother, and then the trial…the learning about these—people…and feeling so helpless. I can almost understand why he might…"

"That's a motive, not an excuse."

"I know. But I still feel bad."

I nodded. "Me too."

Our next stop was Hollister's little office at the Congregational Church. We didn't expect to find much there, and the cubicle, tidy and bare, offered little opportunity for a significant discovery: a desk with a password-protected iPad and a notebook with revision notes; a glass full of throw-away fountain pens, a wooden chair, an inspirational black-and-white photograph of Agatha Christie pinned to the wall, a pinking old snapshot of nine- or ten-year-old Hollister and a pretty woman in her mid-thirties, his mother I assumed, at the beach somewhere, smiling and happy. Better days. There was a navy blue windbreaker hanging on a hook, lining intact, pockets empty. The room yawned at us, mute and blank.

I checked the trash on the way out—crumpled papers, takeout coffee cups, used yogurt containers, plastic cutlery, a Claritin package...and the haunted can of keyboard cleaner. It was back. Almost full, thrown away, with no keyboard to clean. I didn't believe in ghosts and I wasn't going to waste any time looking for Eugene O'Neill's shoes.

Instead, I pulled on another pair of surgical gloves, plucked the can out of the trash and gave it my undivided attention. I was reading the directions and warnings when the final one jumped out at me so hard I reared my head backward. "Jesus."

"Chief?"

"If this spray comes into contact with your skin, it causes frostbite."

"Wait, what? It's keyboard cleaner. All it has to do is blow air at the keys."

I handed it over. "See for yourself."

She skimmed the text. "This is crazy. Who makes a product like this? And why would you? Unless it's cheaper, somehow. It's like...some kind of absurdist critique of capitalist economics."

She was drifting off-topic. "Karen. We need to take a scraping from Refn's face. I'll bet my pension the specimen will show the presence of this product. Bag the can and let's get out of here."

My pension was safe. Monica had the results in less than twenty minutes. I sent Karen and Charlie to make the arrest. They left Hollister in a holding cell, but I waited a couple of hours before I went to see him. I wanted him tense, off-balance, scared, and hungry.

Hollister was handcuffed to the table in the interrogation room when I walked in.

"Chief!" he tried to rise but the cuff caught him and he sat down awkwardly. "What's going on? What am I doing here? These two storm troopers showed up at the Theater Lab office and—"

"Storm troopers?"

"They barged in, and—"

"Did they threaten you?"

"Uh, no…"

"Did they injure you?"

"No, but—"

"Did they even handcuff you? They're legally permitted to restrain a felony suspect."

"No, they didn't, but—felony suspect? I'm a felony suspect?"

I sat down opposite him. "We're being recorded, Blair. So, first of all, I have to make sure that my officers informed you of your rights."

"Yes. Yes, they did."

"Do you want a lawyer present today?"

"No, I'm good." He smiled. "Funny phrase, isn't it? People use it all the time now. 'I'm going for coffee, want one?' 'No, I'm good.' But at this moment I mean it literally. I'm *good*, Chief. Not evil, not a felon, not a killer."

"Killer?"

"Come on. Jesus! There's been exactly one crime on this island since I got here. You've already interrogated me about it."

I spoke to the room, the hidden microphones. "Suspect has waived his right to counsel."

"Can you talk to me instead of the tape recorder?"

"Sorry. I'm done. Formalities complete."

"Good."

"So…"

"So I didn't kill anyone!"

"Ever?"

"I hit a dog with my car once. But he lived."

"An accident, I'm sure. But you had good reason to kill Refn. And Judge Galassi."

"Is he dead, too? Is that what this is about?"

"No. Not yet."

"And every minute I'm in here and no one's getting killed makes me look more even more guilty."

I nodded. "Sitting with me would be an excellent alibi if someone were killing Victor right now."

"But they're not."

"To the best of my knowledge."

"Oh, well. A boy can dream."

"A lawyer would have counseled you to avoid statements like that."

"Lawyers have no sense of humor."

"And you keep yours, even under duress."

"One of my finer traits. Besides—only an innocent man would make a remark that incriminating."

"Unless he wanted to get caught."

"Then count me out." He leaned across the desk. "In fact, this is my worst nightmare. Literally. I've been having this dream since I was twelve years old—being arrested for a crime I didn't commit. Like Joseph K."

I offered him the first sentence of Kafka's novel: "Someone must have been lying about Joseph K., because without having done anything wrong he was arrested one fine morning."

"Exactly. So just let me go."

"As soon as you give me a new alibi."

"What's wrong with my old alibi?"

"Blair."

"I'm serious. What's wrong with it?"

I exhaled, trying to clear the lies and bad intentions out of my lungs. "No one corroborates it."

"You mean the WAVE bus driver—"

"Toby Vollans. He has no recollection of you."

"And the cab driver—Chris something—"

"Christopher Felleman. He was at the airport, using the Bank of America ATM machine in the terminal that afternoon, almost exactly when you say he was driving you to Cisco. He has the time-stamped receipt to prove it."

"But—"

"One of my detectives checked the surveillance video. It was him, all right—wedding ring, cracked Timex watch, Patriots cap, and all. What he remembers is taking you to drop off Joseph Little's cell phone—at six in the morning, a week ago last Sunday."

"Joe Little's cell phone?"

"Come on, Blair."

"What would I want with Joe Little's cell phone?"

"You cloned it. So it would look like Joe sent Don Harcourt to the crime scene, and he was the one giving orders to your Bulgarians."

He reared back, then snagged his wrist on the cuff again. "Wait, wait, hold it—just stop it. Stop. I never…gave orders to anyone. I don't even give actors line readings. How could I send anyone to a crime scene? I didn't even know it existed until two days later! And I can't clone a phone. I don't even know what that means."

"I couldn't put together an Ikea bed. That's what YouTube is for."

"I never watched any YouTube phone clone videos! Check my search history."

"We will."

"Good! And—and…I don't have any Bulgarians. How do you even 'have' a Bulgarian? Are people adopting them now?"

I stood and walked over to the entry. I saw Haden Krakauer through the small, square wire-meshed glass of the door's window. He tilted his head; I shook mine. I didn't need help and I wasn't done.

I turned back to Hollister, dropped the bomb. "We found the sim card cloning equipment in your apartment."

"Then someone planted it!"

"And who might have done that?"

"I don't know! How should I know? Why do cops ask questions like that? If I knew I could solve your case for you. I'm not a detective, I'm not a criminal. I have nothing to do with this. I don't have any theories. It's none of my business! Anyway, it's nuts—I live in NTL housing, six other people live there, maybe thirty people are in and out every day, everybody has keys, there's no privacy. It could have been anyone! You get a theory, you figure it out!"

I let his tirade crumble into the air conditioner rasp of the interrogation room. "No one else had counterfeit hundred-dollar bills in their room. Just you—and Refn and Galassi."

"Counterfeit—what does that have to do with anything?"

"We know about your court case, Blair. We know what Refn did to your mother, or should I say, what Barry Pomeroy did to her, and why Galassi let him off. We know about the casino and Refn's Columbian counterfeiters, and the money-laundering scheme. All of it."

Hollister studied me, putting it together. "You talked to Rob Roman."

"He's on-island right now."

"Yeah? Did he tell you I had a chance to kill Galassi and didn't do it?"

"Because you realized you were aiming your gun at his twin

brother. Galassi himself showing up at the house was just hap-
penstance. Or luck."

"Or fate. That's how it felt to me."

"You should have googled him, Blair."

He rubbed his eye with the palm of his hand. "That's what
I get for using real life in my play. Nothing's quite as implau-
sible as real life. People who write bad plays always say, 'It's a
true story! It happened to me.' And I always think, 'I don't care
what happened to you. Your job is to make something happen
to *me*.' Anyway, coming that close to pulling the trigger was a
real wake-up call. It pulled me back from the brink, you know?
Like—what the fuck did you almost do? Who are you? What
did these fucking people do to your head? You're better than this.
You're better than them."

Silence settled between us. It felt like stepping inside, out of
the wind. Hollister thought we were finished. I thought he was
giving the performance of a lifetime. "So," I said finally, "how
do you explain the counterfeit money?"

"I can't."

"Here's my theory. You stole it from Galassi, but not to spend.
You wanted a calling card only he and Refn would understand.
A warning. A threat."

"No, listen, that's not—"

"True or false?"

"False! Well, I mean…mostly false, all right? Yeah, I took the
money, to scare those two crooks—the same reason I wrote the
play. To freak them out and maybe…get them to confess? I know
it sounds stupid. It wasn't part of some weird murder plan. I just
needed to mess with them."

"The play's the thing, wherein I'll catch the conscience of
the king."

He looked down. "Something like that."

I felt a swift twinge of regret for what I was about to tell him.
I was starting to like Hollister, against my better judgment, and

the cruelty of the facts arrayed against him seemed intentional, even sadistic. But he had brought this on himself. I set the next jagged piece of reality in front of him. "We spoke to Judith Barsch's housecleaner, as you suggested. She never saw you the day Rafn died. And Mrs. Barsch mentioned that you had more or less begged her to go along with whatever story you were going to tell. At the time she had no idea what you were talking about. But it's very clear now."

"No, I—she...Judy—I never—"

"I'm amazed you trusted her."

"I didn't! I'd never say anything like that!"

"Maybe she misunderstood."

"No! She didn't misunderstand what I said because I never said anything."

Time to read him the final number on his winning lottery ticket. Congratulations! You've just won a life sentence in a federal maximum security prison. "We found the can of keyboard cleaner in your office."

His blank look was almost comical. "What?"

"The keyboard cleaner you used when you killed Refn."

"How—? You're losing it, Chief. You're saying I killed Refn with a computer keyboard...and then cleaned the blood off the keys with some kind of spray?"

"I'm saying you used the spray to torture him before you killed him. There was frostbite on Refn's face—antemortem. Skin specimens match the tissue samples to the product we found in your wastebasket."

"Wait, what? Keyboard cleaner can give you frostbite?"

"You knew that. You read the label, just like I did."

We stared at each other as he tried to gather his thoughts. "I don't have a keyboard. I use an iPad. What would I be doing with a can of keyboard cleaner?"

"We asked ourselves that very question, Blair. But you knew Refn was phobic about the cold."

"How could I know that?"

"I assume you did your research. Writers are good at research."

"Now, wait a second. If I really used this—thing, this spray can…to torture Refn, why would I throw it away in my own office trash? Why wouldn't I bury it a million miles away? Or plant it on someone else?"

"Because you're cocky. And careless. And crazy. For cops, that's the trifecta, Blair. That's Son of Sam's parking tickets. That's Ted Bundy driving with a broken headlight."

I watched it all sink in. Then he made his final plea. "These people—Carmen and Chris Felleman and that bus driver—they're all lying. They're lying! You have to find out why. There must be a reason! Someone made them do that, and he planted that stuff in my home and my office…that's the real killer. Not me! I'm innocent!" He caught my calm steady pitiless look, and sagged backward in his chair. "What's the use? You don't believe me."

He was right.

God help me, I didn't believe a word he said.

Chapter Seventeen

The Eye of the Storm

With Blair Hollister in custody, his bail set at half a million dollars, island life resumed its usual pace, like a jogger tripping over an uneven sidewalk and lurching to recover—without even an embarrassed "I meant to do that" for the jaded onlookers. And there were quite a few of them. The story had engaged the attention of the national press, already piqued by a famous actor's sexual indiscretions at a local restaurant. The island had become a rich fudge of scandal and the public had a sweet tooth for privileged people acting badly.

Nantucket in the new gilded age could trigger a case of type-two diabetes.

The publicity helped an odd selection of people. David Trezize, who ran our local alternative newspaper, was once again out in front of the bigger news outlets with a sensational expose. And the Theater Lab was looking at a possible Broadway production of *Who Dun It*. I received a little of the "reflected gory," as my father once called it, after he'd spent the afternoon strolling the streets of Manhattan with Boris Karloff. I was being touted as a small town Sherlock Holmes, an activist lawman who refused to spend his days behind a desk issuing press releases. My connection with Jane Stiles spiked the sales of her Nantucket-based cozy mysteries. And Nantucket branded merchandise was flying off the shelves at Murray's Toggery and the Nobby Shop.

All was right with the world. The good guys had won. You could feel the holiday atmosphere at the police station and I was happy for the respite.

I had another crime to solve, and it was strictly personal.

I was sitting at home on Darling Street one balmy Saturday morning, enjoying a rare late breakfast, the kids roaming the island on their bikes with a blissful lack of parental supervision. My one constraint: "Be home by dinner." I knew there were many communities where this laissez faire attitude would be considered a misdemeanor if not a felony.

There was a famous case a few years before, when parents in Maryland had their children taken by Protective Services after Silver Spring Police found them playing unsupervised in a nearby park. Maybe those concerns made sense elsewhere, but Nantucket remained a sanctuary for a different era's style of child-rearing. I remembered reading an editorial in the *New York Times* in which the writer described memorizing her daughter's clothes before she went to school every day so she could provide a useful "last seen wearing…" report to the police. Such concerns seemed tragic but bizarrely remote thirty miles out at sea. I had never flinched—as I might have in a big city—when my kids dashed out of sight around a corner. I knew they were most likely to crash headlong into any one of two dozen adults who adored them.

That was a luxury, and I was feeling luxurious on this peerless late June day. Jane had taken her second coffee upstairs to her office, where she was determined to get her thousand words written on the new Maddie Clark mystery. Often in my life I had felt a loneliness more acute because I was surrounded by people—bitter wife, disapproving inlaws, tiresome acquaintances. This feeling was exactly the opposite—solitary at my kitchen table, but comfortably tethered at various distances to delightful children, steadfast colleagues, and the brilliant, funny, gorgeous woman upstairs, two-finger tapping her way toward the end of Chapter Six.

The mild breeze smelled of cut grass and the harbor. I took a deep breath, pushed my coffee aside and took out my phone. I found the pictures I had taken in Hector Cruz's bedroom and started scrolling through them.

Walking through a big job at the "punch list" stage with Mike Henderson a couple of years before, he had made a point that came back to me now.

"It takes at least three people to do a good latex touch-up. You know why? Because people don't really look—more than that, they don't want to look. The eye skips over any anomaly. Maybe it's just laziness—noticing stuff means work. Like the other day, I spent the morning painting trim with wall paint. They were the same color, but still—that meant I was painting over gloss oil with eggshell latex…for four hours! I've been doing this job since I was a teenager, Chief. So what the hell happened? I really thought about it and I remember some little twinge in the back of my head, like the tickle in your throat before you cough. But I ignored it because the paint was going on glossy—it was wet, of course it looked glossy—and I don't make those kinds of mistakes. Except, obviously I do.

"So I think the trick is to focus on those anomalies, not ignore them…to put the brakes on, and ask—what's going on here? Which is kind of like police work, don't you think? I mean, that's really your whole job, in a way—looking for the little things that don't feel right, the stuff that people naturally ignore, stopping where the natural momentum of life tells you to keep moving. It's so counterintuitive. It must be tough to train yourself to think that way."

Mike was right, and that was exactly what I had to do now. I had to look for the scuff mark above the baseboard, the faint speckle of paint on the doorknob. There was some anomaly in the pictures I had taken of Hector's room, and I was determined to find it.

When I finally did, fifteen minutes later, it felt a big rich cough from the bottom of your lungs, when you finally feel a tenacious cold loosening in your chest. I was on the mend.

And Hector was off the hook.

I left Jane a note, slipped out of the house, and drove to Hector's house. His parents were out, of course. His mother was working double shifts at Cottage Hospital, and Sebastian was charging through the height of his landscaping season, with dozens of lawns to cut, gardens to weed and deadhead against upcoming weddings and fundraisers, hedges to install, stone walls to build, and God-knows-how-many metric tons of fertilizer to lay down before the Fourth of July. He worked side by side with his crew and worked rings around most of them, once famously offering double pay to any pair of guys who could dig as many split-rail fence post holes as he could in four hours. Like all those long-forgotten first-out-of-the gate horses in all those Triple Crown races, they started strong but faded against the relentless energy of a great competitor.

"Sprinters lose," was Sebastian's summary. He had a point. I'd always been a plodder and it paid off for me. Today was a perfect example.

Hector came to the door wearing board shorts, flip-flops, and a Cruz Land Design t-shirt, his eyes bleary from a lengthy X-Box session. I could see past his shoulder to the frozen image on the big flat-screen TV in the living room—his platoon clearing the rubble in some cyber Baghdad or Fallujah.

I clamped down on the urge to lecture him about getting off the couch and into the sunshine. Hector got more exercise than most kids his age, if only from the demanding summer practice schedule. Anyway, he wasn't my kid and it wasn't my problem. I'd already solved the only problem between us.

He looked at me warily. "What's up, Chief?"

"Can I come in?"

"Sure."

He stepped back.

"I'd like to go up to your room for a second."

"It's kind of a mess."

"I'm used to that."

He grinned. He knew what a cyclone my daughter was.

As we walked upstairs I said, "I know that…picture on Carrie's phone isn't you, Hector. And I understand why you don't want you own picture taken."

"That's private, like I said."

"Absolutely. And it's also not necessary."

He opened the door to his room for me and I stepped across the piles of clothes, magazines, and powercords to the bookshelf. The Coke can was still there, with the same white cursive writing on the same red background, in the same iconic font.

But the letters were unrecognizable. To me anyway—I don't read Hebrew.

I picked up the can. It was unopened. "This isn't a soft drink. It's a souvenir."

He looked down, needlessly, absurdly embarrassed. He understood.

"When was your last trip to Israel?"

"Last summer. My big brother is working on a kibbutz in Kalia. On the Dead Sea, forty minutes north of Jerusalem."

"So your dad is a Sephardic Jew."

"His dad was. Pops wanted no part of it."

"But your brother felt differently."

"You don't stop being a Jew, Chief. It don't work that way. Whatever Pops might think."

"Still…you're keeping the secret."

"I go to shul. We have one here, you know."

"But under the radar."

"I have enough problems on this rock without adding that one, Chief. 'Hey, the wetback spic is also a kike!'"

I had to smile. "That reminds me of something Sammy Davis, Jr. once said."

"Who?"

Oh, boy. "Just—an entertainer from way back in the twentieth century. He said, 'I'm a one-eyed, black Jewish midget—at least I don't live in the Valley.' He was talking about the San Fernando Valley."

"Where the real housewives live!"

"Right." I released a breath. "So your circumcision is none of anyone's business. Including mine."

He smiled. "You get a pass, Chief. You figured it out on your own."

He stepped back toward the door, the body language ending the conversation. But we weren't quite done. "There's still one question, Hector."

He nodded. "Who did it? Who done it, just like that dude's play. My dad says the two most important questions in his life are 'When are they coming?' and 'Did you send the check?' For him it's all about the customers. Their schedules and their bank accounts. But 'who done it'—that's your number one question. Am I right?"

"Actually, most of the time, it's more 'What's wrong with this picture?' Like a Coke can with the wrong script on the can. So what do you think? Who did this? Any theories?"

He leaned against the door casing. "I wouldn't know where to start."

"How about…someone with access to your phone? Someone with a crush on Carrie. Someone jealous of your position on the team. Someone raised wrong—single parent, latch key kid, lots of booze in the house. Someone with a chip on his shoulder and a bad attitude. A shoplifter, a joy-rider, a bully, a braggart, a cheater. But insecure and scared. Cocky like a coward. Sound familiar?"

I saw the tension in his face, the swift look down. He had someone in mind. I pushed on. "I don't have enough evidence for a warrant, I can't prove anything and your gut instinct isn't admissible. But this shit has to stop."

"So what you gonna do?"

"Nothing. This one's on you, Hector."

"Me?"

"You're going to be team captain next year, Carrie tells me."

"Yeah, so?"

"So show some leadership. I don't want to ruin some poor kid's life for an idiotic mistake and no wants to hear a lecture from the Police Chief. But he'll listen to you. He'll expect an ass-kicking. Give him a warning instead. Get him back on the straight and narrow. Do a little good—for the kid, for the team, for the school. Think you can handle that?" Hector looked up, met my eyes, nodded. "Good."

"So I'm your deputy now?"

"Something like that." And I thought—you, Boiko, and Dimo, what a group!

Did he sense what I was thinking? I got the flash of a smile, like the sun glittering on the underside of maple leaves in a sudden gust of wind. "You are one weird-ass police officer, Chief Kennis."

I smiled back. "I'll take that as a compliment."

My reward was waiting for me at home. Jane had left for a walk, the kids were still AWOL, but I found the Tarrant sisters sitting in my kitchen, straight and stiff as the ladderback chairs, as if I were the visitor. They had even made themselves a pot of tea.

Edith, the smaller one, squat and compact in a white blouse, long blue skirt, and running shoes, said, "Would you like a cup of this very nice Darjeeling, Chief Kennis? You seem to be out of sugar, unfortunately. And there's nothing but that awful two percent milk in the icebox."

"The tea may be a little bit strong by now," Paula added. She wore a plaid shirt, faded blue jeans, and well-worn hiking boots. I guessed she was the walker and Edith was the recluse. "We've been waiting quite a while!"

I almost apologized. This was home invasion, Nantucket-style. Two bossy old ladies whose ancestors stole the place from the

Wampanoags amble into your unlocked house, take over your kitchen, and scold you gently for the sorry state of your pantry. At least they approved my choice of tea.

I took one of the remaining chairs. "What can I do for you, ladies?"

Paula took a sip and set her cup down carefully in the saucer. "It's so nice to see people living in the Fraker house again."

"Jane always loved this place," Edith added. "Poor thing—she's been doing the Nantucket shuffle since the divorce."

"Summer rental, winter rental, moving twice a year. Ghastly. I don't know how anyone manages. I could hardly stand moving into the guest bedroom when Aunt Gladys came to visit."

"Which is why I usually wound up there," Edith said.

The two sisters glared at each other for a second, and clearly decided not to "wash the dirty linen in public." Their ancient family squabbles were none of my business—just like Hector Cruz' religious beliefs, Kelly Ramos' sexual orientation, or half the other stuff I found out in the course of my working week.

Paula huffed and sat up straighter in the ladder back chair. "We've actually come to talk about Jane."

"Well, about the two of you."

I cringed—what nightmarish item of gossip had migrated to their little house in the moors? Had someone seen Jane's car parked at Joe's house and assumed they were getting back together? Maybe someone had seen her eating alone at the Rose & Crown and assumed we were breaking up.

But it was nothing like that.

Paula removed the item from her purse, with the delicate awe and respect of a child picking up a ladybug. She set it on the table. "This has come back to us. But we have no use for it. And you do."

I was stunned. "How did you—?"

"Carl Bender was at the auction, Chief Kennis. So were quite a few other people. Word gets around."

"On Nantucket, a secret is something you don't know everyone else knows you know. That's what my father used to say."

I thought of that great old John Prine song—"There's Nowhere to Hide, in a Town This Size." So true.

"Jane has always been like a daughter to us."

"When her parents were transferred overseas, we took her in for the last two years of high school, so she wouldn't have to leave the island."

"She took care of our horses for years. Back in the old days."

"We had a little barn out by Eel Point Road."

"She loved those horses."

"So this seems right. We're the end of the line for the Tarrant family and something ought to be passed along to the next generation."

I reached over and picked up their gift. "Are you sure?"

Edith smiled. "If you are."

I slipped it into my pocket. Then I helped them stand, gave them each a hug, and walked them to the door.

Edith took my arm in a surprisingly strong grip before she stepped outside. "Live up to it, boy!"

I met her stern gaze. "Yes, ma'am."

She smiled, turned away, and hurried to catch up with her sister.

Watching them bustle up Darling Street in the dappled shade of the old maple trees, I felt like I'd finally arrived on Nantucket. Their small gift had conferred some profound affiliation and so did the familial exigence of that parting demand. I belonged here. I was no longer just a washashore from around the point.

I know now that Edith would have been amused by that idea. "You?" she would have answered gently. "No, sorry, Chief. Your children, maybe. If they don't run off away to America and leave us all behind."

Oh, well—one step at a time. I was good at taking things slowly. I was even starting to enjoy it that summer—the languid pace of petty crimes and half days at the beach, in the lingering glow of my big case closed and nothing on the horizon but the Fourth of July fireworks.

Then I got the phone call from Joe Stiles.

What he had to show me caused a drastic shift, not in my situation, but in my perception of it. I thought of driving to Providence a few years before, coming off the Bourne Bridge, missing the turnoff for Route 25 that would have taken me to 195, then 95 and eventually into Rhode Island. Instead, chatting away about some case, or arguing about some political nonsense, I wound up on Route 3, heading north toward Boston. I recall laughing about the bumper-to-bumper traffic on the other side of the highway as we sailed along on the open road.

Then I noticed a sign for Plymouth.

Plymouth?

I'd taken the kids to Plimouth Plantation a couple of times. I suddenly knew exactly where we were—on the wrong road, thirty miles in the wrong direction and about to lock ourselves into the giant traffic jam we'd been laughing about five minutes before.

What do you do in that situation? Grit your teeth and turn yourself around. That was exactly what I had to do now. My case had flipped one hundred-eighty degrees. I had to find my way back and get going in the right direction and do it fast, even if it meant driving in the breakdown lane. Because if I wasted more time, more people would die, and it would be my fault. A moment of distraction was all it took. Chuck Obremski would have dropped one of his patented weary frowns and repeated his most basic advice to young detectives: Pay attention.

And when you think your case is solved?

Pay attention more.

Chapter Eighteen

The Killing Bottle

"Can you come over to the house?" Joe Stiles' voice sounded pinched and squeaky, but it could have been the connection. "I found something you need to see, and we can't talk about it on the phone."

"Hey, we're just making dinner, and—"

"Turn the stove off, Chief. This can't wait."

"Listen, Joe—"

But he was gone.

Jane turned from the Instant Pot on the counter, where she was searing a pair of veal chops. "My Joe?"

"I thought you'd donated him to charity."

She shook her head, flipped the chops. "Naaah, not worth it. No tax deduction for ex-husbands."

"He sounded scared."

"That's odd. But he has been browsing the Dark Web lately."

"He was using a burner phone. I didn't recognize the number. He wants to see me right now."

She tonged the browned chops out of the pot and set them on a folded paper towel. "This can wait."

"You sure?"

"Joe never sounds scared. You should go, Henry. I'll have another glass of wine and watch the news."

My kids were with Miranda, and Sam had a sleep-over with a friend. It was a rare night to ourselves and I couldn't help the petty thought that Joe was happy to wreck it for us. But Jane's serious stare banished my suspicions.

I gave her a hug and kissed her cheek. "Be back soon."

Joe was waiting for me in his study. I noticed that he had stuck a piece of electrician's tape on his Chrome Book's camera lens.

"Thanks for coming, Chief." He tipped his head toward the little laptop. "I use that for the Dark Web and nothing else. Keeps me safe. There are some bad actors out there."

"What did you find, Joe?"

"I have some keywords flagged on the TOR network. I'm always checking the sites and blogs. You never know what's going to turn up. I flagged 'Nantucket,' 'Kennis,' and 'Refn' a while ago. And today I hit the trifecta." He handed me a printout. "Whoever wrote this had to be pretty certain no one who mattered would ever be able to access it. Criminals like to brag on the Dark Web. They think they're safe. But you'd need a much more sophisticated encryption to be safe from me. Just saying."

I read the post—around twelve hundred words. A few of them jumped up like crickets on a bedspread:

This—

I heard Nantucket Police Chief Kennis in an interview on the local radio station confessing that he never knows how a poem will end, and that it always feels like a minor miracle when the last verse comes to him. He pointed out crime-solving works the same way.

So does committing a crime, that's what he fails to realize. We have something in common after all—we're mirror images! But which one is reversed, and which one is real?

Glad to meet you, Police Chief Kennis. I'm your evil twin.

And this—

Another person had to be tricked into the investigator's killing bottle: the empty vessel of time, the precise duration of the murder, in which they would have no way to explain their whereabouts. But who? Propinquity figured into the equation—the hapless individual would need to be "on-site" as it were, and available to participate. But they also needed to have a motivation. That was the essential qualification.

Indeed, the individual I selected had to want Horst Refn dead just as much as I did.

And finally...this—

I had known all along that the process of getting away with murder would be absorbing and heuristic, I hoped it would be gratifying.

But I never for a moment imagined it would be this much fun.

I handed the pages back to Joe. "Is this real?"

"Real as roadkill, Chief. It's just a screengrab. The post was deleted an hour after I found it. Someone knew I was there. But they can't ID me any more than I can ID them. Luckily. "

"Jesus Christ."

A bleak little smile. "I doubt he'd approve."

I sat, half fell, into the cat-scratched corduroy armchair by the door. "Hollister..."

"Framed. By an expert. Unless he posted this himself for us to find."

"From jail?"

Joe bit his lip. "Right, yeah. Good point. I'm not thinking."

"You're doing great, Joe, Thank you for this. Now it's time for my leg of the relay race."

"What are you going to do?"

I stood. "I'm going to play pick-up sticks."

Another tight little smile. "Just like Maddie Clark."

"Yeah."

He still read his ex-wife's books. I admired that. Miranda hadn't read a poem of mine in years, and that required a lot less commitment. On the other hand, Jane's books were fun, and her advice was sound.

I started the second round of the game the same way as the first, poking at the edges of Hollister's alibi...assuming the Dark

Web poster's plan had worked and Hollister actually was innocent. I didn't want to re-interview anyone unless it was absolutely necessary. Word would get back to my quarry and I didn't want to give myself away.

The key to Chris Felleman's story: he was at the airport ATM getting cash when Hollister claimed they were driving to Cisco. I went to the bank, pulled the surveillance tape again, and printed out the best frames as still photographs. Then I had Joe Stiles perform a simple hack into Felleman's Facebook account and send me a couple of dozen photographs. I printed them out and laid them on my office floor next to the ATM video captures.

Same guy?

Same hat, same shirt, same wristwatch, but the face was conveniently obscured. No rings, no tattoos, no scars on the hands in both sets of pictures. But I was still suspicious. Maybe that was why I kept at it. If you think you *may have* dropped your phone in your car, you'll rummage for a while and then give up. If you *know for certain* it's there, you'll look until you find it. That's just human nature. I wasn't absolutely certain, but the smug arrogant tone of that blog post goaded me. It was an insult and a challenge. The law enforcement community was beneath contempt for this person—a group of officious dimwits to manipulate for fun and profit.

Not if I could help it.

I made myself a cup of coffee and set the Facebook candids and selfies on my desk against the screen grabs from the bank. This time I looked twice at a shadow on the ATM man's hand. On his thumbnail, to be exact. A true shadow would be a kind of peninsula—connected back to the source that blocked the light.

This was an island. The shadow that connected to the rest of the finger had a different shade and texture, probably thrown by the edge of the ATM machine itself. It had been easy to miss in the bad resolution of the surveillance tape. But I recognized the mark—the bruise from a hammer blow. This guy was a carpenter, and not a very good one. He had been banging nails and missed. I went back through the Facebook images.

No bruise.

It was time to talk to Chris Felleman, and let him take the news of my interrogation back to whoever gave the orders. Fuck it, let the chips fall. It occurred to me that making the blogger nervous might be a useful tactic. If I flushed him out of hiding or forced his hand, I'd be watching, and any unusual behavior among my flock of suspects would constitute another clue.

I dug out Felleman's card, called his cab for a ride.

I was waiting in the cop shop parking lot when the taxi pulled up. I climbed in the back and Felleman said, "Uh oh."

"Nice to see you, too, Christopher."

He hacked out a quick unhappy laugh. "The last person who called me that was Superintendent Bissel, just before he suspended me."

"Sorry, Chris."

"Where to?"

"Just drive around."

He took a left out on to Fairgrounds Road, heading for Surfside. "How did you figure it out?"

No stalling, I liked that. "Your friend had a blood bruise under his thumb."

"He was probably running his lines in his head. Sometimes when he does something stupid, Pat or Billy'll say, 'Got that speech memorized yet?' or 'Don't forget to mention this one in your Oscar speech.'"

"Pat Folger and Billy Delavane?"

"Yeah. C.J.'s the new kid on the crew. Pat said if he worked a year and paid attention, he'd be able to build his own house. Somehow I doubt it. The trick is the 'paying attention' part."

"So why did he do the withdrawal for you?"

"Hey, I cover for him, he covers for me. He needs a jump I drive out with cables. I need a loan he finds the cash. We're pals."

"So you made him an accessory to murder. Some pal."

"Hey wait, slow down there, Chief. Only thing C.J.'s an accessory to is a little old-fashioned small-town cheating. That was my afternoon delight, that's all."

He had managed to surprise me. I kept my face blank in case he glanced in the rearview. "Go on."

"I have a girlfriend, Hallie Conway? She cleans houses in Madaket. The people are off-island until the Fourth. So I meet her there, daytimes. My wife works at the bank, she's the fat blond teller who never smiles at anyone. I know she can get a look at the videofeed, she's having her own little thing with the branch manager. So the withdrawal time-stamps the fact that I couldn't have been anywhere but halfway across the island from Hallie's love nest on Starbuck Road. The hat and wristwatch clinch it, in case she checks the footage."

"And it just so happens that a murder was happening at exactly that moment."

"Why not? Lots of things were happening at exactly that moment, Chief. Probably some bigger crimes than mine. And a million other things. They could do one of those big picture books: *One Hour in the Life of America* or something like that."

I let him drive for a minute or two. He pulled into the Surfside Beach parking lot. Every space was taken and there was big crowd around the new overpriced gourmet concession stand. He followed my look. "Yeah, right? You can't even get a regular old hot dog at the beach no more."

"Hallie will back you up on this story of yours? C.J., too?"

"Sure."

"Call them."

He did, and they did.

I didn't like it. The stories sounded pat and rehearsed. They fit together like neatly machined puzzle pieces. Who was holding the jigsaw? That was my question. All my cop instincts told me Chris and his cohorts were lying, but they had told me Hollister was a killer, also. My instincts were unreliable these days, and I liked that least of all.

There was nothing to do but press on. My next target was Toby Vollans, the WAVE bus driver who had claimed no recollection of Hollister among his passengers on the afternoon of the murder.

I found him having an early beer at the Chicken Box, and got a small concession.

"Look, maybe he was on the bus and maybe not. Maybe it was that day and maybe it was a different day. I don't pay that much attention, okay? I just want to drive out my shift and get home." I looked around the seedy bar, from the pool tables to the bandstand, lifted an inquiring eyebrow. "Yeah, okay, I stop off here first. Here or the Muse. Like nine-tenths of everybody else who works for a living around here. So what?"

"Chris Felleman told me Hollister promised him a part in a play if he'd lie about that day. It wasn't Hollister, but someone made that promise—to both of you. A production of *True West*. At the time it seemed like a great deal, but now you're both accessories to murder and you're thinking your best bet is to stonewall the cops."

"Nobody promised me anything. Besides, if the Lab did *True West*, they'd bring in a couple of Equity actors from New York, anyway. That's what they do now. Fucking 'community theater.' What a joke."

"But you believed it. And now you're trapped."

"One more word and I'm calling a lawyer."

I stood up. "That's a good idea, Toby. Have your parents hire a criminal attorney out of Boston or New York. There's no one around here smart enough to get you out of this one."

If the plan was in fact to stonewall me, Toby had done a good job. Something smelled bad, but as anyone who's had a mouse die in their house can tell you, it's often hard to locate the source of the smell. Billy Delavane had wound up taking a sawzall to his living room wall a couple of years ago, and I was prepared to take my entire house apart one room at a time if I had to, until there was nothing left but rubble.

One room at a time.

My next target was Carmen Delgado, Judith Barsch's maid. Perhaps some pressure would change her story. She could have any number of reasons for lying, including her own guilt. She was friends with Sebastian Cruz, her paperwork was flimsy, Refn could have threatened to turn her into Immigration and Customs Enforcement. He could have taken advantage of her in other ways. It wasn't tough to conjure reasons why anyone would have wanted to kill Refn. I couldn't see her colluding with Toby Vollans and Chris Felleman, but that was just one more reminder of how little I knew about my adopted island, and its complex tangle of social networks. Anything was possible, and after close to a decade on Nantucket, surprise was practically dereliction of duty.

The driveway was empty and the door was open when I arrived, with carpets and runners draped over Finnish beating racks outside, while Carmen mopped the floors. The polished ash wood front hall was still drying.

I stuck my head inside. "Hello? Hello?"

Carmen called from upstairs. "Missus not home!"

"I want to talk to you! Carmen? It's Chief Kennis!"

A moment of silence, then, "Come on up."

I found Carmen in the master bath, scrubbing the claw-foot tub with a scouring powder called Barkeeper's Friend. I made a note of it—rich people found all the best products. I looked around. Something was wrong.

"Chief Kennis?"

"Shhhhh."

What was it? I knew it was something I'd seen in Hamburger's video, and failed to register, just as Hector's Israeli Coke can had failed to register when I studied the photographs I'd taken of his room. I scanned the closets, cabinets, counters, sink and bath, mirrored doors, racks of shoes and glasses. It didn't help, looking could only take me so far.

Then I hung my head and stared down at the floor—white hexagons, beige grout. I sensed Carmen rising to her feet, but I ignored her. I let my mind disengage, studying the ceramic tiles. If you imagined a "Y," with lines drawn from the bottom legs of the top triangle and a vertical stroke down to the apex of the bottom triangle, the hexagons turned into cubes, stacks of cubes. I released the tension of focus and they turned back into hexagons again. Squint, push—cubes; relax, hexagons. From two dimensions to three, popped and flattened, reversed, made opposite, restored—because of nothing more than a tiny wrench of perception.

Just like this case.

When I looked up, I knew exactly what I was looking for and exactly where to find it.

I grabbed what I needed from the counter and, in a linked moment of inspiration, from the cabinet above the sink. Carmen was saying something to me. I barely heard her and didn't answer. I left her standing there. I didn't need to talk to her anymore.

Time was running out and I had work to do.

Chapter Nineteen
Malice and Forethought

I drove back to the station too fast, running stop signs with my flashers on, pushing cars and SUVs and painters' vans, tour buses, taxis and gardeners' trucks with their trailers of clanking lawnmowers to the side of the road like a blast wave, moving like a bullet through soft tissue.

I pulled into my space behind the station and was upstairs in my office with the door shut three minutes later. I spoke to no one and no one dared speak to me.

I grabbed my chair, rolled it up the desk, and booted the computer. The full set of scanned files Karen Gifford had compiled for me popped up—court records, transcripts, depositions tied to a time line of Refn/Pomeroy's movements east across the country over the previous decade.

His slogan under both names could have been "Often Indicted, Never Convicted." He always managed to skate on some technicality, missing witness, dropped charge, or recanted testimony. Then there were all the cases where he was never even charged, but Karen had found his mark. She followed the trail of counterfeit hundred-dollar bills, paid blackmail, broken marriages, and looted nonprofits. None of it helped me. I was looking for one particular case, one special swindle. I didn't know what it was, and I wasn't even sure of the victim's name. I hoped I'd recognize it when I saw it. I skimmed half a dozen dismissed civil suits, and even more litigations deemed frivolous, findings against the plaintiff, court costs paid by the complainant. All small-time stuff, bricks through a window.

I was looking for the wrecking ball.

It was dark out when I finally found it.

The company was called Beckham Studios, and it billed itself as the first major film production entity to locate in the Midwest. Located in Elk City, Oklahoma, named after the city's home county of Beckham, the brand new distributor arrived in town with a carpetbag full of tax breaks from the state government and a substantial, but never fully disclosed, initial operating budget. They bought a bankrupt industrial park on the outskirts of the city and launched into a spectacular renovation—repaved parking lot, remodeled offices, and ground cleared for a pair of sound stages. Their motto was "Twenty-first century entertainment— Twentieth Century Entertainments." They meant it. They had the rights to remake or revamp a slew of old TV shows, from *Mr. Ed* to *The Gale Storm Show*, *Topper* and *My Little Margie*. They had purchased solid properties that no one else seemed much interested in—Chuck Norris films (they were actively seeking "the new Chuck Norris"), Steven Seagal films, old Western serials like *The Lone Ranger* and *Zorro*. "Wholesome old-fashioned stories," the CEO told a city council meeting as they were breaking ground for the first of the soundstages. "Rousers!"

By all accounts he was charismatic, charming, and—most of all—convincing. City managers saw new revenue streams pouring into the city, leading to a new cachet—Elk City would become the Hollywood of the Plains. And there was more—a new string of drive-in movie theaters, upgraded with the latest technology, as well as surf parks tied to their collection of old beach movies, from *Gidget* to *Beach Blanket Bingo*.

But they weren't just blowing into town on a gust of tax

incentives, cheap and star-struck local politicians. It was a heart-land company and wanted heartland men and women involved with the day-to-day running of the business. They wanted to "Put America back into American movies."

Beckham Studios offered stock options and investment oppor-tunities. Shareholders, if they put enough skin in the game and enough money on the line, would be brought into the highest level of decision-making at the studio. They would be "green lighting" major motion pictures and partnerships with streaming companies like Hulu and Netflix, signing off on financing for giant movie-themed amusement park construction across three states. More importantly, they would be helping to shape national culture as their nation sailed into the new uncharted century.

Heady stuff. It seemed too good to be true.

And of course it was.

The CEO was one Horst Refn.

Karen had scanned news photographs and TV screen grabs. It was Refn, all right. His phony film company practically bank-rupted the city and ruined a number of its more prominent citizens. But the biggest investor, who was only allowed to par-ticipate after an exhaustive "due diligence" that included ten years of tax audits and a month-by-month review of his company's ledgers as well as his own credit history, family holdings, and capital acquisitions, was one Gregory Fillion of Fillion Oil. That was his grandfather's name for the company, outdated now since their primary business had become extracting natural gas through hydraulic fracturing.

Fillion was so busy proving himself to Refn that it never occurred to him make Refn prove himself to his investors. It would only have been needlessly discouraging—"looking a gift horse in the mouth" and this glamorous stallion had a fine set of choppers. Fillion was sure of it. He said so in his deposition.

It made sense at the time. Beckham Studios was demonstrating strength and solvency every day, pumping much needed money into the city, changing the landscape emotionally as well as physically. Elk City was turning into a boomtown and the giddy imminence of impending wealth lent a party atmosphere to the early spring days as winter faded and the last patches of dirty snow started to melt on the newly patched sidewalks.

Fillion was given an office suite and a seat on the board of directors. All he had to do in return was wire what turned out to be his life savings, along with his liquidated stock holdings and the family funds held in trust (he was the designated beneficiary) into a numbered account in the Cayman Islands.

His wife begged him not to do it—as wives often do.

He ignored her, as husbands often do.

A week later the construction had stopped, the half-renovated offices were empty and Beckham Studios had ceased to exist, the loans they had taken out to start construction defaulted, the ownership of their intellectual properties proved fraudulent, the operating officers vanished. Everything turned out to be a lie, even the supposed tax breaks from the state government. It was a teetering construction of outrageous fabrications and it couldn't have lasted long, but it didn't need to.

It struck me that Beckham Studios resembled one of those L.A. bank robberies where the thieves were in and out in under two minutes, just ahead of an LAPD three-minute response time. Speed was everything—speed and a posture of absolute confidence. The robbers achieved it with masks and automatic weapons.

All Refn needed was a good story and a smile.

The city recovered, but Gregory Fillion committed suicide.

In the State Attorney General's investigation, Fillion's widow described confronting Refn and demanding their money back. He gave her cash.

In the transcript the Deputy AG asks,

"Cash? Didn't that make you suspicious?"
"Indeed, it did. But he had a good explanation."
"Will you share it with us?"

"Very well. He told me, and I later verified this, that
New Mexico and Colorado to the west, and Missouri and
Arkansas to the east, all had much more lenient policies
concerning marijuana. New Mexico and Missouri had
decriminalized the drug, it was okayed for medical use in
Arkansas, and Colorado, of course, had legalized it. But
the states were at odds with the federal government and
banks were reluctant to take deposits from these people.
Consequently, they had a great deal of cash on hand and
they were actively looking to invest it."

"Or launder it."

"Yes, I was sure that some of this activity was indeed
illegal. But I confess I was happy to take the money."

"Which turned out to be counterfeit. Mrs. Fillion? I need
a verbal response."

"Yes. Yes, the money was counterfeit. One more lie. And
there was nothing anyone could do about it. Refn vanished
into thin air. And left us with nothing."

I pushed back my chair and stood.

It all fit, even the initials: Judith Lane Fillion.

On a stationery monogram that would read: JFL.

A quick search gave me the rest of it. Barsch was Judith Lane
Fillion's maiden name. She had never stopped hunting for Refn
and she had finally managed to find him. She could have tracked
him by his MO, which was always the same, or by a trail of news
photographs, since Refn wasn't shy and liked seeing his picture
in the papers. It couldn't have been cheap, but Barsch had family
money. Determining how much of it was left, how much of it
her husband had put into Beckham Studios would be a job for
a team of FBI forensic accountants, somewhere down the line.

Right now I had more urgent problems. Hollister's glasses,
hiding in plain sight on Hamburger's video, pale-red plastic
frames stuck among the pink ones in Barsch's bathroom, most
likely by Carmen tidying up after Hollister's visit on the day of
the murder and mistaking them for one of Barsch's many pairs,
proved he had been at the house. Which meant Felleman and

Vollans were lying. Now I know who had offered them roles in the Sam Shepherd play. She saw through them with icy contempt and used them with pragmatic indifference. By the time their white lies turned black it was too late to recant. They were already part of a murder conspiracy and their only hope was that no one would figure it out.

I picked up the bottle of Elizabeth Arden Mariah Carey Eau de Parfum, thinking all the Oklahoma oil money in the world doesn't give you good taste. Hollister had been right about that. I pulled the crystal stopper. But I already knew what it would smell like.

Marshmallows.

That was the perfume Kelly Ramos had smelled on the day when Barsch planted the keyboard cleaner in Hollister's office at the theater. Her hand was everywhere. She had taken Joe Little's phone that day at Ventuno, and had her favorite cab driver return it. I'd be fascinated to find out how she pulled that one off.

But first things first. I had to get Hollister out of my jail and offer my most heartfelt apologies, and hope or, better yet, pray, that he would chose not to sue the town for harassment and false arrest.

Oh, and I could also return his glasses.

But when I got to the holding cells, Hollister was gone. Thick-necked, potato-faced, crew-cutted Quentin Swan was manning the booking desk, absorbed with his iPhone in the big empty room. He always had the look of a State Police storm trooper; maybe he was studying for the exam online. The room was silent except for the faint rasp of the air conditioning and the rhythmic tapping of his heel against the linoleum—restless leg syndrome. The mass of him visible above the desk seemed alarmingly still, a pour of fresh cement staring to cure in a footing. Soon to be a fully weight-bearing slab!

"Swan," I said. He looked up from his phone, eyes only, head motionless. "Where's Hollister?"

"They bailed him out."

"They? Who? When did this happen?"

"Couple hours ago. Just before my shift. Didn't you get the text? Johnson said he texted you."

"I had my phone turned off. Let me see the paperwork."

He set his cell down and pulled a file folder out of a drawer. Call me a dinosaur, but I liked keeping hard copies of all arraignments, bench warrants, and pre-trial release outcomes. We've had some spectacular computer crashes, some of them suspicious in origin. I wasn't a hundred percent sure our records had been tampered with, but paper was backup and insurance.

I crossed the room and picked up the file, feeling a queasy tremor of premonition. I flipped to the last page looking for the co-signer and surety. The Nantucket Theater Lab, third-party custody assigned to NTL Board President J. Barsch.

I dropped the file on the desk, my head pinwheeling like a car on black ice. Stay on the road, steer with the skid, foot off the brakes, round and round, scanning for oncoming headlights. Why would she do this? What could possibly be the point? It wasn't forgiveness, I was sure of that.

Swan must have caught my stunned expression. "Johnson said they wanted him at the theater. I guess his play opens tonight? He's like the guest of honor. So it looks bad if he's in jail, supposedly. Anyway, that's what Johnson told me."

"Right. Of course. The play."

"Chief?"

"Thanks, Quentin."

"Everything okay?"

"Everything's fine. Keep your eyes open and have a good shift."

This new piece of information completed the picture. It reminded me of the night I figured out Joe Arbogast was sleeping with my ex-wife.

I wanted to sell my ring back to Rebecca Harper's jewelry store where I'd bought it in the first place. Getting rid of the thing felt like an essential act. I needed to purge the totems of my marriage.

Tim and I had run into Becky at the Stop & Shop one afternoon. I stood chatting with her in the dairy aisle while Tim investigated the gaudy packages of kids' yogurt. I mentioned the ring of pale flesh on my ring finger and the conversation went on from there. Becky offered to buy the wedding band back. I had no idea that Tim was even listening.

But he was. He had taken the divorce much harder than his sister, who seemed to cruise through life's entanglements like a yacht through kelp. Timmy was the opposite: he got caught in the seaweed. It wrapped around him and immobilized him, and even if he made it out of the water, he was picking the stuff out of his hair for days afterward. The thought that his father might sell the sacred symbol of his parents' marriage, of their family, of his home, just for money, for forty pieces of silver, horrified him. The things that mattered most to him meant nothing to his father, that was the worst part. He was alone. He felt like an orphan. He couldn't say all this, of course. He was seven years old. Instead, he stood in front of the Sponge Bob yogurt boxes and started sobbing.

I got the message.

I apologized to Becky Harper, and hustled Tim out of the store as fast as I could. We spent the better part of two hours, first in the car driving around the island and then at home, talking about it. I apologized a couple of dozen times. The crying chugged to a halt. Finally, we compromised. I didn't want the ring and Timmy did, so I'd just give it to him. Timmy liked that idea, but when I described the incident to Miranda a few days later, she said Timmy might lose it, as he lost everything else from his band trumpet to his math homework to his left sneaker.

"I'll hold it for him," she said. "Until he's old enough to take care of it himself."

That had seemed like a reasonable solution.

Everything had seemed startlingly reasonable, in fact—until the evening when the actual hand-off occurred. It was after the

Christmas band-chorus concert. Carrie was in the chorus and Timmy was in the band, so I had to be there for the duration.

I found Miranda in the lobby outside, afterward. She was chatting with her yoga teacher and some dowdy woman from the Land Bank. Joe Arbogast was hovering nearby. There was a break in the conversation and it seemed like a perfect opportunity. I dug into my pocket as I approached.

"Hey, Miranda—before I forget." I handed her the ring. "I figure you could put it on the mantel or something, where he could see it but not actually put his hands on it. Or whatever. It's up to you."

"Okay," she said. She seemed off-balance, tricked into silence.

I dove through the gap. "Well, okay then…see you around. Ladies," I nodded to the two women. I ignored Joe. Twenty seconds later I was outside in the clean, biting cold of the December night, congratulating myself on handling a potentially awkward situation with skill and grace.

I should have known better.

The phone was ringing when I got home. I picked it up and Miranda started in before I could say a word. "I can't believe you did that."

"Excuse me?"

"How could you?"

"I'm not sure what—"

"In public that way? In front of my friends? That is so sick."

"Miranda—"

"Was it just to humiliate me? Well, it worked. Congratulations. Throwing your wedding ring at me as if it was a piece of trash, as if our whole marriage was nothing but some—"

"Wait a second. I didn't throw it at you. I just—"

"Joe thought it was childish. That's what he said. Pathetic and childish."

"Joe?"

"He saw the whole thing."

"What the hell does he have to do with—?"

"He happens to be a very shrewd judge of character."

I took a breath. "Look, that ring means nothing to me. I didn't want to do the whole ring thing in the first place. That was your idea, remember? I've been meaning to give the ring to you and this was the first chance I got. Period."

"Fine. Whatever. I have to go."

She hung up.

Thinking about it later, the thing that struck me most about the conversation was Joe Arbogast's comment. It was overly emphatic, bizarrely partisan. In my experience there was only one reason why a man would adopt a woman's point of view with such strident zeal. It wasn't because he had suddenly discovered a mutual interest in the arcane protocols of divorce. It wasn't because he was a chivalrous debater who liked standing up for over-matched losers, or because he believed what she was saying and felt a moral obligation to fight for the truth.

No, it was because he was fucking her. It was the only sensible explanation.

Joe Arbogast was fucking my ex-wife.

And Judith Barsch had big plans for Blair Hollister. Human nature carves these channels through the rock of observed behavior, like a million years of stream water, following gravity, twisting downhill. The motives were always the same, the opportunities found or self-created. Sex and death, passion and revenge, malice and forethought. Barsch needed Hollister on the loose because she was going to frame him for another murder. As soon as I knew why, I knew who.

And as soon as I knew who, I knew how.

I tumbled into my cruiser, burned rubber squealing out of the lot, hit the flashers, and stamped on the gas. The clock on the dash read 8:51. How long was the first act of Hollister's play? I had no idea. All I knew for sure was I had to get to the theater, and I might already be too late.

Chapter Twenty

Stagecraft

Kelly Ramos was clearing away the intermission drinks table when I burst through the front door of Bennett Hall.

The bang of the door struck her like a gunshot. "Jesus, Chief—you scared the crap out of me."

"Can you get me backstage?"

"Did you get my message?"

"I need to—what?"

"I called you."

I picked a great day to turn my phone off. "No, sorry. What's going on?"

"I smelled it again—that marshmallow smell. In the prop room, just before curtain. You said to tell you if—"

That was all the confirmation I needed. "When does he drink the poison?"

"He? Who—? Oh, in the play…Oh, my God. How can—?"

"When does that scene happen?"

"It…I don't know. Right now, basically."

"Shit!"

I didn't organize a plan, I didn't call for backup, I just ran. Back out the door, around the church, along the narrow alley beside it into the wide-sloped parking lot at the back, and down through the double doors that led to the backstage area—the dressing rooms, prop and costume storage, and the wings.

I paused for a second trying to get control of my breath. I could hear the actors talking from the stage beyond the blackout curtain. I skirted a table of first act props, picked my way past some pieces of broken furniture, and slipped through the heavy drapes. I stood still listening.

"Is that a threat?"

"People only ask that question when they already know the answer."

I remembered the scene. Galassi was seconds away from pouring his drink and making his toast. When he fell convulsing to the boards it wouldn't be an act.

My time was up. I charged the stage.

The judge had the wine in his hand. "Here's to weakness," he said, lifting his glass.

The stage lights blinded me for a second. "Stop! Don't drink that!"

The younger actor, Jon, was frozen for a second, then he blurted, "You're too late, McPherson!" and rushed me. His shoulder struck my chest and we both staggered into Galassi.

McPherson?

Jon rasped at the judge, "Fucking Toland! Improv on opening night? Really?"

Galassi grinned and mouthed the words, "Let's do it."

Jon kicked my heel backward and slammed me to the stage on my back.

"Is this your new idea, McPherson? That young Fenwick plans to murder me? Don't concern yourself. It's all bluster. He's not capable of it, and in any case, killing me just digs his hole deeper. In fact, that hole is starting to look like…my grave!"

Jon and I thrashed on the stage. He had twenty pounds on me, all of it muscle and he was at least fifteen years younger.

Galassi poured more wine. "To deep holes and graves!"

He was flushed, riding a giant black wave of adrenaline, making it up as he went along, hearing the tumbling thunder as the wall of water crashed behind him and the smooth face firmed and steepened in front of him. He was flying. This might be the finest moment of his acting career.

And the last.

He lifted the glass.

I thrashed an arm free, and twisted Jon's ear. He shrieked in pain and I lunged past him, Galassi's ankle filling my field of vision. I reached out and yanked it as hard as I could. He staggered back and the glass went flying. He hit the drinks table and slid to the floor.

I scrambled over to him, rasping in his ear. "That. Wine. Is. Poison. This is real."

His face went as white as the skin under your wristwatch. "Barsch."

I nodded. "Barsch."

"Oh, my God." His eyes went wide, the name was a truck bearing down on him, headlights filling his world. Then it hit him and he passed out.

The audience was applauding wildly. Most them were on their feet, cutting loose with a standing ovation. They knew something extraordinary had happened, they just didn't know what. Which was just what I wanted. I helped Jon up. The noise covered my words. "Don't touch that wine. The poison is real. This stage is a crime scene now. Do not taint it."

"But it—I—"

"Get back on track. Wake up the judge and finish. Take your curtain call. Fit the action to the word. Make it work. The play must go on. Right? Right?"

"Right."

"This is your big moment, Jon. Don't blow it. You could wind up on Broadway after all."

I took a quick bow and dashed off the stage. As I scanned

the audience in that moment, I saw Karen Gifford in the front row and it struck me that she might very possibly be the only person in the theater who understood what had just happened. Or perhaps not. It would all depend on how far she had travelled down the twisted path of misinformation and deception I had followed myself. It didn't matter anyway. The important thing was that I had a trusted officer at the scene.

As I wound my way down the twisted cobblestone lane, from the church to Centre Street, I phoned Haden Krakauer. I wanted the theater sealed and the stage and prop room taped off as soon as the audience had left the theater. There had to be other board members in attendance and one stray tweet, Facebook post, text, or even (most of them were quite elderly, after all) phone call could set my quarry on the run. I remembered years before, when I had startled a stately deer in the Polpis woods with the sound of unwrapping a cookie from my pocket. All it took was the faint crackle of plastic in that huge stillness to snap the fight-or-flight alarm in the deer's central nervous system.

I had no doubt that Barsch's reflexes were just as sensitive.

I ran down her options as I hurtled south on Hummock Pond Road. No boats until the morning and she had already missed the last commercial flight. That would trap most people on the island until morning, but the wealthy always had other options. I called Sean Pollack at the Fixed Base Operator general aviation terminal and told him to ground all flights. That was Barsch's most likely escape route from the island and the fleets of private jets coming in out of Nantucket Memorial Airport in the summer made it the busiest airfield in New England, and that included Logan. If Barsch didn't have her own plane she surely had half a dozen friends who did. Most of their mansions had a suite of rooms for their pilots. It was a good life. It certainly beat puddle-jumping for Cape Air.

Pollack was upset at the request.

"It's not a request, Sean."

The silence on the line was more dramatic than an argument. He was having the argument all by himself in his head. I didn't have to say a word.

"How long are we talking about?" he asked finally.

"Two or three hours, tops. Just until midnight, at the latest."

"Okay. But you owe me one." I said nothing, as I swerved around a slow-moving minivan. "Fine. You don't owe me one." I slowed for the turn into the Nanahumacke Preserve. "Shit! I still owe you one, all right?" Never underestimate the power of silence. I was pulling into Barsch's driveway when Pollack gave up and said. "Okay, ten. I owe you ten. Now let me get to work over here."

"Thanks, Sean."

Barsch's Audi SUV was parked in the driveway with the hatchback up, and a couple of suitcases already stacked. The door was open, she was obviously moving back and forth, loading up for the trip. She was taking a trip, all right. But not the one she was planning on.

I stepped inside. It was quiet, but I heard movement from above. I took the stairs two at a time and followed the second-floor passageway to the master bedroom. Barsch was inside, laying an armful of dresses, still on their wooden hangers, across the bed, next to an open Louis Vuitton suitcase. The wheels and retractable handle—with its attendant image of Barsch trundling through an endless airport concourse, pulling the bag behind her—struck an oddly jarring note. Didn't people like her have minions to lug their luggage for them? Maybe not.

I stood in the door, watching her for a moment or two, choosing my opening gambit.

"Going somewhere?"

She looked up, startled for a second but back in control instantly, as if she'd just met an acquaintance and blanked on their name. But she would never forget for long. A quick scan of her interior files and archives and she'd be introducing everyone with a cordial smile, kind of like the one she was giving me right now.

"Hello, Chief Kennis. It's customary to knock."

"The door was open."

"I'm loading the car, so…I have a house on Mount Desert Island."

"But you're missing the end of the play."

Another chilly little smile. "I know how it comes out."

"Yeah…fans like to leave early when the game's in the bag. They beat the traffic that way. But sometimes you wind up with a Heidi Bowl situation. Do you remember the Heidi Bowl?"

"No."

"Neither do I. But my dad always talked about it. Late November, 1968—Jets, Raiders. The game ran long and the network cut to the regularly scheduled program for the next time slot—the movie *Heidi*. Ooops. Kind of a bad call, because the Raiders went on to score two touchdowns in the final minute, and no one on the East Coast got to watch."

"And the point is?"

"You never know."

"I play the odds. And I usually win."

"Fair enough. So tell me—why leave the island at the height of the season? I wouldn't have bet on anyone doing that."

She turned back to the closet for a folded pile of shirts. "You know what the old 'Sconset biddies used to say—"No one goes to Nantucket anymore. It's too crowded."

I watched her load the shirts into the suitcase and zip it up. "Looks like you're going to be gone for a while."

"I like having my options open, and I'm an expert packer. My husband could never get all his clothes back in the suitcase when he came home from business trips. We used to joke about it."

"That's your mutant power. Packing?"

"No, puzzles. Fitting things together perfectly in unique ways that cannot be reproduced. That's my real talent."

"I'll give you that. You're the best."

"Indeed, I am. And you are remarkably observant."

"It's my job."

"I suppose."

She pulled another suitcase from the closet. The matching set must have cost close to ten thousand dollars. I pushed on. "So your husband traveled a lot? On business?"

"Yes, he did."

"Was he planning to travel a lot for Beckham Studios?" She looked up—a first flicker of alarm, as if shuffling across the carpet she had touched something and gotten a static electricity sting. Once again, her face cleared into a calm but combative neutrality. "Trips to L.A. and New York?" I continued. "Sundance and Cannes? All the glamour locations. I can just see him, walking the red carpet a few steps behind the stars, but expecting to notch some thank you's in the Oscar speeches."

"I have no idea what you're talking about."

"Most of all I want to thank Greg Fillion and his team at Beckwith for their unfailing support. You're my heroes!"

"I think you should leave."

"I can understand he was tempted. All that glamour. But glamour is a function of distance. As Greg found out."

She stood in front of the unzipped empty suitcase with her fists on her hips. "All right, very well. Congratulations. You did your research. Or some unheralded worker bee you employ did your research. That was a terrible time in our lives and I prefer not to think about it."

"Nope. My bet is, you haven't thought about anything else since your husband's death. Or suicide, to be more accurate."

"Yes, Gregory did indeed commit suicide. Not that it's any business of yours."

"They swindled your husband. They left him broke and disgraced. They ruined both your lives and made you a widow. Anyone would want revenge. I don't blame you for that."

"I appreciate your sympathy, Chief Kennis. If that was the purpose of your visit, consider it... mission accomplished. Now, if you'll excuse me—"

"Your plan failed."

"Excuse me?"

"It failed. I stopped it."

"Now see here, what exactly are you—?"

"The plan to poison Judge Victor Galassi on stage and frame Blair Hollister for the murder."

"Oh, that plan."

"This amuses you?"

"It flabbergasts me. I find you and your accusations ludicrous and insulting and very possibly actionable in a court of law."

"Stagehands smelled your perfume in the prop room before the play. You changed out the fake poison for the real thing. The other time they smelled it you'd just planted the keyboard cleaner in Hollister's office."

Her look was a small masterpiece of incredulous bewilderment. "Keyboard cleaner? Chief Kennis, you sound deranged. Have you been drinking?"

"It's over, Judy. I feel comfortable with using your first name now, I've spent so much time in your head."

"—because I will happily report this to the selectmen and the State Attorney General. Chief Kennis came to my house in a state of advanced intoxication, harassed me, accused me of capital crimes, and generally slandered my good name in order to attempt some—"

"I have you for the Refn murder, too. The frame on Hollister is history. All your shills are flipping on you. I have proof that one of them was lying. Chris Felleman isn't going to jail for you. And neither is his pal—the one who helped him with the ATM machine masquerade. Nice idea, by the way. It almost worked."

"Wait one moment—"

"Here's what really happened. Felleman drove Hollister here on the afternoon of Refn's murder. There should have been no sign of Hollister's presence in the house. But unfortunately for you, he left his glasses here. And Carmen put them back in your closet, without even thinking about it, assuming they were yours. They're easy to spot in Hamburger's video. And Carmen will testify to the fact that Hollister was here, and that she lied about it for you. She can't afford to play games with the law anymore. Her legal status in the country depends on it. ICE tends to frown on green card holders who get charged with accessory to murder and obstruction of justice."

Now I had gotten a rise out of her. Her face flushed red under the heavy makeup. "I refuse to listen to this! I will not hear—"

"You will not hear anything but this for the next two years! This is a big story. Judy. David Trezize is going to write a true-crime book about it. He has my blessing. It's a story that deserves to be told. I'll give him all the research and evidence. All the depositons and interrogation transcripts. I may even put him in touch with my dad's old agent. Rich people doing bad things? That's right up his alley."

Her voice was a quiet rasp. "Evidence?"

"Nice. You picked the one important word out of everything I just said."

"What evidence?"

"You made mistakes, Judy. Don't feel bad, it was inevitable. You built a big machine with too many moving parts. For instance, you gave yourself no alibi for Refn's killing. Well, of course not, since you couldn't be in two places at once. You called the dog officer but that only placed you in range of one of the island's two cell towers. You could have been anywhere this side of 'Sconset. Then there's the fact that you stole Joe Little's phone and cloned the sim card."

"You can't prove that! It's—this is all conjecture! It's circumstantial. It's beyond circumstantial! It's crazy. No one could possibly—"

"Stop. We have Felleman's testimony. That's right. He told us everything." Well, of course he hadn't yet, but I knew he would. "He returned Joe's phone for you. And I think we'll see how you pulled off the switch if we dig a little. For instance...I'll bet my pension Hollister was at Ventuno that day at your request. And whatever got into Joe's food, you paid or bribed or threatened someone on the kitchen staff to put it there. You see, Judy? You pull one string and the whole fabric unravels. Everyone talks. Everyone wants to get as far away from you as possible."

"But—"

"Ships deserting a sinking rat. That's what my son used to say when he was little. It was so funny the way he mixed things up. Not this time, though. Then there's your blog on the Dark Web."

"You can't trace that back to me!"

I had to smile. "I think I just did."

"You can't prove I said anything! You're not wearing a wire! This conversation isn't admissible, you never read me my Miranda rights!"

"It doesn't matter. The NSA has new algorithms that can identify Internet posters by the way they write. The rhythms in their language. It's a high-tech version of the Unabomber's brother recognizing his writing in the *New York Times* letter. David knew Ted's prose style instantly, Judy. And I recognized yours. How hard will it be for an NSA supercomputer?"

"You couldn't—"

"Indeed, I could. Indeed."

"That's one word!"

"Right. One of many, all fit together in a unique way, just like one of your puzzles. But you made other mistakes, too—like dropping those counterfeit bills. No one has them but you and Hollister. The cops never recovered the main stash. The most amazing thing is you never even bothered to cover your tracks. Going back to your maiden name? Did you really think that was enough? Yeah, we have your stationery, and I have a feeling it will show your prints when we test it. Galassi let Refn go. They were up to their necks in half a dozen criminal conspiracies, but he was too smart and no one could ever prove anything. Still, the fact remains. He let Refn walk and he walked right into your life and blew it apart. You needed to get both of them."

"So why didn't I just kill Galassi first?"

I released the bomb casually, dropping the hand grenade like a scrap of litter. "He knew all this. He'd assembled his own dossier on you. For insurance. If he died, his lawyer had instructions to release it and connect the dots for the half-wit local police. That would be me."

"Mutually assured destruction."

"Except you had your Bulgarians steal his safe-deposit box key. You went into his box and messed with the file, maybe just replaced it and resealed it. They put the key back and it worked. He didn't know it but you'd stripped away his last defense. The only question at that point was how and when to kill him. That was why you had to get Hollister out of jail. So he could take the fall for the killing."

"You're diabolical."

"High praise from my evil twin." She glared at me. It always disarms writers when you quote their work back to them. "Why Hollister?" I asked.

"Why not? He fit the profile. He had a grudge. And he had written that play! What an idiot. A useful idiot, as Vladimir Lenin might have said."

"So you'd destroy his life without a second thought?"

"How many thoughts would you suggest? Hollister is simply collateral damage."

I shook my head. "I should have listened to my daughter. She had your number, just from looking at your groceries. Unsweetened yogurt, Fresca, and chicken livers? Pork spleens? And what did you want that plastic spoon for anyway?"

Her squint tightened. "Let me ask you a question, Chief Kennis. As I watch you strut and brag about your little discoveries, I wonder, has anyone else managed to follow your little trail of breadcrumbs? No? I thought not. My reading of you, from your groceries—the Icelandic Skyr—even Siggi's yogurt isn't authentic enough for you…the two-percent milk, the 'organic' chicken, the kale, dear God, the wormy apples from the healthy bin, the bags of black beans and chickpeas—no cans for Chief Kennis! It was obvious. You think of yourself as very special, indeed. The most progressive dad, the smartest man in the room."

"What's your point?"

"I had a professor in college. Brilliant man, cocky and arrogant and smug, just like you. He wrote dense unreadable symbolic novels that won obscure prizes. I detested him and the feeling was mutual. I wasn't pretty enough to be worth 'mentoring'—or taking advantage of. Greg said to me, you don't like it that he's smarter than you, and I said something that still makes me smile. 'Smarter than me? He's smarter than himself!' I would say the same applies to you, Chief Kennis. Why else come here alone?"

"For the same reason that I waited until the play was finished and the audience was gone before I sealed Bennett Hall as a crime scene. I know this town. They'll want your arrest handled with as little publicity as possible. You're a stain on this island. Like a wine stain on a silk couch. The Board of Selectmen wants to flip the pillow and dryclean the slipcover later. After Labor Day, preferably. That's fine with me. I don't want to ruin Nantucket's reputation, and spoil it as a haven for the rich people who pay the taxes and keep the place going. I just want to arrest the bad guys."

"So you come alone, into the house of a dangerous sociopath who eats raw chicken livers in the Stop & Shop parking lot with a plastic spoon—"

"I knew it wasn't the yogurt!"

"—without my confession—which can never be used in court now, you have nothing against me but your preposterous spec-ulations and the testimony of some trifling peons who will say anything to save their sweaty little necks."

"Not quite. We'll have DNA evidence, also. We have samples

from the crime scene—hair and blood that didn't belong to the victim. All we need to do is swab your cheek and you're finished."

She took a step toward me. "But that will never happen! Never!"

"Sorry, but I'm afraid—"

The words caught halfway up my throat as her knee drove up into my crotch. A glassy white-hot wave of pain rolled through me and I dropped to my hands and knees. I heard a pathetic high-pitched keening and realized it was me. I tried to stand and felt the first kick in my ribs. She punted me like a football, tipped me over on my side, and she kept on kicking—my stomach, my legs, my neck. I covered my face as best I could.

Kick, kick, kick, kick. "Never! Never! Never! Never!"

I curled into a ball, still disoriented, half blind, every part of my body shrieking in pain.

"Never! Never! Never! Never!"

My head, my thigh, my butt, my back, my stomach again, right where I clutched myself with my hands. It felt like she broke a finger. Maybe more than one. I was bellowing and squealing in pain, rolling on the floor to get away from her. It was impossible. She was crazed, feral, unstoppable.

"Never! Never! Never!"

I felt a rib crack. She connected with my temple and I blacked out for a second. When I came to, she lurched off me, planted one more kick and flipped me over on my back. I wanted to kick at her, but I couldn't seem to move my legs. There was blood in my eyes. I saw everything through a red scrim. It occurred to me through twisting jabs of pain that she was right. She hadn't outsmarted me. I had outsmarted myself.

And I was going to pay for my hubris with my life.

She disappeared into the bathroom and came out with a syringe full of some clear liquid. She stood over me, feet planted on either side of my waist, out of range of my useless legs.

She tilted the needle against the light, savoring the clarity of the toxin as if it were some fine wine.

"Succinylcholine," she said. "Have you ever heard of it? It remains in many ways the perfect poison. I've made quite a study of these things. It's even better than the aconitine I put into the wine for Galassi. Aconitine works more slowly, but that was the whole point. I wanted him to suffer. The process starts with numbness—paresthesia, the doctors call it. It takes a few hours for the vomiting, the difficulty breathing and the paralysis. By the time the ventricular tachycardia set in, he would have had plenty of time to contemplate the folly of his life choices. For you, I have something different."

I wrenched myself sideways into her leg, hoping to knock her off balance. It was my only move and it did nothing. She booted me over onto my back again and placed a foot between my legs. A small nudge sent another vibrating bulge of agony chunking through me. The pain was bigger than my body, it was going to split me open. I was panting and whimpering. She put a vertical manicured finger to her lips. She wanted silence. Finally, she got it, except for the rough sawing of my breath. "The best thing about succinylcholine is they don't test for it in toxicology screens. It paralyzes the entire breathing apparatus. You'll suffocate to death and it will look like a heart attack. I'll explain that you injured yourself in the course of a preliminary seizure. A tragic early death, followed in short order by the conviction and sentencing of Blair Hollister."

"But Galassi is still alive," I wheezed.

Another grim little smile. "Not for long."

"You'll have to frame someone else for it, with Hollister gone."

"Why don't you leave that to me, Chief Kennis? We both know I'm quite adept at these games. And in any case, you'll be well out of it and long gone." She pushed the plunger, releasing a single clear drop of the poison. She knelt down beside me. "Any last words?"

"Fuck you."

"Spoken like a true poet."

She was about to jab me with the needle when Karen Gifford's voice rang out. "Stop! Drop the needle and step back."

There was a serene madness in Barsch's face when she responded, simply, "No."

She thrust at me with the needle and Karen's gun went off, deafening in the enclosed space. The round caught Barsch in the shoulder and knocked her back against the bed, bright arterial blood spurting from the wound. Splashing on my neck and chest. Barsch gaped at Karen in furious disbelief. She'd be going into shock soon. But she still held the syringe.

Karen advanced slowly, gun forward in the weaver position. "Judith Barsch, I am placing you under arrest. You have the right to remain silent. If you waive that right, anything you say can and will be used against you in a court of law."

Another step forward.

"You have the right to an attorney. If you cannot afford an attorney one will be appointed for you by the court."

She stepped gingerly over my body, gun steady, and reached down for the needle.

"Do you understand these rights as I have read them to you?"

I saw it coming, a split second too late. "Karen—no!"

Barsch let out a guttural roar of rage and pitched herself over me into Karen's knees. Karen reeled backward, dropping her gun, and Barsch was after her like a terrier on a rat, lifting her syringe for the strike. She landed with her knees on Karen's chest, blowing the breath out of her body. I twisted over, scrabbled across the carpet for the gun.

"I have enough of this for both of you!" Barsch crowed. She pushed Karen's sleeve up, looking for the perfect injection spot. I grabbed the gun and wrenched myself over, peering through bloody double vision, triple vision, trying to pick a Barsch to shoot. The needle touched flesh and I pulled the trigger.

The first shot missed and so did the second. But the battering noise and the stink of cordite stopped her for a critical heartbeat.

My last round blew her head into a pink mist and tossed her through the door like a sack of trash into a dumpster.

The syringe rested on the carpet, lethal as a snake. I stared at Karen. She stared back.

"Get Monica Terwilliger. We need an ambulance and a hearse," I said. "Call Dave Carmichael at home, the number's in my wallet. He'll get the Medical Examiner out here by morning. While we're waiting, find me an Advil or six. Nice shooting, by the way. And excellent police work."

I gave her my best encouraging smile.

Then I fainted.

Epilogue

The Fake and the Real

I spent two days in the hospital while the State Attorney General's force review committee conducted its officer-involved shooting investigation. Apparently, Karen Gifford was eloquent in my defense, and the syringe of poison, covered with Barsch's fingerprints, supported Karen's reconstruction of the incident. It turned out that Carmen Delgado had been cowering in one of the second-floor guest bedrooms when the shooting happened, and part of her deal with the DoJ and the immigration enforcement people included sworn testimony that exonerated both me and Karen.

I heard about it all secondhand, from Dave Carmichael. From the way he talked to me on the phone I could tell he had never taken the administrative inquiry seriously. "The officials reviewed the play, and the ruling on the field stands! Both feet in bounds and no offensive pass interference. The only question is—kick the extra point or go for the two-point conversion."

"Jesus, Dave."

"There must be someone else over there you want to nail with a righteous shoot."

"Not really."

"I can think of a couple. I'll text you a list. Meanwhile, heal up and start thinking about a cushy job in Boston. It's a hell of a lot safer. No one's ever tried to poison me—except my wife. And she used her mother's cheesecake recipe."

I spent another couple hours giving David Trezize the story, from the day Refn died to the shootout in Cisco. Once again, he'd be scooping the big papers and his plans to write a book about the case were coming together nicely. My father's old agent, Sheldon Meisel, was thrilled. "I love this kid!" Anyone under seventy was a kid to Sheldon. "He's gonna be the new Dominick Dunne!"

"I'll settle for being the new Joe McGinnis," David said, sitting by my bedside the next day, fussing over me like my long-dead Jewish grandmother. His opening salvo would have made Bessie proud: "What are they feeding you in here?"

I must have looked flimsy. I couldn't eat much with my jaw wired shut, and that combined with the thirty stitches in my scalp, the three broken fingers, four cracked ribs, and a broken nose flanked by two black eyes gave me the look of a mournful raccoon, starving to death with my paw in a trap.

Still, all things considered, I felt pretty good. The Tylenol codeine helped, but so did the news. The ancillary arrests had gone smoothly, the murder investigation closed without wrecking the island tourist trade, and Haden Krakauer was handling things impeccably in my absence. Victor Galassi, who should have been in jail on at least seven counts of grand larceny, fraud, and racketeering, was at least still alive, out and about, still just as prone to criminal activity, and still just as likely to make a mistake.

If he ever did, I'd be waiting.

Meanwhile, no one had accidentally dosed themselves with Barsch's aconitine. That was a plus.

Hector Cruz had talked his teammate into confessing and Superintendent Bissel had shown unusual restraint in limiting punishment to a two-week suspension and a hundred hours of community service. A cynic might say that he just wanted to keep his championship Whalers football team intact and, as usual, a cynic would be right. I didn't care about that. Any excuse to give a teenage kid a second chance was fine with me.

Carrie and Hector were happier than ever and she was delighted to see that her Grocery Gumshoe deductions had been so accurate. "Maybe you'll listen to me next time," she chided gently, patting my intact left hand. Tim had good news, too. He'd finally managed to catch a few waves, impressing Debbie Garrison, using Billy Delavane's secret trick. "Which is what?" I asked him.

"Smiling," Tim said.

"Smiling?"

"The biggest, sappiest goofiest smile you can manage."

"And that helps you catch waves?"

"Totally. Billy says smiling rewires your brain. It relaxes you. You're not as nervous or scared and you have more fun. It's like your face is giving your brain orders. But it really works. It's awesome."

Equally awesome—Tim Hobbes had been named the Artistic Director of the Theater Lab and his first announced production for the new season was Sebastian Cruz's play, *Fundamental Attribution Error.* In a lovely tip of the hat to the history of the organization, he had persuaded Howard Anderwald, the founder, to direct the play and Tag Reemer, the Lab's movie star figurehead, to play one of the leads. Best of all, he had rehired Marcia Stoddard as Production Designer.

She was our first visitor when I got home from the hospital.

"Oh, my God, you look terrible," she blurted, right at the front door.

"You should have seen me two days ago."

"How many were there? The men who did this to you?"

As I may have mentioned, the precise details of the incident at the Nanhumacke Preserve hadn't quite filtered out to the general public yet.

"You wouldn't believe it," I said. But she probably would. My combat skills were not exactly the subject of legend.

Jane offered her coffee and we all sat down in the living room. While we caught up with each other's news and passed along the requisite congratulations, I studied the two women seated next to each other on the big couch—virtual twins, supposedly. In fact they scarcely looked alike apart from some basic Identikit details: short, slim, frizzy haired, long as opposed to round or squared-off faces. It was tragic and peculiar that two women who shared so many basic features could look so different. Marcia was just shy of homely and Jane was gorgeous. Don't take my word for it—check out her dust jacket photographs.

I was musing about this, not really listening to the conversation, when Marcia got to the point of her visit.

"I know where Refn hid his blackmail money."

That got my attention. "Really?"

She dug into her big canvas purse and pulled out a cascade of pearls, at least five strings of them. These were sitting in the Theater Lab jewelry collection."

I picked one up, held it to the light as if I could discern anything special about them.

"They're natural," Marcia said. "As opposed to cultured. I had them tested to be sure. Look at the rose-green overtones. That was the giveaway for me."

I handed them back. "You're a detective, too, Marcia."

Jane grinned. "I'm using this in my next book."

"These strands can go for anywhere from seventy thousand dollars to half a million or more. And Refn just…left them, in a pile next to the rhinestones and the cubic zirconia."

"I guess he figured no one would notice."

"Big mistake. That's my domain, Chief Kennis. I notice everything."

"Wow."

"So…what do I do with them?"

Jane shrugged. Both women studied my battered face. The King Solomon of South Shore Road. I think I came up with a workable idea. "Five strands, total? I say we put four of them up for sale at some respected New York auction house and split the proceeds among the blackmail victims."

"Sounds fair," Jane said.

"What about the fifth strand?" Marcia asked.

"That's your finder's fee."

"Wait, that's—"

"We'd never have recovered anything if not for you. And no one would have ever seen a dime. As to how many strands you actually found? Who can say?"

"Is that legal?"

"Not strictly. But it will make everyone happy. And your secret is safe with me."

She glanced nervously over at Jane.

Jane lifted her right hand. "Me, too!"

"Oh, my God. Really?"

I nodded. "Put them somewhere safe. Or just back with the costume jewelry."

She smiled. "Good idea."

As she was leaving, she turned in the doorway and gave me an impulsive hug. I felt her lips on my neck for a second, then she scurried away.

We watched her go. Was she actually walking on air? It was hard to tell. "Kissing my twin, in plain sight of half the town!" Jane said. "That's a very confusing way to commit adultery."

"How about killing your enemy's twin brother? That's a weird way to commit murder. And Hollister was about ten seconds from doing exactly that."

"And then Galassi plays himself and his brother in a play about Hollister almost killing him. And almost gets killed himself. By a guy playing Hollister so Hollister can take the fall for the killing. Or something. This gives me a headache. And I write this crazy shit for a living."

I shrugged. "Truth is stranger than fiction."

"Or in this case fiction is stranger than fact based on fiction based on fictionalized fact."

"Ouch."

I hobbled back to the living room behind her, and sat down while she poured out the last of the coffee.

She settled in next to me. "I'll tell you what bothers me the most. Everything's fake. Everything's counterfeit. Refn's hundred-dollar bills, Refn himself. And Galassi and Barsch, or Fillion, or whatever her real name was…and the wine on stage that's really poison, and the keyboard cleaner that's really some kind of frost-bite mace weapon, and the faked sim card…and the evidence against Barsch in Galassi's safe-deposit box—that's fake now, too…and all those stories about what Hollister was doing the day of the murder…and…and even the pearls! The fake pearls aren't even real fakes! You start to wonder…is there anything that's not a counterfeit?"

I saw my moment. I was never going to get a better one. I set my coffee down carefully. "Well…technically, those pearls are real. And so is this."

I pulled the engagement ring out of my pocket and held it out to her with my good left hand.

"Henry…"

I got down on my knees in front of the couch, awkwardly nudging the coffee table backward. "Will you marry me?"

She took the ring between two fingers, examining it like a jeweler. "This is Dot Tarrant's engagement ring."

"The sisters wanted you to have it. And it was the red herring in an actual mystery so I thought—perfect for you."

She didn't smile at my little joke. "You're perfect for me, Henry Kennis." She gave me her hand and let me slip on the ring. "It's beautiful, but you could have given me a loop of string, and it wouldn't have made any difference."

"So, you will marry me?"

She took my hand in both of hers. "I would have married you the first day we met."

"I should have asked."

"No. This is better. I wanted your kids' approval."

"Well, you've got it."

"And Sam thinks you're a super hero."

"It's the siren and the flashers."

"No, it's not."

She slid down onto the floor beside me, and folded herself into my arms. I kissed her, and she kissed me back hard and sweet and it hurt like a punch but I didn't care. And speaking of the kids, after a while, I glanced over her shoulder and saw all three of them standing in the living room door, studiously licking ice cream cones from the Juice Bar, watching us like we were zoo animals.

Carrie nodded sagely at Tim. "Told you so."

Jane pulled away an inch or two, pushed the coffee table clear with one foot, spilling magazines and the philodendron in its china lightship basket to the floor. "Get over here, all three of you."

There was one second of hesitation, then the kids bounded at us and pounced into a gleeful five-way hug.

I thought I was going to pass out from the pain in my ribs, but I got my feet under me, stood up, and said, "Let's keep our priorities straight. Back to the Juice Bar! Grown-ups need ice cream, too."

To see more Poisoned Pen Press titles:

Visit our website:
poisonedpenpress.com
Request a digital catalog:
info@poisonedpenpress.com

31901063730602